PREJUDICES
FIFTH SERIES

PREJUDICES
FIFTH SERIES

By H. L. MENCKEN

OCTAGON BOOKS

A DIVISION OF FARRAR, STRAUS AND GIROUX

New York   1977

Reprinted 1977
by special arrangement with Alfred A. Knopf, Inc.

OCTAGON BOOKS
A DIVISION OF FARRAR, STRAUS & GIROUX, INC.
19 Union Square West
New York, N.Y. 10003

Library of Congress Cataloging in Publication Data

Mencken, Henry Louis, 1880-1956.
    Prejudices: fifth series.

    Reprint of the ed. published by Knopf, New York.
    Includes index.
    I. Title.
PS3525.E43P85   1977   818'.5'209   76-30379
ISBN 0-374-95578-6

Manufactured by Braun-Brumfield, Inc.
Ann Arbor, Michigan
Printed in the United States of America

CONTENTS

CONTENTS

PREJUDICES
FIFTH SERIES

PREJUDICES: FIFTH SERIES

I. FOUR MORAL CAUSES

1

Birth Control

THE grotesque failure of the campaign to put down propaganda for birth control in the Republic has a lesson in it for those romantic optimists who believe that in the long run, by some mysterious hook or crook and perhaps with divine help, Prohibition will be enforced. They will not heed that lesson, but it is there nevertheless. Church and state combine to baffle and exterminate the birth controllers. They are threatened with penal servitude and their customers are threatened with hell fire. Yet it must be obvious that they are making progress in the land, for the national birth-rate continues to slide downhill, steadily and rapidly.

Incidentally, it is amusing and instructive to observe that it diminishes with greatest celerity among the educated and highly respectable classes, which is to say, among those who are ordinarily most law-abiding. The same thing is to be noted when one turns to Prohibition. The majority of professional criminals, now as in the old days of sin, are tee-totalers, but when one comes to the good citizens who scorn them and demand incessantly that the *Polizei* butcher them and so have done with them, one comes at once upon a high density of scofflaws. I know many Americans of easy means, some of them greatly respected and even eminent. Not two per cent make any pretense of obeying the Volstead Act. And not two per cent of their wives are innocent of birth control. The reason is not far to seek. Both the Volstead Act and the statute aimed at birth control invade the sanctity of the domestic hearth. They take the roof off a man's house, and invite the world to look in. Obviously, that looking in is unpleasant in proportion as the man himself is dignified. If he is a low fellow, he doesn't care much, for he is used to such snooping by his low neighbors. But if he is one who has a high opinion of himself, and is accustomed to seeing it ratified by others, then he is outraged. And if he has any natural bellicosity in him and resistance seems reasonably safe, he resists with great diligence and vigor.

Here, perhaps, we come upon an explanation of the fact that Prohibition and all other such devices for making men good by force are far less opposed in the country than they are in the cities. The yokel is trained from infancy to suffer espionage. He has scarcely any privacy at all. His neighbors know everything that is to be known about him, including what he eats and what he feeds his quadrupedal colleagues. His religious ideas are matters of public discussion; if he is recusant the village pastor prays for him by name. When his wife begins the sublime biological process of giving him an heir, the news flies around. If he inherits $200 from an uncle in Idaho everyone knows it instantly. If he skins his shin, or buys a new plow, or sees a ghost, or takes a bath it is a public event. Thus living like a goldfish in a glass globe, he acquires a large tolerance of snoutery, for if he resisted it his neighbors would set him down as an enemy of their happiness, and probably burn his barn. When an official spy or two are added to the volunteer pack he scarcely notices it. It seems natural and inevitable to him that everyone outside his house should be interested in what goes on inside, and that this interest should be accompanied by definite notions as to what is nice and what is not nice, supported by pressure. So he submits to governmental tyranny as he submits to the village inquisition, and when he hears that city men resist, it only confirms his general feeling that they are scoundrels. They are scoundrels because they have a better time than he has—the sempiternal human reason. The city man is differently trained. He is used to being let alone. Save when he lives in the slums, his neighbors show no interest in him. He would regard it as outrageous for them to have opinions about what goes on within the four walls of his house. If they offered him advice he would invite them to go to hell; if they tried force he would bawl for the police. So he is doubly affronted when the police themselves stalk in. And he resists them with every means at his command, and believes it is his high duty to do so, that liberty may not perish from the earth.

The birth control fanatics profit by this elemental fact. It is their great good fortune that their enemies have tried to put them down, not by refuting their ideas, but by seeking to shove them into jail. What they argue for, at bottom, remains very dubious, and multitudes of quite honest and intelligent persons are against it. They have by no means proved that a high birth-rate is dangerous, and they have certainly not shown that they know of any sure and safe way to reduce it—that is, any way not already known to every corner druggist. But when an attempt is made to put them down by law, the question whether they are wise falls into the background, and the question whether their rights are invaded comes forward. At once the crowd on their side is immensely reinforced. It now includes not only all the persons who believe in birth control, but also all the persons who believe in free ideas and free speech, and this second group, it quickly appears, is far larger than the first one, and far more formidable. So the birth controllers suddenly find themselves supported by heavy battalions, and that support is sufficient to make them almost invulnerable. Personally, I am inclined to be against them. I believe that the ignorant should be permitted to spawn *ad libitum,* that there may be a steady supply of slaves, and that those of us who are more prudent and sanitary may be relieved of unpleasant work. If the debate were open and fair, I'd oppose the birth controllers with all the subtlest devices of rhetoric, including bogus statistics and billingsgate. But so long as they are denied their plain rights—and, in particular, so long as those rights are denied them by an evil combination of theologians and politicians,—I am for them, and shall remain so until the last galoot's ashore. They have got many more allies on the same terms. And I believe that they are winning.

The law which forbids them to send their brummagem tracts through the mails is obviously disingenuous and oppressive. It is a part of the notorious Postal Act, put on the books by Comstock himself, executed by bureaucratic numskulls, and supported by every variety of witch-burner. I know of no intelligent man or woman who is in favor of the principal of such grotesque legislation; even the worst enemies of the birth controllers would not venture to argue that it should be applied generally.   The way to dispose of such laws is to flout them and make a mock of them.   The theory that they can be got rid of by enforcing them is nonsense.   Enforcing them simply inspires the sadists who advocate them to fresh excesses.   Worse, it accustoms the people to oppression, and so tends to make them bear it uncomplainingly.   Wherever, in the United States, there has been any sincere effort to enforce Prohibition, the anti-evolutionists are already on the warpath, and the Lord's Day Alliance is drumming up recruits.   No, the way to deal with such laws is to defy them, and thus make them ridiculous.   This is being done in the case of the Volstead Act by millions of patriots, clerical and lay.   It is being done in the case of the Comstock Act by a small band, but one full of praiseworthy resolution.

Thus I deliver myself of a whoop for the birth controllers, and pass on to pleasanter concerns.   Their specific Great Cause, it seems to me, is full of holes. They draw extremely questionable conclusions from a highly dubious body of so-called facts.   But they are profoundly right at bottom.   They are right when they argue that anyone who tries to silence them by force is the common enemy of all of us.   And they are right when they hold that the best way to get rid of such opposition is to thumb the nose at it.

2

Comstockery

In 1873, when the late Anthony Comstock began his great Christian work, the American flapper, or, as she was then called, the young lady, read *Godey's Ladies' Book*. To-day she reads—but if you want to find out what she reads simply take a look at the cheap fiction magazines which rise mountain-high from every news-stand. It is an amusing and at the same time highly instructive commentary upon the effectiveness of moral legislation. The net result of fifty years of Comstockery is complete and ignominious failure. All its gaudy raids and alarms have simply gone for naught.

Comstock, of course, was an imbecile; his sayings and doings were of such sort that they inevitably excited the public mirth, and so injured the cause he labored for. But it would be inaccurate, I believe, to put all the blame for its failure upon his imbecility. His successor, in New York, John S. Sumner, is by no means another such unwitting comedian; on the contrary, he shows discretion and even a certain wistful dignity. Nevertheless, he has failed just as miserably. When he took office "Three Weeks" was still regarded as a very salacious book. The wives of Babbitts read it in the kitchen, with the blinds down;

it was hidden under every pillow in every finishing-school in the land.   To-day "Three Weeks" is dismissed as intolerably banal by school girls of thirteen.   To make a genuine sensation it is not sufficient that a new book be naughty; it must be downright pathological.

I have been reviewing current American fiction pretty steadily since 1908.   The change that I note is immense.   When I began, a new novel dealing frankly with the physiology and pathology of sex was still something of a novelty.   It was, indeed, so rare that I always called attention to it.   To-day it is a commonplace.   The surprise now comes when a new novel turns out to be chemically pure.   Try to imagine an American publisher, in these days, getting alarmed about Dreiser's "Sister Carrie" and suppressing it before publication!   The oldest and most dignified houses would print it without question; they print far worse every day.   Yet in 1900 it seemed so lewd and lascivious that the publisher who put it into type got into a panic of fright, and hid the whole edition in the cellar.   To-day that same publisher is advertising a new edition of Walt Whitman's "Leaves of Grass," with "A Woman Waits for Me" printed in full!

What ruined the cause of the Comstocks, I believe, was the campaign of their brethren of sex hygiene. The whole Comstockian case, as good Anthony himself used to explain frankly, was grounded upon the doctrine that virtue and ignorance were identical— that the slightest knowledge of sin was fatal to virtue. Comstock believed and argued that the only way to keep girls pure was to forbid them to think about sex at all. He expounded that doctrine often and at great length. No woman, he was convinced, could be trusted. The instant she was allowed to peek over the fence she was off to the Bad Lands. This notion he supported with many texts from Holy Writ, chiefly from the Old Testament. He was a Puritan of the old school, and had no belief whatever in virtue *per se*. A good woman, to him, was simply one who was efficiently policed. Unfortunately for him, there rose up, within the bounds of his own sect, a school of uplifters who began to merchant quite contrary ideas. They believed that sin was often caused by ignorance—that many a virtuous girl was undone simply because she didn't know what she was doing. These uplifters held that unchastity was not the product of a congenital tendency to it in the female, but of the sinister enterprise of the male, flowing out of his superior knowledge and sophistication. So they set out to spread the enlightenment. If all girls of sixteen, they argued not unplausibly, knew as much about the dreadful consequences of sin as the average police lieutenant or midwife, there would be no more seductions, and in accordance with that theory, they began printing books describing the discomforts of parturition and the terminal symptoms of lues. These books they broadcasted in numerous and immense editions. Comstock, of course, was bitterly against the scheme. He had no faith in the solemn warnings; he saw only the new and startling frankness, and he believed firmly that its one effect would be to "arouse a libidinous passion . . . in the mind of a modest woman." But he was spiked and hamstrung by the impeccable respectability of the sex hygienists. Most of them were Puritans like himself; some were towering giants of Christian rectitude. One of the most active, the Rev. Dr. Sylvanus Stall, was a clergyman of the first chop—a sorcerer who had notoriously saved thousands of immortal souls. To raid such men, to cast them into jail and denounce them as scoundrels, was palpably impossible. Comstock fretted and fumed, but the thing got beyond him. Of Pastor Stall's books alone, millions were sold. Others were almost as successful; the country was flooded from coast to coast.

Whether Comstock was right or wrong I don't know —that is, whether these sex hygiene books increased or diminished loose living in the Republic I don't know. Some say one thing and some another. But this I *do* know; they had a quick and tremendous influence upon the content of American fiction. In the old-time novel what are now called the Facts of Life were glossed over mellifluously, and no one complained about it, for the great majority of fiction readers, being young and female, had no notion of what they were missing. But after they had read the sex hygiene books they began to observe that what was set out in novels was very evasive, and that much of it was downright untrue. So they began to murmur, to snicker, to boo. One by one the old-time novelists went on the shelf. I could make up a long and melancholy roll of them. Their sales dropped off; they began to be laughed at. In place of them rose a new school, and its aim was to tell it all. With this new school Comstock and his heirs have been wrestling ever since, and with steadily increasing bad fortune. Every year they make raids, perform in the newspapers and predict the end of the world, but every year the average is worse than the worst of the year before. As a practicing reviewer, I have got so used to lewd and lascivious books that I no longer notice them. They pour in from all directions. The most virtuous lady novelists write things that would have made a bartender blush to death two decades ago. If I open a new novel and find nothing about Freudian suppressions in it, I suspect at once that it is simply a reprint of some forgotten novel of 1885, with a new name. When I began reviewing I used to send my review copies, after I had sweated through them, to the Y. M. C. A. Now I send them to a medical college.

The Comstocks labor against this stream gallantly, but, it seems to me, very ineptly. They can't, of course, proceed against every naughty book that comes out, for there are far too many, but they could at least choose their marks far more sagaciously than they do. Instead of tackling the books that are frankly pornographic and have no other excuse for being, they almost always tackle books that have obvious literary merit, and are thus relatively easily defended. In consequence, they lose most of their cases. They lost with "Jurgen," they lost with "The 'Genius,'" they lost with "Mlle. de Maupin," and they have lost countless other times. And every time they lose they grow more impotent and absurd. Why do they pick out such books? Simply because raiding them gets more publicity than raiding more obscure stuff. The Comstock Society, like all other such pious organizations, is chronically short of money, and the way to raise it is to make a noise in the newspapers. A raid on "Night Life in Chicago," or "Confessions of an Escaped Nun" would get but a few lines; an attack on "Jurgen" is first-page stuff for days on end. Christian virtuosi, their libido aroused, send in their money, and so the society is saved. But when the trial is called and the case is lost, contributions fall off again, and another conspicuous victim must be found.

Well, what is the Comstocks' own remedy for this difficulty? It is to be found in what they call the Clean Books Bill. The aim of this bill is to make it impossible for a publisher accused of publishing an immoral book to make any defense at all. If it ever becomes a law the Comstocks will be able to pick out a single sentence from a Dreiser novel of 10,000 pages and base their whole case upon it; the author and publisher will be forbidden to offer the rest of the book as evidence that the whole has no pornographic purpose. Under such a law anyone printing or selling the Bible will run dreadful risks. One typographical error of a stimulating character will suffice to send a publisher to jail. But will the law actually achieve its purpose? I doubt it. Such extravagant and palpably unjust statutes never accomplish anything. Juries revolt against them; even judges punch holes in them. The Volstead Act is an excellent specimen. Has it made the Republic dry?

3

Capital Punishment

Having argued against the death penalty with great heat and eloquence for more than twenty years, I

hope I do not go beyond my rights when I now an-
nounce that I have begun to wobble, and feel a strong
temptation to take the other side.   My doubts, in all
seriousness, I ascribe to the arguments of the current
abolitionists.   The more earnestly they set forth those
arguments, the more I am harassed by suspicions
that they are full of folly.   A humane and Christian spirit, to be sure, is in them; but is there any
sense?   As I hint, I begin to doubt it.   Consider
the two that are oftenest heard:

1. That hanging a man (or doing him to death in any
other such coldblooded way) is a dreadful business, de-
grading to those who have to do it and revolting to those
who have to witness it.

2. That it is useless, for it does not deter others from the
same crime.

The first of these arguments, it seems to me, is
plainly too weak to need serious refutation.   All
it says, in brief, is that the work of the hangman is
unpleasant.   Granted.   But suppose it is?   It may
be quite necessary to society for all that.   There are,
indeed, many other jobs that are unpleasant, and
yet no one thinks of abolishing them.   I pass over
those connected with surgery, obstetrics, plumbing,
military science, journalism and the sacred office,
and point to one which, like that of the hangman,
has to do with the execution of the laws: to wit, the
post of Federal judge under Prohibition.   Consider

what a judge executing the Volstead Act must do
nearly every day. He must assume that men whom
he esteems and loves, men of his own profession,
even his fellow judges—in brief, the great body of
wet and enlightened Christian men—are all criminals. And he must assume that a pack of spies
and blackmailers whose mere presence, in private
life, would gag him—in brief, the corps of Anti-
Saloon League snouters and Prohibition agents—
are truth-seekers and altruists. These assumptions
are obviously hard to make. Not a few judges, unable to make them, resign from the bench; at
least one has committed suicide. But the remaining
judges, so long as they sit, must make them as in duty
bound, whatever the outrage to their feelings. Many
grow callous and suffer no more. So with the hangman, and his even more disagreeable offices. A man
of delicate sensibilities, confronting them, would die
of horror, but there is no evidence that they are
revolting to the men who actually discharge them.
I have known hangmen, indeed, who delighted in
their art, and practiced it proudly. I have never
heard of one who threw up his job.

In the second argument of the abolitionists there
is more force, but even here, I believe, the ground
under them is very shaky. Their fundamental error
consists in assuming that the whole aim of punish-
ing criminals is to deter other (potential) criminals

—that we hang or electrocute A simply in order to so alarm B that he will not kill C. This, I believe, is an assumption almost as inaccurate as those which must be made by a Federal judge. It confuses a part with the whole. Deterrence, obviously, is *one* of the aims of punishment, but it is surely not the only one. On the contrary, there are at least half a dozen, and some of them are probably quite as important. At least one of them, practically considered, is *more* important. Commonly, it is described as revenge, but revenge is really not the word for it. I borrow a better term from the late Aristotle: *katharsis*. *Katharsis*, so used, means a salubrious discharge of emotions, a healthy letting off of steam. A schoolboy, disliking his teacher, deposits a tack upon the pedagogical chair; the teacher jumps and the boy laughs. This is *katharsis*. A bootlegger, paying off a Prohibition agent, gives him a counterfeit $10 bill; the agent, dropping it in the collection plate on Sunday, is arrested and jailed. This is also *katharsis*. A subscriber to a newspaper, observing his name spelled incorrectly in the report of a lodge meeting, spreads a report that the editor of the paper did not buy Liberty Bonds. This again is *katharsis*.

What I contend is that one of the prime objects of judicial punishments is to afford this grateful *katharsis* (a) to the immediate victims of the criminal punished, and (b) to the general body of moral

and timorous men. These persons, and particularly
the first group, are concerned only indirectly with
deterring other criminals. The thing they crave
primarily is the satisfaction of seeing the criminal
before them suffer as he made them suffer. What
they want is the peace of mind that goes with the
feeling that accounts are squared. Until they get
that satisfaction they are in a state of emotional
tension, and hence unhappy. The instant they get
it they are comfortable. I do not argue that this
yearning is noble; I simply argue that it is almost
universal among human beings. In the face of in-
juries that are unimportant and can be borne without damage it may yield to higher impulses; that is
to say, it may yield to what is called Christian
charity. But it never so yields when the injury
is serious, and gives substantial permanent satisfaction to the person inflicting it. Here Christianity
is adjourned, and even saints reach for their side-
arms. The better the Christian, in fact, the more
violent his demand for *katharsis*—once he has un-
loaded the Beatitudes. At the time of the Leopold-
Loeb trial in Chicago the evangelical pastors of the
town bawled for blood unanimously, and even a
Catholic priest joined them. On lower levels, it is
plainly asking too much of human nature to expect
it to conquer so natural an impulse. A keeps a
store and has a bookkeeper, B. B steals $700, in-

vests it in Texas oil stocks, and is cleaned out. What is A to do? Let B go? If he does so he will be unable to sleep at night. The sense of injury, of injustice, will keep him awake. So he turns B over to the police, and they send him to prison. Thereafter A can sleep. More, he has pleasant dreams. He pictures B chained to the wall of a dungeon a hundred feet underground, devoured by rats. It is so agreeable that it makes him forget his $700. He has got his *katharsis*.

The same thing precisely takes place on a larger scale when there is a crime which destroys a whole community's feeling of security. Every law-abiding citizen feels menaced and frustrated until the criminals have been struck down—until the communal capacity to get even with them, and more than even, has been dramatically demonstrated. Here the business of deterring others is no more than an afterthought. The main thing is to destroy the scoundrels whose act has alarmed everyone, and thus made everyone unhappy. Until they are brought to book that unhappiness continues; when the law has been executed upon them there is a sigh of relief. In other words, there is *katharsis*.

There is no public demand for the death penalty for ordinary crimes, even for ordinary homicides. Its infliction, say, for necking, for playing poker or for bootlegging would shock all men of normal decency of feeling—that is to say, practically all men save the evangelical clergy and their lay catchpolls. But for crimes involving the deliberate and inexcusable taking of human life, by men openly defiant of all civilized order—for such crimes it seems, to nine men out of ten, a just and proper punishment. Any lesser punishment leaves them feeling that the criminal has got the better of society—that he can add insult to injury by laughing. That feeling is intensely unpleasant, and no wonder! It can be dissipated only by a recourse to *katharsis,* the invention of the aforesaid Aristotle. That *katharsis* is most effectively and economically achieved, as human nature now is, by wafting the criminal to realms of bliss.

4

War

My mail is flooded with the briefs and broadsides of pacifist organizations, damning war as a curse and those who make it as scoundrels. Such literature I always read attentively, for it is full of racy satire against the military, a class of men inevitably more or less ludicrous in time of peace. But does it convert me to the pacifist cause, which, as the pacifists contend, is the cause of God? I can only report simply that it does not. I read it, enjoy it, pass it on to my pastor—and go on believing in war myself.

War is the only sport, so far as I know, that **is** genuinely amusing. And it is the only sport that has any intelligible use.

The arguments that are brought against it are chiefly arguments, not against the thing itself, but only against its political accompaniments and consequences, most of them transient and gratuitous. They reached a high tide of obnoxiousness, revolting to all self-respecting men, during the last great moral combat. That combat was carried on, at least from this side of the fence, in a grossly hysterical, disingenuous, cowardly and sordid manner. The high participating parties were vastly alarmed by the foe, and insanely eager to keep business going as usual, and even better than usual. The result was that the thing began as a sort of Methodist revival and ended as a raid on a gentleman's winecellar, with the Prohibition agents fighting among themselves for the best jugs. The richest of them, once peace came, began sending the others extortionate bills for the brass-knuckles, Bibles and jimmies that all had used in common, and the heroes serving this usurer began demanding tips in cash. But all that swinishness, I submit, had no necessary connection with war itself. It is perfectly possible to conduct war in a gallant and honorable manner, and without using it as a mere cloak to rob noncombatants. More, the thing has been done, and many times in the history of the world. If it has been seldom done by democratic nations, then blame democracy, not war. In democratic nations everything noble and of good account tends to decay and smell badly.

War itself, in its pure form, is something quite different. It is a combat of men who believe that a short and adventurous life, full of changing scenes and high hazards, is better than a safe and dull one —in other words, that it is better to have lived magnificently than to have lived long. In this doctrine I am unable to discern anything properly describable as fallacy. If you argue that, assuming every man to embrace it, the human race would come to an end, I reply at once that you assume something wholly impossible. And if you argue that the life of a warrior is not actually magnificent, then I report that the warrior should be permitted to judge of that himself. Against all such arguments lie the plain facts that the great races of the world have always been more or less warlike, and that war has attracted the talent and satisfied the aspiration of some of their best men. I do not speak of antiquity alone; I speak of our own time. The English, the Germans and the French are all warlike, to-day as always—and if you took away the English, the Germans and the French *Homo sapiens* would be shorn of his stomach, his liver and his ductless glands. If war is immoral, then these great races are all immoral, and so are their greatest men. The pacifists, of course, do not shrink from that absurd argument. But the more they maintain it the more it becomes evident that, as logicians, they are on all fours with the Prohibitionists.

War, so conducted by warriors, is a superb business and full of high uses. It makes for resolution, endurance, enterprise, courage. It puts down the sordid yearnings of ignoble men. Does it, incidentally, shed some blood? Does it cost lives? The pacifists, discussing those lives, always enmesh themselves in the theory that, without war, they would go on forever. It is, I believe, not so. War, at worst, shortens them somewhat. But at the same stroke it speeds up their tempo. The net result is simply a matter of bookkeeping. A man killed at thirty, after six months of war, has lived far longer than a man dead of a bellyache at sixty, after forty-five years on an office stool.

But I am not on my legs to-day to sing the charms and glories of war; my purpose is to argue that, whether glorious or not, it will remain inevitable on this sad mud-pie so long as the great races of men retain the view of it that I have described, and to deduce therefrom the doctrine that pacifism, as a scheme of practical politics, is thus not only unsound but also very dangerous. All that it could conceivably accomplish, imagining it to succeed anywhere, would be to make the nation embracing it highly vulnerable—in brief, a sort of boozy idealist or un-armored butter-and-egg man, roaming the world un-protected, and so holding out irresistible temptations to less moral and more realistic nations.

War, under the sorry scheme that now passes for civilization, has been degraded—transiently only, I hope and believe—to the uses of robbery. Whoever has gold must have an army to guard it, or resign him-self to losing it. Especially must he have a guard for it if his public repute is that of one with a not too fine understanding of the difference between *meum* and *tuum*. Such a reputation, it must be manifest, is precisely that of the United States to-day. The rest of the world is so passionately convinced that it is a thief that robbing it would take on the high virtue and dignity of a constabulary act. It is not robbed be-cause it is strong. It will not be robbed until it grows weak.

But armed strength, argue the pacifists, does not prevent war: it causes it. Who, reading history, could believe in such transparent nonsense? Let us turn to the late enemy. What kept the peace in Europe for forty-four years if it was not the mighty German army? If it had been weak, France would have struck in 1875, and again in 1882, and again in

1887, and again every two years thereafter. It took nearly half a century to roll up a force sufficient to tackle the colossus, and it took four years to bring it down even then. Our own history is full of examples to the same effect. In 1867 Napoleon III, believing that the United States was war weary and its army disbanded, prepared to move into Mexico and tear the Monroe Doctrine to tatters. He overlooked the large forces engaged in burning barns, robbing hen-roosts and raiding cellars in the late Confederacy. When General Sheridan marched upon the Rio Grande at the head of this army of heroes, Napoleon changed his mind. Three years later he was disposed of by the Germans, and the Continent settled down to forty-four years of peace.

Consider, again, the Venezuela episode. When President Cleveland sent his message to Congress on December 17, 1895, war with England became imminent overnight. What prevented it? Was it the fact that the United States had no army worthy of the name? Or the fact that the United States had a brand-new, highly effective and immensely pugnacious navy, notoriously eager to try its guns? Come, now, to 1898. Of all the nations of Europe, only England sided with us against Spain. The Germans, at Manila, went to great lengths to show their hostility. Did they refrain from attacking Dewey because his fleet was smaller and weaker than theirs, or because it was larger and stronger?

I could multiply instances, but observe the time-keeper reaching for the gong. So far as I know, there is no record in history of a nation that ever gained anything valuable by being unable to defend itself. Such nations, true enough, have sometimes managed to exist for a time—but at what cost! There is the case of Denmark to-day. It is discussing disbanding its army on the ground that any probable or even possible foe could dispose of that army in five days. But what does this mean? It means that the Danes must reconcile themselves to living by the sheer grace of their stronger neighbors —that they must be willing, when the time comes, to see their country made a battle-ground by those neighbors, and without raising a hand. Here I do not indulge in idle talk: I am quoting almost literally a member of the Danish cabinet.

I can't imagine the people of a truly great nation submitting to any such ignominious destiny. The Danes have been forced into acquiescence by their weakness. But why should the United States invite the same fate by putting off its strength?

II. FOUR MAKERS OF TALES

1

Conrad

SOME time ago I put in a blue afternoon rereading Joseph Conrad's "Youth." A *blue* afternoon? What nonsense! The touch of the man is like the touch of Schubert. One approaches him in various and unhappy moods: depressed, dubious, despairing; one leaves him in the clear, yellow sunshine that Nietzsche found in Bizet's music. But here again the phrase is inept. Sunshine suggests the imbecile, barnyard joy of the human kohlrabi—the official optimism of a steadily delighted and increasingly insane Republic. What the enigmatical Pole has to offer is something quite different. If its parallel is to be found in music, it is not in Schubert, but in Beethoven—perhaps even more accurately in Johann Sebastian Bach. It is the joy, not of mere satisfaction, but of understanding— the profound but surely not merry delight which goes with the comprehension of a fundamental fact—above all, of a fact that has been coy and elusive. Certainly the order of the world that Conrad sets forth with such diabolical eloquence and plausibility is no banal moral order, no childish sequence of virtuous causes and edifying effects. Rather it has an atheistic and even demoniacal smack: to the earnest Bible student it must be more than a little disconcerting. The God he visualizes is no loving papa in a house-coat and carpet-slippers, inculcating the great principles of Christian ethics by applying occasional strokes *a posteriori*. What he sees is something quite different: an extremely ingenious and humorous Improvisatore and Comedian, with a dab of red on His nose and maybe somewhat the worse for drink—a furious and far from amiable banjoist upon the human spine, and rattler of human bones. Kurtz, in "Youth," makes a capital banjo for that exalted and cynical talent. And the music that issues forth—what a superb *Hexentanz* it is!

One of the curiosities of critical stupidity is the doctrine that Conrad is without humor. No doubt it flows out of a more general error; to wit, the assumption that tragedy is always pathetic, that death itself is inevitably a gloomy business. That error, I suppose, will persist in the world until some extraordinary astute mime conceives the plan of playing "King Lear" as a farce—I mean deliberately. That it *is* a farce seems to me quite as obvious as the fact that "Romeo and Juliet" is another, this time lamentably coarse. To adopt the contrary theory—to

view it as a great moral and spiritual spectacle,
capable of purging and uplifting the psyche like
marriage to a red-haired widow or a month in the
trenches—to toy with such notions is to borrow the
critical standards of a party of old ladies weeping
over the damnation of the heathen.   In point of fact,
death, like love, is intrinsically farcical—a solemn
kicking of a brick under a plug-hat—, and most other
human agonies, once they transcend the physical—
i. e., the unescapably real—have far more of irony
in them than of pathos.   Looking back upon them
after they have eased one seldom shivers: one smiles
—perhaps sourly but nevertheless spontaneously.
This, at all events, is the notion that seems to me
implicit in every line of Conrad.   I give you "Heart
of Darkness" as the archetype of his whole work and
the keystone of his metaphysical system.   Here we
have all imaginable human hopes and aspirations
reduced to one common denominator of folly and
failure, and here we have a play of humor that is
infinitely mordant and searching.   Turn to pages 136
and 137 of the American edition—the story is in the
volume called "Youth"—: the burial of the helms-
man.   Turn then to 178–184: Marlow's last inter-
view with Kurtz's intended.   The farce mounts by
slow stages to dizzy and breath-taking heights.   One
hears harsh roars of cosmic laughter, vast splutter-
ings of transcendental mirth, echoing and reëchoing

down the black corridors of empty space. The curtain descends at last upon a wild dance in a dissecting-room. The mutilated dead rise up and jig. . . .

It is curious, re-reading a thrice-familiar story, how often one finds surprises in it. I have been amazed, toward the close of "The End of the Tether," to discover that the *Fair Maid* was wrecked, not by the deliberate act of Captain Whalley, but by the machination of the unspeakable Massy. How is one to account for so preposterous an error? Certainly I thought I knew "The End of the Tether" as well as I knew anything in this world—and yet there was that incredible misunderstanding of it, lodged firmly in my mind. Perhaps there is criticism of a sort in my blunder: it may be a fact that the old skipper willed the thing himself—that his willing it is visible in all that goes before—that Conrad, in introducing Massy's puerile infamy at the end, made some sacrifice of inner veracity to the exigencies of what, at bottom, is somewhat too neat and well-made a tale. The story, in fact, belongs to the author's earlier manner; I guess that it was written before "Youth" and surely before "Heart of Darkness." But for all that, its proportions remain truly colossal. It is one of the most magnificent narratives, long or short, old or new, in the English language, and with "Youth" and "Heart of Darkness" it makes up what is probably the best book of imaginative writing that the English literature of the Twientieth Century can yet show. Conrad learned a great deal after he wrote it, true enough. In "Lord Jim," in "Victory," and, above all, in a "A Personal Record," there are momentary illuminations, blinding flashes of brilliance that he was incapable of in those days of experiment; but no other book of his seems to me to hold so steadily to so high a general level—none other, as a whole, is more satisfying and more marvelous. There is in "Heart of Darkness" a perfection of design which one encounters only rarely and miraculously in prose fiction: it belongs rather to music. I can't imagine taking a single sentence out of that stupendous tale without leaving a visible gap; it is as thoroughly *durch componiert* as a fugue. And I can't imagine adding anything to it, even so little as a word, without doing it damage. As it stands it is austerely and beautifully perfect, just as the slow movement of the Unfinished Symphony is perfect.

I observe of late a tendency to examine the English of Conrad rather biliously. This folly is cultivated chiefly in England, where, I suppose, chauvinistic motives enter into the matter. It is the just boast of great empires that they draw in talents from near and far, exhausting the little nations to augment their own puissance; it is their misfortune that these talents often remain defectively assimilated. Conrad remained the Slav to the end. The people of his tales, whatever he calls them, are always as much Slavs as he is; the language in which he describes them retains a sharp, exotic flavor. But to say that this flavor constitutes a blemish is to say something so preposterous that only schoolmasters and their dupes may be thought of as giving it credit. The truly first-rate writer is not one who uses the language as such dolts demand that it be used; he is one who reworks it in spite of their prohibitions. It is his distinction that he thinks in a manner different from the thinking of ordinary men; that he is free from that slavery to embalmed ideas which makes them so respectable and so dull. Obviously, he cannot translate his notions into terms of everyday without doing violence to their inner integrity; as well ask a Richard Strauss to funnel all his music into the chaste jugs of Prof. Dr. Jadassohn. What Conrad brought into English literature was a new concept of the relations between fact and fact, idea and idea, and what he contributed to the complex and difficult art of writing English was a new way of putting words together. His style now amazes and irritates pedants because it does not roll along in the old ruts. Well, it is precisely that rolling along in the old ruts that he tried to avoid—and it was precisely that

avoidance which made him what he is.   What lies
under most of his alleged sins seems to me to be simple
enough: he views English logically and analytically,
and not through a haze of senseless traditions and
arbitrary taboos.   No Oxford mincing is in him.
If he cannot find his phrase above the salt, he seeks
it below.   His English, in a word, is innocent.   And
if, at times, there gets into it a color that is strange
and even bizarre, then the fact is something to rejoice
over, for a living language is like a man suffering
incessantly from small internal hemorrhages, and what
it needs above all else is constant transfusions of new
blood from other tongues.   The day the gates go up,
that day it begins to die.

A very great man, this Mr. Conrad.   As yet, I
believe decidedly underestimated, even by many of
his post-mortem advocates.   Most of his first ac-
claimers mistook him for a mere romantic—a talented
but somewhat uncouth follower of the Stevenson tradition, with the orthodox cutlass exchanged for a Malay
kris.   Later on he began to be heard of as a linguistic
and vocational marvel: it was astonishing that any
man bred to Polish should write English at all, and
more astonishing that a country gentleman from the
Ukraine should hold a master's certificate in the
British merchant marine.   Such banal attitudes are
now archaic, but I suspect that they have been largely

responsible for the slowness with which his fame has spread in the world. At all events, he is vastly less read and esteemed in foreign parts than he ought to be, and very few Continental Europeans have risen to any genuine comprehension of his stature. When one reflects that the Nobel Prize was given to such third-raters as Benavente, Heidenstam, Gjellerup and Tagore, with Conrad passed over, one begins to grasp the depth and density of the ignorance prevailing in the world, even among the relatively enlightened. One "Lord Jim," as human document and as work of art, is worth all the works produced by all the Benaventes and Gjellerups since the time of Rameses II. It is, indeed, an indecency of criticism to speak of such unlike things in the same breath: as well talk of Brahms in terms of Mendelssohn. Nor is "Lord Jim" a chance masterpiece, an isolated peak. On the contrary, it is but one unit in a long series of extraordinary and almost incomparable works—a series sprung suddenly and overwhelmingly into full dignity with "Almayer's Folly." I challenge the nobility and gentry of Christendom to point to another Opus 1 as magnificently planned and turned out as "Almayer's Folly." The more one studies it, the more it seems miraculous. If it is not a work of absolute genius then no work of absolute genius exists on this earth.

2

Hergesheimer

This gentleman, like Conrad, has been slated very waspishly because his English is sometimes in contempt of Lindley Murray. Once, a few years back, a grammarian writing in the *New Republic* formally excommunicated him for it. A number of his offending locutions were cited, all of them, it must be admitted, instantly recognizable as pathological and against God by any suburban schoolma'm. *Soit!* The plain truth is that Hergesheimer, when it comes to the ultimate delicacies of English grammar, is an ignoramus, as he is when it comes to the niceties of Swedenborgian theology. I doubt that he could tell a noun in the nominative case from a noun in the objective. But neither could any other man who writes as well as he does. Such esoteric knowledge is the exclusive possesion of grammarians, whose pride in it runs in direct ratio to its inaccuracy, unimportance and imbecility. English grammar as a science thus takes its place with phrenology and the New Thought: the more a grammarian knows of it, the less he is worth listening to. Mastering such blowsy nonsense is one thing, and writing sound English is quite another thing, and the two achievements seem to be impossible to the same man.

As Anatole France once remarked, nearly all first-rate writers write "bad French"—or "bad English." Joseph Conrad did. France himself did. Dreiser does. Henry James did. Dickens did. Shakespeare did. Thus Hergesheimer need not repine. He is sinful, but in good company. He writes English that is "bad," but also English that is curiously musical, fluent, chromatic, various and caressing. There is in even the worst of his *Saturday Evening Post* novelettes for Main Street a fine feeling for the inner savor of words—a keen ear for their subtler and more fragile harmonies. In "Cytherea," which I like beyond all his works—even beyond "The Three Black Pennys" and "Java Head" —they are handled in so adept and ingenious a way, with so much delicacy and originality, that it is no wonder they offer an intolerable affront to pedagogues.

This novel, as I say, seems to me to be the best that Hergesheimer has yet done. His best writing is in it, and his best observation. What interests him fundamentally is the conflict between the natural impulses of men and women and the conventions of the society that they are parts of. The struggles he depicts are not between heroes and villains, dukes and peasants, patriots and spies, but between the desire to be happy and the desire to be respected. It is, perhaps, a tribute to the sly humor of God that whichever way the battle goes, the result is bound to be

disastrous to the man himself.   If, seeking happiness
in a world that is jealous of it and so frowns upon it,
he sacrifices the good will of his fellow men, he always finds in the end that happiness is not happiness
at all without it.   And if, grabbing the other horn of
the dilemma, he sacrifices the free play of his instincts to the respect of those fellow men, he finds that
he has also sacrificed his respect for himself.   Hergesheimer is no seer.   He does not presume to solve
the problem; he merely states it with agreeable variations and in the light of a compassionate irony.   In
"Cytherea" it takes the ancient form of the sexual
triangle—old material, but here treated, despite the
underlying skepticism, with a new illumination.
What we are asked to observe is a marriage in which
all the customary causes follow instead of precede
their customary effects.   To the eye of the world,
and even, perhaps, to the eye of the secondary figures
in it, the Randon-Grove affair is no more than a
standard-model adultery, orthodox in its origin and
in its course.   Lee Randon, with an amiable and
faithful wife, Fanny, at home in Eastlake, Pa., in the
Country-Club Belt, with two charming children at
her knee, goes to the hell-hole known as New York,
falls in love with the sinister Mrs. Savina Grove, and
forthwith bolts with her to Cuba, there to encounter a
just retribution in the form of her grotesque death.
But that is precisely what does *not* happen—that is,

interiorly. Savina actually has little more to do with the flight of Randon than the Pullman Company which hauls him southward. It is already inevitable when he leaves Eastlake for New York, almost unaware of her existence. Its springs are to be sought in the very normalcy that it so profoundly outrages. He is the victim, like Fanny, his wife, of a marriage that has turned upon and devoured itself.

Hergesheimer was never more convincing than in his anatomizing of this *débâcle*. He is too impatient, and perhaps too fine an artist, to do it in the conventional realistic manner of piling up small detail. Instead he launches into it with a bold sagittal section, and at once the play of forces becomes comprehensible. What ails Randon, in brief, is that he has a wife who is a shade too good. Beautiful, dutiful, amiable, virtuous, yes. But not provocative enough —not sufficiently the lady of scarlet in the chemise of snowy white. Worse, a touch of stupid blindness is in her: she can see the honest business man, but she can't see the romantic lurking within him. When Randon, at a country-club dance, sits out a hoe-down with some flashy houri on the stairs, all that Fanny can see in it is a vulgar matter, like kissing a chambermaid behind the door. Even when Randon brings home the doll, Cytherea, and gives it a place of honor in their house, and begins mooning over it strangely, she is unable to account for the business in any terms save those of transient silliness. The truth is that Cytherea is to Randon what La Belle Ettarre is to Cabell's Felix Kennaston—his altar-flame in a dun world, his visualization of the unattainable, his symbol of what might have been. In her presence he communes secretly with the outlaw hidden beneath the chairman of executive committees, the gypsy concealed in the sound Americano. One day, bent upon God's work (specifically, upon breaking up a nefarious affair between a neighboring Rotarian and a moving-picture lady), he encounters the aforesaid Savina Grove, accidentally brushes her patella with his own, gets an incandescent glare in return, discovers to his horror that she is the living image of Cytherea—and ten days later is aboard the Key West Express with her, bound for San Cristobal de la Habaña, and the fires eternal.

A matter, fundamentally, of coincidence. Savina, too, has her Cytherea, though not projected into a doll. She too has toiled up the long slope of a flabby marriage, and come at last to the high crags where the air is thin, and a sudden giddiness may be looked for. To call the thing a love affair, in the ordinary sense, is rather fantastic; its very endearments are forced and mawkish. What Randon wants is not more love, but an escape from the bonds and penalties of love—a leap into pure adventure. And what Savina wants, as she very frankly confesses, is the same thing. If a concrete lover must go with it, then that lover must be everything that the decorous William Loyd Grove is not—violent, exigent, savage, inordinate, even a bit gross. I doubt that Savina gets her wish any more than Randon gets his. Good business men make but indifferent Grand Turks, even when they are in revolt: it is the tragedy of Western civilization. And there is no deliverance from the bonds of habit and appearance, even with a mistress. Ten days after he reaches Havana, Randon is almost as securely married as he was at Eastlake. Worse, Eastlake itself reaches out its long arm and begins to punish him, and Savina with him. The conventions of Christendom, alas, are not to be spat upon. Far back in the Cuban hinterland, in a squalid little sugar town, it is a photograph of Fanny that gives a final touch of gruesomeness to the drama of Randon and Savina. There, overtaken in her sin by that banal likeness of the enemy she has never seen, she dies her preposterous death. An ending profoundly ironical. A curtain that gives a final touch of macabre humor to a tale that, from first to last, is full of the spirit of high comedy. Hergesheimer never devised one more sardonically amusing, and he never told one with greater skill.

The reviewers, contemplating it, were shocked by his hedonism in trivialities—his unctuous manner of recording the flavor of a drink, the sheen of a fabric, the set of a skirt, the furnishings of a room. In all that, I suppose, they saw something Babylonish, and against the Constitution. But this hedonism is really as essential a part of Hergesheimer as moral purpose is part of a Puritan. He looks upon the world, not as a trial of virtue, but as a beautiful experience—in part, indeed, as a downright voluptuous experience. If it is elevating to the soul to observe the fine colors of a sunset, then why is it not quite as elevating to observe the fine colors of a woman's hair, the silk of her frock, a piece of old mahogany, a Jack Rose cocktail? Here it is not actually Hergesheimer's delight in beauty that gives offense, but his inability to differentiate between the beauty that is also the good and the true, and the beauty that is simply beauty. As for me, I incline to go with him in his heresy. It constitutes a valuable antidote to the moral obsession which still hangs over American letters, despite the collapse of the Puritan *Kultur*. It still seems a bit foreign and bizarre, but that is because we have yet to achieve a complete emancipation from the International Sunday-school Lessons. In "Cytherea," as in "Java Head," it gives a warm and exotic glow to the narrative. That narrative is always recounted, not by a moralist, but by an artist. He knows how to give an episode color and reality by the artful use of words and the images that they bring up—how to manage the tempo, the play of light, the surrounding harmonies. This investiture is always as much a part of his story as his tale itself. So is his English style, so abhorrent to grammarians. When he writes a sentence that is a bit artificial and complex, it is because he is describing something that is itself a bit artificial and complex. When he varies his rhythms suddenly and sharply, it is not because he is unable to write in the monotonous sing-song of a rhetoric professor, but because he doesn't want to write that way. Whatever such a man writes is *ipso facto* good English. It is not for pedagogues to criticise it, but to try to comprehend it and teach it. The delusion to the contrary is the cause of much folly.

3

Lardner

A few years ago a young college professor, eager to make a name for himself, brought out a laborious "critical" edition of "Sam Slick," by Judge Thomas C. Haliburton, eighty-seven years after its first publication. It turned out to be quite unreadable—a dreadful series of archaic jocosities about varieties of *Homo americanus* long perished and forgotten, in a dialect now intelligible only to paleophilologists. Sometimes I have a fear that the same fate awaits Ring Lardner. The professors of his own day, of course, are quite unaware of him, save perhaps as a low zany to be enjoyed behind the door.   They would no more venture to whoop him up publicly and officially than their predecessors of 1880 would have ventured to whoop up Mark Twain, or their remoter predecessors of 1837 would have dared to say anything for Haliburton.   In such matters the academic mind, being chiefly animated by a fear of sneers, works very slowly.   So slowly, indeed, does it work that it usually works too late.   By the time Mark Twain got into the text-books for sophomores two-thirds of his compositions, as the Young Intellectuals say, had already begun to date; by the time Haliburton was served up as a sandwich between introduction and notes he was already dead.   As I say, I suspect sadly that Lardner is doomed to go the same route. His stories, it seems to me, are superbly adroit and amusing; no other contemporary American, sober or gay, writes better.   But I doubt that they last: our grandchildren will wonder what they are about.   It is not only, or even mainly, that the dialect that fills them will pass, though that fact is obviously a serious handicap in itself.   It is principally that the people they depict will pass, that Lardner's Low Down Americans—his incomparable baseball players, pugs, song-writers, Elks, small-town Rotarians and golf caddies—are flitting figures of a transient civilization, and doomed to be as puzzling and soporific, in the year 2000, as Haliburton's Yankee clock peddler is to-day.

The fact—if I may assume it to be a fact—is certain not to be set against Lardner's account; on the contrary, it is, in its way, highly complimentary to him. For he has deliberately applied himself, not to the anatomizing of the general human soul, but to the meticulous histological study of a few salient individuals of his time and nation, and he has done it with such subtle and penetrating skill that one must belong to his time and nation to follow him. I doubt that anyone who is not familiar with professional ball players, intimately and at first hand, will ever comprehend the full merit of the amazing sketches in "You Know Me, Al"; I doubt that anyone who has not given close and deliberate attention to the American vulgate will ever realize how magnificently Lardner handles it. He has had more imitators, I suppose, than any other living American writer, but has he any actual rivals? If so, I have yet to hear of them. They all try to write the speech of the streets as adeptly and as amusingly as he writes it, and they all fall short of him; the next best is miles and miles behind him. And they are all inferior in observation, in sense of character, in shrewdness and insight. His studies, to be sure, are never very profound; he makes no attempt to get at the primary springs of human motive; all his people share the same amiable stupidity, the same transparent vanity, the same shallow swinishness; they are all human Fords in bad repair, and alike at bottom. But if he thus confines himself to the surface, it yet remains a fact that his investigations on that surface are extraordinarily alert, ingenious and brilliant—that the character he finally sets before us, however roughly articulated as to bones, is so astoundingly realistic as to epidermis that the effect is indistinguishable from that of life itself. The old man in "The Golden Honeymoon" is not merely well done; he is perfect. And so is the girl in "Some Like Them Cold." And so, even, is the idiotic Frank X. Farrell in "Alibi Ike"—an extravagant grotesque and yet quite real from glabella to calcaneus.

Lardner knows more about the management of the short story than all of its professors. His stories are built very carefully, and yet they seem to be wholly spontaneous, and even formless. He has grasped the primary fact that no conceivable ingenuity can save a story that fails to show a recognizable and interesting character; he knows that a good character sketch is always a good story, no matter what its structure. Perhaps he gets less attention than he ought to get, even among the anti-academic critics, because his people are all lowly boors. For your reviewer of books, like every other sort of American, is always vastly impressed by fashionable pretensions. He belongs to the white collar class of labor, and shares its prejudices. He praises F. Scott Fitzgerald's stories of country-club flappers eloquently, and overlooks Fitzgerald's other stories, most of which are much better. He can't rid himself of the feeling that Edith Wharton, whose people have butlers, is a better novelist than Willa Cather, whose people, in the main, dine in their kitchens. He lingers under the spell of Henry James, whose most humble character, at any rate of the later years, was at least an Englishman, and hence superior. Lardner, so to speak, hits such critics under the belt. He not only fills his stories with people who read the tabloids, say "Shake hands with my friend," and buy diamond rings on the instalment plan; he also shows them having a good time in the world, and quite devoid of inferiority complexes. They amuse him sardonically, but he does not pity them. A fatal error! The moron, perhaps, has a place in fiction, as in life, but he is not to be treated too easily and casually. It must be shown that he suffers tragically because he cannot abandon the plow to write poetry, or the sample-case to study for opera. Lardner is more realistic. If his typical hero has a secret sorrow it is that he is too old to take up osteopathy and too much in dread of his wife to venture into bootlegging.

Of late a sharply acrid flavor has got into Lardner's

buffoonery. His baseball players and fifth-rate pugilists, beginning in his first stories as harmless jackasses, gradually convert themselves into loathsome scoundrels. The same change shows itself in Sinclair Lewis; it is difficult, even for an American, to contemplate the American without yielding to something hard to distinguish from moral indignation. Turn, for example, to the sketches in the volume called "The Love Nest." The first tells the story of a cinema queen married to a magnate of the films. On the surface she seems to be nothing but a noodle, but underneath there is a sewer; the woman is such a pig that she makes one shudder. Again, he investigates another familiar type: the village practical joker. The fellow in one form or other, has been laughed at since the days of Aristophanes. But here is a mercilessly realistic examination of his dunghill humor, and of its effects upon decent people. A third figure is a successful theatrical manager: he turns out to have the professional competence of a chiropractor and the honor of a Prohibition agent. A fourth is a writer of popular songs: stealing other men's ideas has become so fixed a habit with him that he comes to believe that he has an actual right to them. A fourth is a trained nurse—but I spare you this dreadful nurse. The rest are bores of the homicidal type. One gets the effect, communing with the whole gang, of visiting a museum of anatomy. They are as shocking as what one encounters there—but in every detail they are as unmistakably real.

Lardner conceals his new savagery, of course, beneath his old humor. It does not flag. No man writing among us has greater skill at the more extravagant varieties of jocosity. He sees startling and revelatory likeness between immensely disparate things, and he is full of pawky observations and bizarre comments. Two baseball-players are palavering, and one of them, Young Jake, is boasting of his conquests during Spring practice below the Potomac. "Down South ain't here!" replies the other. "Those dames in some of those swamps, they lose their head when they see a man with shoes on!" The two proceed to the discussion of a third imbecile, guilty of some obscure tort. "Why," inquires Young Jake, "didn't you break his nose or bust him in the chin?" "His nose was already broke," replied the other, "and he didn't have no chin." Such wise cracks seem easy to devise. Broadway diverts itself by manufacturing them. They constitute the substance of half the town shows. But in those made by Lardner there is something far more than mere facile humor: they are all rigidly in character, and they illuminate that character. Few American novelists, great or small, have character more firmly in hand. Lardner does not see situations; he sees people. And what people! They are all as revolting as so many

Methodist evangelists, and they are all as thoroughly American.

4

Masters

The case of Masters remains mysterious; more, even, than Sherwood Anderson, his fellow fugitive from a Chicago in decay, he presents an enigma to the prayerful critic. On the one hand there stands "The Spoon River Anthology," unquestionably the most eloquent, the most profound and the most thoroughly national volume of poetry published in America since "Leaves of Grass"; on the other hand stands a great mass of feeble doggerel—imitations of Byron, of Browning, of Lowell, of George H. Boker, of all the bad poets since the dawn of the Nineteenth Century. Of late he turns to prose, and with results almost as confusing. In all of his books there are fine touches, and in one of them, "Mitch Miller," there are many of them. But in all of them there are also banalities so crass and so vast that it is almost impossible to imagine a literate man letting them go by. Consider, for example, the novel, "Mirage." It seems to me to be one of the most idiotic and yet one of the most interesting American novels that I have ever read. Whole pages of it are given over to philosophical discussions that recall nothing so much as the palavers of neighboring barbers between shaves, and yet they are intermingled with observations that are shrewd and sound, and that are set forth with excellent grace and no little eloquence.   Some of the characters in the book are mere stuffed dummies, creaking in every joint; others stand out as brilliantly alive as the people of Dreiser or Miss Cather.   My suspicion is that there are actually two Masterses, that the man is a sort of literary diplococcus.   At his worst, he is intolerably affected, arty and artificial—almost a fit companion for the occult, unintelligible geniuses hymned in the *Dial*. At his best he probably gets nearer to the essential truth about the civilization we suffer under than any other contemporary literatus.

"Mirage," I daresay, is already forgotten, though it was published only in 1924.   In substance, it is the story of Skeeters Kirby's quest for the Wonder Woman that all sentimentalists seek, and that none of them finds until drink has brought him to his death-bed, and he sees the fat, affable nurse through a purple haze.   Skeeters comes from the town of Mitch Miller, and when we first encounter him he is a lawyer in Chicago.   Already the search for the Perfect Doll has begun to leave scars upon his psyche. First there was the sweet one who died before he could get her to the altar; then there was the naughty Alicia, his lawful wife, but, as he would say himself, a lemon. As the story opens, Alicia, divorcing him, had just blackmailed him out of $70,000, almost his whole fortune, as the price of her silence about Mrs. Becky Morris. Becky is the widow of a rich old man, and now enjoys the usufruct of his tenements and hereditaments. She has red hair and a charming manner, and is a great liar. She falsely pretends to have read Schopenhauer's "The World as Will and Idea," and passes in her circle as an intellectual on the strength of it. She tells Skeeters that she is virtuous, or, rather, that she *has* been virtuous, and all the while she is carrying on with one Delaher, a handsome frequenter of the Hotel Ritzdorf in New York. A saucy and poisonous baggage, this Becky, but Skeeters falls violently in love with her, and gladly pays Alicia the $70,000 in order to protect her from scandal. But then she leaves him, writes him a letter of farewell, and refuses flatly to marry him, and when he pursues her to New York, confronts her with her adulteries, and throws up to her the fact that he has gone broke for her, she requites him only with a dreadful slanging. I quote the exact text:

Kirby took a drink of brandy from the flask and came to her, taking her in his arms. "Tell, me, dear, what shall we do? Are we engaged?"

Becky shook her head.

"What do you wish? Shall I treat you as my bride-to-be, or shall we go on as we are now?"

"Go on as we are now!"

"You know I am free now—and it cost me, too, to be free."

"How much?"

"Seventy thousand dollars."

"That's not much."

"It's practically all I have."

"Well, *Alicia won't have such a large income out of it.*"

"And I paid it for you."

Becky opened her eyes. Her face became a bonfire of rage. Her red hair bristled like a wild animal's.

"You're just a liar to say that! And you can't say such things in my room. This is my room; *I pay for it.* And *you can be respectful to me here, or you can go.*"

Kirby did not betray his anger. He concentrated it and went on: *"I beg your pardon."*

In a voice as soft as oil he asked:

"Did you see Delaher?"

"Yes, I did, and he's a rough-neck."

"Well?"

"None of your business!"

"None of my business, eh?" Kirby said, with a bitter intonation.

"Leave my room," Becky said.

"No, I'll not leave your room."

"I'll have you put out."

"You don't dare, Becky—you don't dare!" . . .

Two pages more of this, and then Becky breaks out grandly:

"What do you want, anyway? You have had everything I have to give: my hospitality, *my bread, my wine, my couch, my affection, gift-tokens of my love*—what do you want?"

Kirby explains that he wants a wife and a soul-mate—"a mind to be the companion of my mind." But Becky refuses to marry him. Instead she goes to her bedroom and then returns with Kirby's letters:

"Here are your letters. You've stayed and had your say out. And now that you've said it, you can see for yourself that *you have no case against me.* . . . Here are your letters."
"I don't want them."
"Very well, I'll tear them up."
She proceeded to do so.
"Now all the evidence is destroyed," he said.

I have thrown in a few italics to point the high spots of this singular colloquy. It goes on for page after page, and the whole book is filled with dialogues like it. What is one to make of such inconceivable banality? Is there worse in "An American Tragedy"? But Masters, you may say, is trying to depict eighth-rate people—frequenters of cabarets and hotel grill-rooms, male and female Elks, dubious hangers-on upon the edges of intelligence and decency—and that is how they actually talk. It may be so, but I note at once two objections to that defense. The first is that Masters does not appear to regard Kirby as eighth-rate; on the contrary, he takes the fellow's moony drabbing quite seriously, and even tries to get a touch of the tragic into it. The second is that precisely the same hollow and meaningless fustian often appears when the author speaks in his own person. The way he tells his story is almost precisely the way it would be told by a somewhat intellectual shoe-drummer in a Pullman smoking-room. Its approach to the eternal sex question, its central theme, is exactly that of such a gentleman; its very phrases, in the main, are his phrases. He actually appears, in fact, as a sort of chorus to the drama, under the name of Bob Haydon. Bob, facing disillusion and death, favors Kirby with many cantos of philosophy. Their general burden is that the prudent man, having marked a sweet one to his taste, uses her person to his wicked ends, and then kicks her out. Kirby's agonies do not move Bob, and neither do they bore him. "Bore me!" he exclaims. "This is better than a circus!"

As I say, I have also enjoyed it myself. It is not, indeed, without its flashes of genuine sagacity; even Bob's stockbroker view of the sexual duel, given such a male as Kirby and such females as Becky, is probably more sound than not. But the chief fascination of the story, I am bound to say, lies in its very deficiencies as a human document and a work of art—in its naïve lack of humor, its elaborate laboring of the obvious, its incredible stiltedness and triteness. There are passages that actually suggest Daisy Ashforth. For example: "She was biting her nails while talking to Delaher, and biting them after he left. *Then she put on white cotton gloves to prevent this nervous habit.*" Again (Kirby has abandoned Becky for another girl, Charlotte, formerly his stenographer):

> *"May I say something to you?"* she whispered at last.
> "What is it, Charlotte?"
> "I want a child, and a child with you."

Somehow, this "May I say something to you?" gives me vast delight: the respectful politeness of the perfect stenographer surviving into the most confidential of moments! No such child is achieved— Charlotte, in fact, dies before it can be born—, and so we miss her courteous request for permission to name it after its father. But she and Kirby, alas, sin the sin, and what is worse, they sin it under his mother's roof. What is still worse, they do it with her knowledge and connivance. She is greatly taken, in fact, with Charlotte, and advises Kirby to marry her. I quote her argument:

> "If Byron had mistresses he was also a rider and a fencer and a poet; and if Webster may have been a drinker, he was great as a lawyer and a speaker. If Charlotte has had extra-marital relationships, she is a capable housekeeper,

a good secretary, a woman skilled in many things; and she has all kinds of virtues, like humor and self-control, and the spirit of happiness, and an essential honesty."

I leave the rest to posterity! What will it make of Masters as novelist? When it turns from the heroic and lovely lines of "Ann Rutledge" to the astounding banalities of "Mirage" what will it say?

III. IN MEMORIAM: W. J. B.

HAS it been duly marked by historians that the late William Jennings Bryan's last secular act on this globe of sin was to catch flies? A curious detail, and not without its sardonic overtones. He was the most sedulous flycatcher in American history, and in many ways the most successful. His quarry, of course, was not *Musca domestica* but *Homo neandertalensis*. For forty years he tracked it with coo and bellow, up and down the rustic backways of the Republic. Wherever the flambeaux of Chautauqua smoked and guttered, and the bilge of Idealism ran in the veins, and Baptist pastors dammed the brooks with the sanctified, and men gathered who were weary and heavy laden, and their wives who were full of Peruna and as fecund as the shad (*Alosa sapidissima*)— there the indefatigable Jennings set up his traps and spread his bait. He knew every country town in the South and West, and he could crowd the most remote of them to suffocation by simply winding his horn. The city proletariat, transiently flustered by him in 1896, quickly penetrated his buncombe and

would have no more of him; the cockney gallery
jeered him at every Democratic national convention
for twenty-five years.   But out where the grass grows
high, and the horned cattle dream away the lazy
afternoons, and men still fear the powers and princi-
palities of the air—out there between the corn-rows
he held his old puissance to the end.   There was no
need of beaters to drive in his game.   The news
that he was coming was enough.   For miles the
flivver dust would choke the roads.   And when he
rose at the end of the day to discharge his Message
there would be such breathless attention, such a rapt
and enchanted ecstasy, such a sweet rustle of amens
as the world had not known since Johann fell to
Herod's ax.

There was something peculiarly fitting in the fact
that his last days were spent in a one-horse Tennessee
village, and that death found him there.   The man
felt at home in such simple and Christian scenes.
He liked people who sweated freely, and were not
debauched by the refinements of the toilet.   Making
his progress up and down the Main street of little
Dayton, surrounded by gaping primates from the
upland valleys of the Cumberland Range, his coat
laid aside, his bare arms and hairy chest shining
damply, his bald head sprinkled with dust—so ac-
coutred and on display he was obviously happy.   He
liked getting up early in the morning, to the tune of

cocks crowing on the dunghill. He liked the heavy, greasy victuals of the farmhouse kitchen. He liked country lawyers, country pastors, all country people. He liked the country sounds and country smells. I believe that this liking was sincere—perhaps the only sincere thing in the man. His nose showed no uneasiness when a hillman in faded overalls and hickory shirt accosted him on the street, and besought him for light upon some mystery of Holy Writ. The simian gabble of the cross-roads was not gabble to him, but wisdom of an occult and superior sort. In the presence of city folks he was palpably uneasy. Their clothes, I suspect, annoyed him, and he was suspicious of their too delicate manners. He knew all the while that they were laughing at him—if not at his baroque theology, then at least at his alpaca pantaloons. But the yokels never laughed at him. To them he was not the huntsman but the prophet, and toward the end, as he gradually forsook mundane politics for more ghostly concerns, they began to elevate him in their hierarchy. When he died he was the peer of Abraham. His old enemy, Wilson, aspiring to the same white and shining robe, came down with a thump. But Bryan made the grade. His place in Tennessee hagiography is secure. If the village barber saved any of his hair, then it is curing gall-stones down there to-day.

But what label will he bear in more urbane regions? One, I fear, of a far less flattering kind. Bryan lived too long, and descended too deeply into the mud, to be taken seriously hereafter by fully literate men, even of the kind who write school-books. There was a scattering of sweet words in his funeral notices, but it was no more than a response to conventional sentimentality. The best verdict the most romantic editorial writer could dredge up, save in the humorless South, was to the general effect that his imbecilities were excused by his earnestness— that under his clowning, as under that of the juggler of Notre Dame, there was the zeal of a steadfast soul. But this was apology, not praise; precisely the same thing might be said of Mary Baker G. Eddy, the late Czar Nicholas, or Czolgosz. The truth is that even Bryan's sincerity will probably yield to what is called, in other fields, definitive criticism. Was he sincere when he opposed imperialism in the Philippines, or when he fed it with deserving Democrats in Santo Domingo? Was he sincere when he tried to shove the Prohibitionists under the table, or when he seized their banner and began to lead them with loud whoops? Was he sincere when he bellowed against war, or when he dreamed of himself as a tin-soldier in uniform, with a grave reserved among the generals? Was he sincere when he denounced the late John W. Davis, or when he swallowed Davis? Was he sincere when he fawned over Champ Clark, or when he betrayed Clark? Was he sincere when he pleaded for tolerance in New York, or when he bawled for the faggot and the stake in Tennessee?

This talk of sincerity, I confess, fatigues me. If the fellow was sincere, then so was P. T. Barnum. The word is disgraced and degraded by such uses. He was, in fact, a charlatan, a mountebank, a zany without shame or dignity. His career brought him into contact with the first men of his time; he preferred the company of rustic ignoramuses. It was hard to believe, watching him at Dayton, that he had traveled, that he had been received in civilized societies, that he had been a high officer of state. He seemed only a poor clod like those around him, deluded by a childish theology, full of an almost pathological hatred of all learning, all human dignity, all beauty, all fine and noble things. He was a peasant come home to the barnyard. Imagine a gentleman, and you have imagined everything that he was not. What animated him from end to end of his grotesque career was simply ambition—the ambition of a common man to get his hand upon the collar of his superiors, or, failing that, to get his thumb into their eyes. He was born with a roaring voice, and it had the trick of inflaming half-wits. His whole career was devoted to raising those half-wits against their betters, that he himself might shine.

His last battle will be grossly misunderstood if it is thought of as a mere exercise in fanaticism—that is, if Bryan the Fundamentalist Pope is mistaken for one of the bucolic Fundamentalists. There was much more in it than that, as everyone knows who saw him on the field. What moved him, at bottom, was simply hatred of the city men who had laughed at him so long, and brought him at last to so tatterdemalion an estate. He lusted for revenge upon them. He yearned to lead the anthropoid rabble against them, to punish them for their execution upon him by attacking the very vitals of their civilization. He went far beyond the bounds of any merely religious frenzy, however inordinate. When he began denouncing the notion that man is a mammal even some of the hinds at Dayton were agape. And when, brought upon Darrow's cruel hook, he writhed and tossed in a very fury of malignancy, bawling against the baldest elements of sense and decency like a man frantic—when he came to that tragic climax of his striving there were snickers among the hinds as well as hosannas.

Upon that hook, in truth, Bryan committed suicide, as a legend as well as in the body. He staggered from the rustic court ready to die, and he staggered from it ready to be forgotten, save as a character in a third-rate farce, witless and in poor taste. It was plain to everyone who knew him, when he came to

Dayton, that his great days were behind him—that, for all the fury of his hatred, he was now definitely an old man, and headed at last for silence. There was a vague, unpleasant manginess about his appearance; he somehow seemed dirty, though a close glance showed him as carefully shaven as an actor, and clad in immaculate linen. All the hair was gone from the dome of his head, and it had begun to fall out, too, behind his ears, in the obscene manner of the late Samuel Gompers. The resonance had departed from his voice; what was once a bugle blast had become reedy and quavering. Who knows that, like Demosthenes, he had a lisp? In the old days, under the magic of his eloquence, no one noticed it. But when he spoke at Dayton it was always audible.

When I first encountered him, on the sidewalk in front of the office of the rustic lawyers who were his associates in the Scopes case, the trial was yet to begin, and so he was still expansive and amiable. I had printed in the *Nation,* a week or so before, an article arguing that the Tennessee anti-evolution law, whatever its wisdom, was at least constitutional —that the rustics of the State had a clear right to have their progeny taught whatever they chose, and kept secure from whatever knowledge violated their superstitions. The old boy professed to be delighted with the argument, and gave the gaping bystanders to

understand that I was a publicist of parts. Not to
be outdone, I admired the preposterous country shirt
that he wore—sleeveless and with the neck cut very
low. We parted in the manner of two ambassadors.
But that was the last touch of amiability that I was
destined to see in Bryan. The next day the battle
joined and his face became hard. By the end of
the week he was simply a walking fever. Hour by
hour he grew more bitter. What the Christian
Scientists call malicious animal magnetism seemed
to radiate from him like heat from a stove. From
my place in the courtroom, standing upon a table,
I looked directly down upon him, sweating horribly
and pumping his palm-leaf fan. His eyes fascinated
me; I watched them all day long. They were blazing
points of hatred. They glittered like occult and
sinister gems. Now and then they wandered to me,
and I got my share, for my reports of the trial had
come back to Dayton, and he had read them. It was
like coming under fire.

Thus he fought his last fight, thirsting savagely
for blood. All sense departed from him. He bit
right and left, like a dog with rabies. He descended
to demagogy so dreadful that his very associates at
the trial table blushed. His one yearning was to
keep his yokels heated up—to lead his forlorn mob
of imbeciles against the foe. That foe, alas, refused
to be alarmed. It insisted upon seeing the whole

battle as a comedy.   Even Darrow, who knew better, occasionally yielded to the prevailing spirit.   One day he lured poor Bryan into the folly I have mentioned: his astounding argument against the notion that man is a mammal.   I am glad I heard it, for otherwise I'd never believe in it.   There stood the man who had been thrice a candidate for the Presidency of the Republic—there he stood in the glare of the world, uttering stuff that a boy of eight would laugh at!   The artful Darrow led him on: he repeated it, ranted for it, bellowed it in his cracked voice.   So he was prepared for the final slaughter.   He came into life a hero, a Galahad, in bright and shining armor.   He was passing out a poor mountebank.

The chances are that history will put the peak of democracy in America in his time; it has been on the downward curve among us since the campaign of 1896.   He will be remembered perhaps, as its supreme impostor, the *reductio ad absurdum* of its pretension.   Bryan came very near being President. In 1896, it is possible, he was actually elected.   He lived long enough to make patriots thank the inscrutable gods for Harding, even for Coolidge. Dullness has got into the White House, and the smell of cabbage boiling, but there is at least nothing to compare to the intolerable buffoonery that went on in Tennessee.   The President of the United States may be an ass, but he at least doesn't believe that the earth is square, and that witches should be put to death, and that Jonah swallowed the whale. The Golden Text is not painted weekly on the White House wall, and there is no need to keep ambassadors waiting while Pastor Simpson, of Smithville, prays for rain in the Blue Room. We have escaped something—by a narrow margin, but still we have escaped.

That is, so far. The Fundamentalists, once apparently sweeping all before them, now face minorities prepared for battle even in the South—here and there with some assurance of success. But it is too early, it seems to me, to send the firemen home; the fire is still burning on many a far-flung hill, and it may begin to roar again at any moment. The evil that men do lives after them. Bryan, in his malice, started something that it will not be easy to stop. In ten thousand country towns his old heelers, the evangelical pastors, are propagating his gospel, and everywhere the yokels are ready for it. When he disappeared from the big cities, the big cities made the capital error of assuming that he was done for. If they heard of him at all, it was only as a crimp for real-estate speculators—the heroic foe of the unearned increment hauling it in with both hands. He seemed preposterous, and hence harmless. But all the while he was busy among his old lieges, preparing for a *jacquerie* that should floor all his enemies at one blow. He did his job competently. He had vast skill as such enterprises. Heave an egg out of a Pullman window, and you will hit a Fundamentalist almost everywhere in the United States to-day. They swarm in the country towns, inflamed by their *shamans,* and with a saint, now, to venerate. They are thick in the mean streets behind the gas-works. They are everywhere where learning is too heavy a burden for mortal minds to carry, even the vague, pathetic learning on tap in little red schoolhouses. They march with the Klan, with the Christian Endeavor Society, with the Junior Order of United American Mechanics, with the Epworth League, with all the rococo bands that poor and unhappy folk organize to bring some light of purpose into their lives. They have had a thrill, and they are ready for more.

Such is Bryan's legacy to his country. He couldn't be President, but he could at least help magnificently in the solemn business of shutting off the Presidency from every intelligent and self-respecting man. The storm, perhaps, won't last long, as time goes in history. It may help, indeed, to break up the democratic delusion, now already showing weakness, and so hasten its own end. But while it lasts it will blow off some roofs.

IV. THE HILLS OF ZION

IT was hot weather when they tried the infidel Scopes at Dayton, but I went down there very willingly, for I had good reports of the sub-Potomac bootleggers, and moreover I was eager to see something of evangelical Christianity as a going concern. In the big cities of the Republic, despite the endless efforts of consecrated men, it is laid up with a wasting disease. The very Sunday-school superintendents, taking jazz from the stealthy radio, shake their fire-proof legs; their pupils, moving into adolescence, no longer respond to the proliferating hormones by enlisting for missionary service in Africa, but resort to necking and petting instead. I know of no evangelical church from Oregon to Maine that is not short of money: the graft begins to peter out, like wire-tapping and three-card monte before it. Even in Dayton, though the mob was up to do execution upon Scopes, there was a strong smell of antinomianism. The nine churches of the village were all half empty on Sunday, and weeds choked their yards. Only two or three of the resident pastors managed to sustain themselves by their ghostly science; the rest had to take orders for mail-order pantaloons or work in the adjacent strawberry fields; one, I heard, was a barber. On the courthouse green a score of sweating theologians debated the darker passages of Holy Writ day and night, but I soon found that they were all volunteers, and that the local faithful, while interested in their exegesis as an intellectual exercise, did not permit it to impede the indigenous debaucheries. Exactly twelve minutes after I reached the village I was taken in tow by a Christian man and introduced to the favorite tipple of the Cumberland Range: half corn liquor and half coco-cola. It seemed a dreadful dose to me, spoiled as I was by the bootleg light wines and beers of the Eastern seaboard, but I found that the Dayton illuminati got it down with gusto, rubbing their tummies and rolling their eyes. I include among them the chief local proponents of the Mosaic cosmogony. They were all hot for Genesis, but their faces were far too florid to belong to teetotalers, and when a pretty girl came tripping down the Main street, which was very often, they reached for the places where their neckties should have been with all the amorous enterprise of movie actors. It seemed somehow strange.

An amiable newspaper woman of Chattanooga, familiar with those uplands, presently enlightened me. Dayton, she explained, was simply a great capital like any other great capital. That is to say, it was to Rhea county what Atlanta was to Georgia or Paris to France. That is to say, it was predominantly epicurean and sinful. A country girl from some remote valley of the county, coming into town for her semi-annual bottle of Lydia Pinkham's Vegetable Compound, shivered on approaching Robinson's drug-store quite as a country girl from up-State New York might shiver on approaching the Metropolitan Opera House or the Ritz Hotel. In every village lout she saw a potential white-slaver. The hard sidewalks hurt her feet. Temptations of the flesh bristled to all sides of her, luring her to hell. This newspaper woman told me of a session with just such a visitor, holden a few days before. The latter waited outside one of the town hot-dog and coco-cola shops while her husband negotiated with a hardware merchant across the street. The newspaper woman, idling along and observing that the stranger was badly used by the heat, invited her to step into the shop for a glass of coca-cola. The invitation brought forth only a gurgle of terror. Coca-cola, it quickly appeared, was prohibited by the country lady's pastor, as a levantine and hell-sent narcotic. He also prohibited coffee and tea—and pies! He had his doubts about white bread and boughten meat. The newspaper woman, interested, inquired about ice-cream. It was, she found, not specifically prohib-

ited, but going into a coca-cola shop to get it would
be clearly sinful. So she offered to get a saucer of
it, and bring it out to the sidewalk. The visitor
vacillated—and came near being lost. But God
saved her in the nick of time. When the newspaper
woman emerged from the place she was in full flight
up the street! Later on her husband, mounted on a
mule, overtook her four miles out the mountain pike.

This newspaper woman, whose kindness covered
city infidels as well as Alpine Christians, offered
to take me back in the hills to a place where the
old-time religion was genuinely on tap. The Scopes
jury, she explained was composed mainly of its customers, with a few Dayton sophisticates added to
leaven the mass. It would thus be instructive to
climb the heights and observe the former at their
ceremonies. The trip, fortunately, might be made
by automobile. There was a road running out of
Dayton to Morgantown, in the mountains to the west-
ward, and thence beyond. But foreigners, it appeared, would have to approach the sacred grove cautiously, for the upland worshipers were very shy,
and at the first sight of a strange face they would ad-
journ their orgy and slink into the forest. They
were not to be feared, for God had long since forbidden them to practice assassination, or even assault,
but if they were alarmed a rough trip would go for
naught. So, after dreadful bumpings up a long and

narrow road, we parked our car in a little woodpath a mile or two beyond the tiny village of Morgantown, and made the rest of the approach on foot, deployed like skirmishers. Far off in a dark, romantic glade a flickering light was visible, and out of the silence came the rumble of exhortation. We could distinguish the figure of the preacher only as a moving mote in the light: it was like looking down the tube of a dark-field microscope. Slowly and cautiously we crossed what seemed to be a pasture, and then we crouched down along the edge of a cornfield, and stealthily edged further and further. The light now grew larger and we could begin to make out what was going on. We went ahead on all fours, like snakes in the grass.

From the great limb of a mighty oak hung a couple of crude torches of the sort that car inspectors thrust under Pullman cars when a train pulls in at night. In the guttering glare was the preacher, and for a while we could see no one else. He was an immensely tall and thin mountaineer in blue jeans, his collarless shirt open at the neck and his hair a tousled mop. As he preached he paced up and down under the smoking flambeaux, and at each turn he thrust his arms into the air and yelled "Glory to God!" We crept nearer in the shadow of the cornfield, and began to hear more of his discourse. He was preaching on the Day of Judgment. The high kings of the earth, he roared, would all fall down and die; only the sanctified would stand up to receive the Lord God of Hosts. One of these kings he mentioned by name, the king of what he called Greece-y. The king of Greece-y, he said, was doomed to hell. We crawled forward a few more yards and began to see the audience. It was seated on benches ranged round the preacher in a circle. Behind him sat a row of elders, men and women. In front were the younger folk. We crept on cautiously, and individuals rose out of the ghostly gloom. A young mother sat suckling her baby, rocking as the preacher paced up and down. Two scared little girls hugged each other, their pigtails down their backs. An immensely huge mountain woman, in a gingham dress, cut in one piece, rolled on her heels at every "Glory to God!" To one side, and but half visible, was what appeared to be a bed. We found afterward that half a dozen babies were asleep upon it.

The preacher stopped at last, and there arose out of the darkness a woman with her hair pulled back into a little tight knot. She began so quietly that we couldn't hear what she said, but soon her voice rose resonantly and we could follow her. She was denouncing the reading of books. Some wandering book agent, it appeared, had come to her cabin and tried to sell her a specimen of his wares. She refused to touch it. Why, indeed, read a book? If what was in it was true, then everything in it was already in the Bible. If it was false, then reading it would imperil the soul. This syllogism from Caliph Omar complete, she sat down. There followed a hymn, led by a somewhat fat brother wearing silver-rimmed country spectacles. It droned on for half a dozen stanzas, and then the first speaker resumed the floor. He argued that the gift of tongues was real and that education was a snare. Once his children could read the Bible, he said, they had enough. Beyond lay only infidelity and damnation. Sin stalked the cities. Dayton itself was a Sodom. Even Morgantown had begun to forget God. He sat down, and a female aurochs in gingham got up. She began quietly, but was soon leaping and roaring, and it was hard to follow her. Under cover of the turmoil we sneaked a bit closer.

A couple of other discourses followed, and there were two or three hymns. Suddenly a change of mood began to make itself felt. The last hymn ran longer than the others, and dropped gradually into a monotonous, unintelligible chant. The leader beat time with his book. The faithful broke out with exultations. When the singing ended there was a brief palaver that we could not hear, and two of the men moved a bench into the circle of light directly under the flambeaux. Then a half-grown girl emerged from the darkness and threw herself upon it. We noticed with astonishment that she had bobbed hair. "This sister," said the leader, "has asked for prayers." We moved a bit closer. We could now see faces plainly, and hear every word. What followed quickly reached such heights of barbaric grotesquerie that it was hard to believe it real. At a signal all the faithful crowded up to the bench and began to pray—not in unison, but each for himself! At another they all fell on their knees, their arms over the penitent. The leader kneeled facing us, his head alternately thrown back dramatically or buried in his hands. Words spouted from his lips like bullets from a machine-gun—appeals to God to pull the penitent back out of hell, defiances of the demons of the air, a vast impassioned jargon of apocalyptic texts. Suddenly he rose to his feet, threw back his head and began to speak in the tongues —blub-blub-blub, gurgle-gurgle-gurgle. His voice rose to a higher register. The climax was a shrill, inarticulate squawk, like that of a man throttled. He fell headlong across the pyramid of suppliants.

A comic scene? Somehow, no. The poor half-wits were too horribly in earnest. It was like peeping through a knothole at the writhings of people in pain. From the squirming and jabbering mass a young woman gradually detached herself—a woman not uncomely, with a pathetic homemade cap on her head. Her head jerked back, the veins of her neck swelled, and her fists went to her throat as if she were fighting for breath. She bent backward until she was like half a hoop. Then she suddenly snapped forward. We caught a flash of the whites of her eyes. Presently her whole body began to be convulsed—great throes that began at the shoulders and ended at the hips. She would leap to her feet, thrust her arms in air, and then hurl herself upon the heap. Her praying flattened out into a mere delirious caterwauling, like that of a Tom cat on a petting party. I describe the thing discreetly, and as a strict behaviorist. The lady's subjective sensations I leave to infidel pathologists, privy to the works of Ellis, Freud and Moll. Whatever they were, they were obviously not painful, for they were accompanied by vast heavings and gurglings of a joyful and even ecstatic nature. And they seemed to be contagious, too, for soon a second penitent, also female, joined the first, and then came a third, and a fourth, and a fifth. The last one had an extraordinary violent attack. She began with mild enough jerks of the head, but in a moment she was bounding all over the place, like a chicken with its head cut off. Every time her head came up a stream of hosannas would issue out of it. Once she collided with a dark, undersized brother, hitherto silent and stolid. Contact with her set him off as if he had been kicked by a mule. He

leaped into the air, threw back his head, and began
to gargle as if with a mouthful of BB shot. Then he
loosed one tremendous, stentorian sentence in the
tongues, and collapsed.

By this time the performers were quite oblivious
to the profane universe and so it was safe to go still
closer. We left our hiding and came up to the
little circle of light. We slipped into the vacant
seats on one of the rickety benches. The heap of
mourners was directly before us. They bounced into
us as they cavorted. The smell that they radiated,
sweating there in that obscene heap, half suffocated
us. Not all of them, of course, did the thing in the
grand manner. Some merely moaned and rolled
their eyes. The female ox in gingham flung her great
bulk on the ground and jabbered an unintelligible
prayer. One of the men, in the intervals between fits,
put on his spectacles and read his Bible. Beside me
on the bench sat the young mother and her baby.
She suckled it through the whole orgy, obviously
fascinated by what was going on, but never venturing
to take any hand in it. On the bed just outside the
light half a dozen other babies slept peacefully. In
the shadows, suddenly appearing and as suddenly
going away, were vague figures, whether of believers
or of scoffers I do not know. They seemed to come
and go in couples. Now and then a couple at the
ringside would step out and vanish into the black

night. After a while some came back, the males
looking somewhat sheepish. There was whispering
outside the circle of vision. A couple of Fords
lurched up the road, cutting holes in the darkness
with their lights. Once some one out of sight loosed
a bray of laughter.

All this went on for an hour or so. The original
penitent, by this time, was buried three deep beneath
the heap. One caught a glimpse, now and then, of
her yellow bobbed hair, but then she would vanish
again. How she breathed down there I don't know;
it was hard enough six feet away, with a strong five-
cent cigar to help. When the praying brothers would
rise up for a bout with the tongues their faces were
streaming with perspiration. The fat harridan in
gingham sweated like a longshoreman. Her hair
got loose and fell down over her face. She fanned
herself with her skirt. A powerful old gal she was,
plainly equal in her day to a bout with obstetrics and
a week's washing on the same morning, but this was
worse than a week's washing. Finally, she fell into
a heap, breathing in great, convulsive gasps.

Finally, we got tired of the show and returned to
Dayton. It was nearly eleven o'clock—an immensely
late hour for those latitudes—but the whole town was
still gathered in the courthouse yard, listening to the
disputes of theologians. The Scopes trial had
brought them in from all directions. There was a

friar wearing a sandwich sign announcing that he
was the Bible champion of the world. There was
a Seventh Day Adventist arguing that Clarence
Darrow was the beast with seven heads and ten horns
described in Revelation xiii, and that the end of
the world was at hand. There was an evangelist
made up like Andy Gump, with the news that atheists
in Cincinnati were preparing to descend upon Dayton,
hang the eminent Judge Raulston, and burn the town.
There was an ancient who maintained that no Catholic
could be a Christian. There was the eloquent Dr.
T. T Martin, of Blue Mountain, Miss., come to town
with a truck-load of torches and hymn-books to put
Darwin in his place. There was a singing brother
bellowing apocalyptic hymns. There was William
Jennings Bryan, followed everywhere by a gaping
crowd. Dayton was having a roaring time. It was
better than the circus. But the note of devotion was
simply not there; the Daytonians, after listening a
while, would slip away to Robinson's drug-store to
regale themselves with coca-cola, or to the lobby of
the Aqua Hotel, where the learned Raulston sat in
state, judicially picking his teeth. The real religion
was not present. It began at the bridge over the
town creek, where the road makes off for the hills.

V. BEETHOVEN

BEETHOVEN was one of those lucky men whose stature, viewed in retrospect, grows steadily. How many movements have there been to put him on the shelf? At least a dozen in the hundred years since his death. There was one only a few years ago in New York, launched by idiot critics and supported by the war fever: his place, it appeared, was to be taken by such prophets of the new enlightenment as Stravinsky! The net result of that movement was simply that the best orchestra in America went to pot—and Beethoven survived unscathed. It is, indeed, almost impossible to imagine displacing him—at all events, in the concert-hall, where the challenge of Bach cannot reach him. Surely the Nineteenth Century was not deficient in master musicians. It produced Schubert, Schumann, Chopin, Wagner and Brahms, to say nothing of a whole horde of Dvořáks, Tschaikowskys, Debussys, Raffs, Verdis and Puccinis. Yet it gave us nothing better than the first movement of the Eroica. That movement, the first challenge of the new music, remains its last word. It is the noblest piece of absolute music ever written in the sonata form, and it is the noblest piece of program music. In Beethoven, indeed, the distinction between the two became purely imaginary. Everything he wrote was, in a way, program music, including even the first two symphonies, and everything was absolute music, including even the Battle grotesquerie. (Is the latter, indeed, as bad as ancient report makes it? Why doesn't some *Kappellmeister* let us hear it?)

It was a bizarre jest of the gods to pit Beethoven, in his first days in Vienna, against Papa Haydn. Haydn was undeniably a genius of the first water, and, after Mozart's death, had no apparent reason to fear a rival. If he did not actually create the symphony as we know it to-day, then he at least enriched the form with its first genuine masterpieces—and not with a scant few, but literally with dozens. Tunes of the utmost loveliness gushed from him like oil from a well. More, he knew how to manage them; he was a master of musical architectonics. If his music is sniffed at to-day, then it is only by fools; there are at least six of his symphonies that are each worth all the cacophony hatched by a whole herd of Schönbergs and Eric Saties, with a couple of Korngolds thrown in to flavor the pot. But when Beethoven stepped in, then poor old Papa had to step down. It was like pitting a gazelle against an aurochs. One colossal bellow, and the combat was over. Musicians are apt to look at it as a mere contest of technicians. They point to the vastly greater skill and ingenuity of Beethoven —his firmer grip upon his materials, his greater daring and resourcefulness, his far better understanding of dynamics, rhythms and clang-tints—in brief, his tremendously superior musicianship. But that was not what made him so much greater than Haydn—for Haydn, too, had his superiorities; for example, his far readier inventiveness, his capacity for making better tunes. What lifted Beethoven above the old master, and above all other men of music save perhaps Bach and Brahms, was simply his greater dignity as a man. The feelings that Haydn put into tone were the feelings of a country pastor, a rather civilized stockbroker, a viola player gently mellowed by Kulmbacher. When he wept it was with the tears of a woman who has discovered another wrinkle; when he rejoiced it was with the joy of a child on Christmas morning. But the feelings that Beethoven put into his music were the feelings of a god. There was something olympian in his snarls and rages, and there was a touch of hell-fire in his mirth.

It is almost a literal fact that there is not a trace of cheapness in the whole body of his music. He is never sweet and romantic; he never sheds conventional tears; he never strikes orthodox attitudes. In his lightest moods there is the immense and inescapable dignity of the ancient Hebrew prophets. He concerns himself, not with the puerile agonies of love, but with the eternal tragedy of man. He is a great tragic poet, and like all great tragic poets, he is obsessed by a sense of the inscrutable meaninglessness of life. From the Eroica onward he seldom departs from that theme. It roars through the first movement of the C minor, and it comes to a stupendous final statement in the Ninth. All this, in his day, was new in music, and so it caused murmurs of surprise and even indignation. The step from Mozart's Jupiter to the first movement of the Eroica was uncomfortable; the Viennese began to wriggle in their stalls. But there was one among them who didn't wriggle, and that was Franz Schubert. Turn to the first movement of his Unfinished or to the slow movement of his Tragic, and you will see how quickly the example of Beethoven was followed—and with what genius! But there was a long hiatus after that, with Mendelssohn, Weber, Chopin and company performing upon their pretty pipes. Eventually the day of November 6, 1876, dawned in Karlsruhe, and with it came the first performance of Brahms' C minor. Once more the gods walked in the concert-hall. They will walk again when another Brahms is born, but not before. For nothing can come out of an artist that is not in the man. What ails the music of all the Tschaikowskys,

Stravinskys—and Strausses? What ails it is that it is the music of shallow men. It is often, in its way, lovely. It bristles with charming musical ideas. It is infinitely ingenious and workmanlike. But it is as hollow, at bottom, as a bull by Bishop Manning. It is the music of second-rate men.

Beethoven disdained all their artifices: he didn't need them. It would be hard to think of a composer, even of the fourth rate, who worked with thematic material of less intrinsic merit. He borrowed tunes wherever he found them; he made them up out of snatches of country jigs; when he lacked one altogether he contented himself with a simple phrase, a few banal notes. All such things he viewed simply as raw materials; his interest was concentrated upon their use. To that use of them he brought the appalling powers of his unrivaled genius. His ingenuity began where that of other men left off. His most complicated structures retained the overwhelming clarity of the Parthenon. And into them he got a kind of feeling that even the Greeks could seldom match; he was preëminently a modern man, with all trace of the barbarian vanished. In his gorgeous music there went all of the high skepticism that was of the essence of the Eighteenth Century, but into it there also went the new enthusiasm, the new determination to challenge and beat the gods, that dawned with the Nineteenth.

The older I grow, the more I am convinced that the most portentous phenomenon in the whole history of music was the first public performance of the Eroica on April 7, 1805. The manufacturers of program notes have swathed that gigantic work in so many layers of childish legend and speculation that its intrinsic merits have been almost forgotten. Was it dedicated to Napoleon I? If so, was the dedication sincere or ironical? Who cares—that is, who with ears? It might have been dedicated, just as well, to Louis XIV, Paracelsus or Pontius Pilate. What makes it worth discussing, to-day and forever, is the fact that on its very first page Beethoven threw his hat into the ring and laid his claim to immortality. Bang!—and he is off! No compromise! No easy bridge from the past! The Second Symphony is already miles behind. A new order of music has been born. The very manner of it is full of challenge. There is no sneaking into the foul business by way of a mellifluous and disarming introduction; no preparatory hemming and hawing to cajole the audience and enable the conductor to find his place in the score. Nay! Out of silence comes the angry crash of the tonic triad, and then at once, with no pause, the first statement of the first subject—grim, domineering, harsh, raucous, and yet curiously lovely—with its astounding collision with that electrical C sharp. The carnage has begun early; we

are only in the seventh measure! In the thirteenth and fourteenth comes the incomparable roll down the simple scale of E flat—and what follows is all that has ever been said, perhaps all that ever *will* be said, about music-making in the grand manner. What was afterward done, even by Beethoven, was done in the light of that perfect example. Every line of modern music that is honestly music bears some sort of relation to that epoch-making first movement.

The rest is Beethovenish, but not quintessence. There is a legend that the funeral march was put in simply because it was a time of wholesale butchery, and funeral marches were in fashion. No doubt the first-night audience in Vienna, shocked and addled by the piled-up defiances of the first movement, found the lugubrious strains grateful. But the *scherzo?* Another felonious assault upon poor Papa Haydn! Two giants boxing clumsily, to a crazy piping by an orchestra of dwarfs. No wonder some honest Viennese in the gallery yelled: "I'd give another kreutzer if the thing would stop!" Well, it stopped finally, and then came something reassuring—a theme with variations. Everyone in Vienna knew and esteemed Beethoven's themes with variations. He was, in fact, the rising master of themes with variations in the town. But a joker remained in the pack. The variations grew more and more complex and surprising. Strange novelties got into them.

The polite exercises became tempestuous, moody, cacophonous, tragic.   At the end a harsh, hammering, exigent row of chords—the C minor Symphony casting its sinister shadow before!

It must have been a great night in Vienna.   But perhaps not for the actual Viennese.   They went to hear "a new grand symphony in D sharp" ·(*sic!*). What they found in the Theater-an-der-Wien was a revolution!

VI. RONDO ON AN ANCIENT
THEME

I T is the economic emancipation of woman, I
suppose, that must be blamed for the present
wholesale discussion of the sex question, so
offensive to the romantic. Eminent authorities have
full often described, and with the utmost heat and
eloquence, her state before she was delivered from
her fetters and turned loose to root or die. Almost
her only feasible trade, in those dark days, was that
of wife. True enough, she might also become a
servant girl, or go to work in a factory, or offer herself upon the streets, but all of those vocations were
so revolting that no rational woman followed them if
she could help it: she would leave any one of them at
a moment's notice at the call of a man, for the call
of a man meant promotion for her, economically and
socially. The males of the time, knowing what a
boon they had to proffer, drove hard bargains. They
demanded a long list of high qualities in the woman
they summoned to their seraglios, but most of all
they demanded what they called virtue. It was not
sufficient that a candidate should be anatomically un-

defiled; she must also be pure in mind.   There was, of course, but one way to keep her so pure, and that was by building a high wall around her mind, and hitting her with a club every time she ventured to peer over it.   It was as dangerous, in that Christian era, for a woman to show any interest in or knowledge of the great physiological farce of sex as it would be to-day for a presidential candidate to reveal himself in his cups on the hustings.   Everyone knew, to be sure, that as a mammal she had sex, and that as a potential wife and mother she probably had some secret interest in its phenomena, but it was felt, perhaps wisely, that even the most academic theorizing had within it the deadly germs of the experimental method, and so she was forbidden to think about the matter at all, and whatever information she acquired at all she had to acquire by a method of bootlegging.

The generation still on its legs has seen the almost total collapse of that naïve and constabulary system, and of the economic structure supporting it.   Beginning with the eighties of the last century, there rose up a harem rebellion which quickly knocked both to pieces.   The women of the Western World not only began to plunge heroically into all of the old professions, hitherto sacred to men; they also began to invent a lot of new professions, many of them unimagined by men.   Worse, they began to succeed in them.   The working woman of the old days worked only until she could snare a man; any man was better than her work. But the working woman of the new days was under no such pressure; her work made her a living and sometimes more than a living; when a man appeared in her net she took two looks at him, one of them usually very searching, before landing him. The result was an enormous augmentation of her feeling of self-sufficiency, her spirit of independence, her natural inclination to get two sides into the bargaining. The result, secondarily, was a revolt against all the old taboos that had surrounded her, all the childish incapacities and ignorances that had been forced upon her. The result, tertiarily, was a vast running amok in the field that, above all others, had been forbidden to her: that of sexual knowledge and experiment.

We now suffer from the effects of that running amok. It is women, not men, who are doing all the current gabbling about sex, and proposing all the new-fangled modifications of the rules and regulations ordained by God, and they are hard at it very largely, I suppose, because being at it at all is a priviilege that is still new to them. The whole order of human females, in other words, is passing through a sort of intellectual adolescence, and it is disturbed as greatly as biological adolescents are by the spouting of the hormones. The attitude of men toward the sex question, it seems to me, has not changed greatly in my time. Barring a few earnest men whose mental processes, here as elsewhere, are essentially womanish, they still view it somewhat jocosely. Taking one with another, they believe that they know all about it that is worth knowing, and so it does not challenge their curiosity, and they do not put in much time discussing it, save mockingly. But among the women, if a bachelor may presume to judge, interest in it is intense. They want to know all that is known about it, all that has been guessed and theorized about it; they bristle with ideas of their own about it. It is hard to find a reflective woman, in these days, who is not harboring some new and startling scheme for curing the evils of monogamous marriage; it is impossible to find any woman who has not given ear to such schemes. Women, not men, read the endless books upon the subject that now rise mountain-high in all the book-stores, and women, not men, discuss and rediscuss the notions in them. An acquaintance of mine, a distinguished critic, owns a copy of one of the most revolutionary of these books, by title "The Art of Love," that was suppressed on the day of its publication by the alert Comstocks. He tells me that he has already lent it to twenty-six women and that he has more than fifty applications for it on file. Yet he has never read it himself!

As a professional fanatic for free thought and free speech, I can only view all this uproar in the *Frauenzimmer* with high satisfaction. It gives me delight to see a taboo violated, and that delight is doubled when the taboo is one that is wholly senseless. Sex is more important to women than to men, and so they ought to be free to discuss it as they please, and to hatch and propagate whatever ideas about it occur to them. Moreover, I can see nothing but nonsense in the doctrine that their concern with such matters damages their charm. So far as I am concerned, a woman who knows precisely what a Graafian follicle is is just as charming as one who doesn't—just as charming, and far less dangerous. Charm in women, indeed, is a variable star, and shows different colors at different times. When their chief mark was ignorance, then the most ignorant was the most charming; now that they begin to think deeply and indignantly there is charm in their singular astuteness. But I am inclined to believe that they have not yet attained to a genuine astuteness in the new field of sex. To the contrary, it seems to me that a fundamental error contaminates their whole dealing with the subject, and that is the error of assuming that sexual questions, whether social, physiological, or pathological, are of vast and even paramount importance to mankind in general—in brief, that sex is really a first-rate matter.

I doubt it. I believe that in this department men show better judgment than women, if only because their information is older and their experience wider.

Their tendency is to dismiss the whole thing lightly, to reduce sex to the lowly estate of an afterthought and a recreation, and under that tendency there is a sound instinct. I do not believe that the lives of normal men are much colored or conditioned, either directly or indirectly, by purely sexual considerations. I believe that nine-tenths of them would carry on all the activities which engage them now, and with precisely the same humorless diligence, if there were not a woman in the world. The notion that man would not work if he lacked an audience, and that the audience must be a woman, seems to me to be a hollow sentimentality. Men work because they want to eat, because they want to feel secure, because they long to shine among their fellows, and for no other reason. A man may crave his wife's approbation, or some other woman's approbation, of his social graces, of his taste, of his generosity and courage, of his general dignity in the world, but long before he ever gives thought to such things and long after he has forgotten them he craves the approbation of his fellow men. Above all, he craves the approbation of his fellow craftsmen—the men who understand exactly what he is trying to do, and are expertly competent to judge his doing of it. Can you imagine a surgeon putting the good opinion of his wife above the good opinion of other surgeons? If you can, then you can do something that I cannot.

Here, of course, I do not argue absurdly that the good opinion of his wife is nothing to him. Obviously, it is a lot, for if it does not constitute the principal reward of his work, then it at least constitutes the principal joy of his hours of ease, when his work is done. He wants his wife to respect and admire him; to be able to make her do it is also a talent. But if he is intelligent he must discover very early that her respect and admiration do not necessarily run in direct ratio to his intrinsic worth, that the qualities and acts that please her are not always the qualities and acts that are most satisfactory to the censor within him—in brief, that the relation between man and woman, however intimate they may seem, must always remain a bit casual and superficial —that sex, at bottom, belongs to comedy and the cool of the evening and not to the sober business that goes on in the heat of the day. That sober business, as I have said, would still go on if woman were abolished and heirs and assigns were manufactured in rolling-mills. Men would not only work as hard as they do to-day; they would also get almost as much satisfaction out of their work. For of all the men that I know on this earth, ranging from poets to ambassadors and from bishops to statisticians, I know none who labors primarily because he wants to please a woman. They are all hard at it because they want to impress other men and so please themselves.

Woman, plainly enough, are in a far different case. Their emancipation has not yet gone to the length of making them genuinely free. They have rid themselves, very largely, of the absolute need to please men, but they have not yet rid themselves of the impulse to please men. Perhaps they never will: one might easily devise a plausible argument to that effect on biological grounds. But sufficient unto the day is the phenomenon before us: they have got rid of the old taboo which forbade them to think and talk about sex, and they still labor under the old superstition that sex is a matter of paramount importance. The result, in my judgment, is an absurd emission of piffle. In every division there is vast and often ludicrous exaggeration. The campaign for birth control takes on the colossal proportions of the war for democracy. The venereal diseases are represented to be as widespread, at least in men, as colds in the head, and as lethal as apoplexy or cancer. Great hordes of viragoes patrol the country, instructing school-girls in the mechanics of reproduction and their mothers in obstetrics. The light-hearted monogamy which produced all of us is denounced as an infamy comparable to cannibalism. Laws are passed regulating the mating of human beings as if they were horned cattle and converting marriage into a sort of coroner's inquest. Over all sounds the battle-cry of quacks and zealots at all times and everywhere: *Veritas liberabit vos!*

The truth? How much of this new gospel is actually truth? Perhaps two per cent. The rest is idle theorizing, doctrinaire nonsense, mere scandalous rubbish. All that is worth knowing about sex—all, that is, that is solidly established and of sound utility —can be taught to any intelligent boy of sixteen in two hours. Is it taught in the current books, so enormously circulated? I doubt it. Absolutely without exception these books admonish the poor apprentice to renounce sex altogether—to sublimate it, as the favorite phrase is, into a passion for free verse, Rotary or the League of Nations. This admonition is silly, and, I believe, dangerous. It is as much a folly to lock up sex in the hold as it is to put it in command on the bridge. Its proper place is in the social hall. As a substitute for all such nonsense I drop a pearl of wisdom, and pass on. To wit: the strict monogamist never gets into trouble.

VII. PROTESTANTISM IN THE REPUBLIC

THAT Protestantism in this great Christian realm is down with a wasting disease must be obvious to every amateur of ghostly pathology. The denominational papers are full of alarming reports from its bedside, and all sorts of projects for the relief of the patient. One authority holds that only more money is needed to work a cure—that if the Christian exploiters and usurers of the country would provide a sufficient slush fund, all the vacant pews could be filled, and the baptismal tanks with them. Another authority argues that the one way to save the churches is to close all other places of resort and amusement on the Sabbath, from delicatessen shops to road-houses, and from movie parlors to jazz palaces. Yet another proposes a mass attack by prayer, apparently in the hope of provoking a miracle. A fourth advocates a vast augmentation of so-called institutional effort, *i. e.*, the scheme of putting bowling alleys and courting cubicles into church cellars, and of giving over the rest of every sacred edifice to debates on the Single Tax, boxing matches, baby shows, mental hygiene clinics, lectures by converted actors, movie shows, raffles, non-voluptuous dances, and evening classes in salesmanship, automobile repairing, birth control, interior decoration, and the art and mystery of the realtor. A fifth, borrowing a leaf from Big Business, maintains that consolidation and reorganization are what is needed—that the existence of half a dozen rival churches in every American village profits the devil a great deal more than it profits God. This last scheme seems to have won a great deal of support among the pious. At least a score of committees are now trying to draw up plans for concrete consolidations, and even the Southern and Northern Methodists, who hate each other violently, have been in peaceful though vain negotiation.

On the merits of these conflicting remedies I attempt no pronouncement, but I have been at some pains to look into the symptoms and nature of the disease. My report is that it seems to me to be analogous to that malady which afflicts a star in the heavens when it splits into two halves and they go slambanging into space in opposite directions. That, in brief, is what appears to be the matter with Protestantism in the United States to-day. One half of it is moving, with slowly accelerating speed, in the direction of the Harlot of the Seven Hills: the other is sliding down into voodooism. The former carries the greater part of Protestant money with it; the latter carries the greater part of Protestant enthusiasm, or, as the word now is, pep. What remains in the middle may be likened to a torso without either brains to think with or legs to dance—in other words, something that begins to be professionally attractive to the mortician, though it still makes shift to breathe. There is no lack of life on the higher levels, where the most solvent Methodists and the like are gradually transmogrified into Episcopalians, and the Episcopalians shin up the ancient bastions of Holy Church, and there is no lack of life on the lower levels, where the rural Baptists, by the route of Fundamentalism, the Anti-Saloon League, and the Ku Klux Klan, rapidly descend to the dogmas and practices of the Congo jungle. But in the middle there is desiccation and decay. Here is where Protestantism was once strongest. Here is the region of the plain and godly Americano, fond of devotion but distrustful of every hint of orgy—the honest fellow who suffers dutifully on Sunday, pays his share, and hopes for a few kind words from the pastor when his time comes to die. He stands to-day on a burning deck. It is no wonder that Sunday automobiling begins to get him in its clutches. If he is not staggered one day by his pastor's appearance in surplice and stole, he is staggered the day following by a file of Ku Kluxers marching up the aisle. So he tends to absent himself from pious exercises, and the news goes about that there is something the matter with the churches, and the denominational papers bristle with schemes to set it right, and many up-and-coming pastors, tiring of preaching and parish work, get excellent jobs as the executive secretaries of these schemes, and go about the country expounding them to the faithful.

The extent to which Protestantism, in its upper reaches, has succumbed to the harlotries of Rome seems to be but little apprehended by the majority of connoisseurs. I was myself unaware of the whole truth until last Christmas, when, in the pursuit of a quite unrelated inquiry, I employed agents to attend all the services held in the principal Protestant basilicas of an eminent American city, and to bring in the best reports they could formulate upon what went on in the lesser churches. The substance of these reports, in so far as they related to churches patronized by the well-to-do, was simple: they revealed a headlong movement to the right, an almost precipitate flight over the mountain. Six so-called Episcopal churches held midnight services on Christmas Eve in obvious imitation of Catholic midnight masses, and one of them actually called its service a solemn high mass. Two invited the nobility and gentry to processions, and a third concealed a procession under the name of a pageant. One offered Gounod's St. Cecilia mass on Christmas morning, and another the

Messe Solennelle by the same composer; three others, somewhat more timorous, contented themselves with parts of masses.   One, throwing off all pretense and euphemism, summoned the faithful to no less than three Christmas masses, naming them by name—two low and one high.   All six churches were aglow with candles, and two employed incense.

But that was not the worst.   Two Presbyterian churches and one Baptist church, not to mention five Lutheran churches of different synods, had choral services in the dawn of Christmas morning, and the one attended by the only one of my agents who got up early enough—it was in a Presbyterian church— was made gay with candles, and had a palpably Roman smack.   Yet worse: a rich and conspicuous Methodist church, patronized by the leading Wesleyan wholesalers and money-lenders of the town, boldly offered a mediæval carol service.   Mediæval? What did that mean?   The Middle Ages ended on July 16, 1453, at 12 o'clock meridian, and the Reformation was not launched by Luther until October 31, 1517, at 10.15 A. M.   If mediæval, in the sense in which it was here used, does not mean Roman Catholic, then I surely went to school in vain.   My agent, born a Methodist, reported that the whole ceremony shocked him excessively.   It began with trumpet blasts from the church spire and it concluded with an Ave Maria by a vested choir!   Candles rose up in glittering ranks behind the chancel rail, and above them glowed a shining electric star. God help us all, indeed! What next? Will the rev. pastor, on some near to-morrow, defy the lightnings of Jahveh by appearing in alb and dalmatic? Will he turn his back upon the faithful? Will he put in a telephone-booth for auricular confession? I shudder to think of what old John Wesley would have said about that vested choir and that shining star. Or Bishop Francis Asbury. Or the Rev. Jabez Bunting. Or Robert Strawbridge, that consecrated man.

Here, of course, I do not venture into the contumacy of criticising; I merely marvel. A student of the sacred sciences all my life, I am well learned in the dogmas and ceremonials of the sects, and know what they affect and what they abhor. Does anyone argue that the use of candles in public worship would have had the sanction of the *Ur*-Weslcyans, or that they would have consented to *Blasmusik* and a vested choir? If so, let the scioist come forward. Down to fifty years ago, in fact, the Methodists prohibited Christmas services altogether, as Romish and heathen. But now we have ceremonies almost operatic, and the sweet masses of Gounod are just around the corner! As I have said, the Episcopalians—who, in most American cities, are largely ex-Methodists or ex-Presbyterians, or, in New York, ex-Jews—go still further. In three of the churches attended by my agents Holy Communion was almost indistinguishable from the mass. Two of these churches, according to information placed at my disposal by the police, are very fashionable; to get into one of them is almost as difficult as ordering a suit of clothes from Poole. But the richer the Episcopalian, the more eager he is to forget that he was once baptized by public outcry or total immersion. The Low Church rectors, in the main, struggle with poor congregations, born to the faith but deficient in buying power. As bank accounts increase the fear of the devil diminishes, and there is bred a sense of beauty. This sense of beauty, in its practical effects, is identical with the work of the Paulist Fathers. To-day, indeed, even the Methodists who remain Methodists begin to wobble. Tiring of the dreadful din that goes with the orthodox Wesleyan demonology, they take to ceremonials that grow more and more stately and voluptuous. The sermon ceases to be a cavalry charge, and becomes soft and *pizzicato*. The choir abandons "Throw Out the Life-Line" and "Are You Ready for the Judgment Day?" and toys with Händel. The rev. pastor throws off the uniform of a bank cashier and puts on a gown. It is an evolution that has, viewed from a tree, a certain merit. The stock of nonsense in the world is sensibly diminished and the stock of beauty augmented. But what would the old-time circuit-riders say of it, imagining them miraculously brought back from hell?

So much for the volatilization that is going on above the diaphragm. What is in progress below? All I can detect is a rapid descent to mere barbaric devil-chasing. In all those parts of the Republic where Beelzebub is still as real as Babe Ruth or Dr. Coolidge, and men drink raw fusel oil hot from the still—for example, in the rural sections of the Middle West and everywhere in the South save a few walled towns—the evangelical sects plunge into an abyss of malignant imbecility, and declare a holy war upon every decency that civilized men cherish. First the Anti-Saloon League, and now the Ku Klux Klan and the various Fundamentalist organizations, have converted them into vast machines for pursuing and butchering unbelievers. They have thrown the New Testament overboard, and gone back to the Old, and particularly to the bloodiest parts of it. Their one aim seems to be to break heads, to spread terror, to propagate hatred. Everywhere they have set up enmities that will not die out for generations. Neighbor looks askance at neighbor, the land is filled with spies, every man of the slightest intelligence is suspect. Christianity becomes a sort of psychic cannibalism. Unfortunately, the doings of the rustic gentlemen of God who furnish steam for this movement have been investigated but imperfectly, and in consequence too little is known about them. Even the sources of their power, so far as I know, have not been looked into. My suspicion is that it has increased as the influence of the old-time country-town newspapers has declined. These newspapers, in large areas of the land, once genuinely molded public opinion. They attracted to their service a shrewd and salty class of rustic philosophers, mainly highly alcoholized; they were outspoken in their views and responded only slightly to the prevailing crazes. In the midst of the Bryan uproar, a quarter of a century ago, scores of little weeklies in the South and Middle West kept up a gallant battle for sound money and the Hanna idealism. There were red-hot Democratic papers in Pennsylvania, and others in Ohio; there were Republican sheets in rural Maryland, and even in Virginia. The growth of the big city dailies is what chiefly reduced them to puerility. As communications improved every yokel began following Brisbane, Dr. Frank Crane, and Mutt and Jeff. The rural mail carrier began leaving a 24-page yellow in every second box. The hinds distrusted and detested the politics of these great organs, but enjoyed their imbecilities. The country weekly could not match the latter, and so it began to decline. It is now in a low state everywhere in America. Half of it is boiler-plate and the other half is cross-roads gossip. The editor is no longer the leading thinker of his town; instead, he is commonly a broken and despairing man, cadging for advertisements and hoping for a political job. He used to aspire to the State Senate; now he is content with the post of town bailiff or road supervisor.

His place has been taken by the village pastor. The pastor got into public affairs by the route of Prohibition. The shrewd shysters who developed the Anti-Saloon League made a politician of him, and once he had got a taste of power he was eager for more. It came very quickly. As industry penetrated to the rural regions the new-blown Babbitts began to sense his capacity for safeguarding the established order, and so he was given the job: he became a local Billy Sunday. And, simultaneously the old-line politicians, taught a lesson by the Anti-Saloon League, began to defer to him in general, as they had yielded to him in particular. He was consulted about candidacies; he had his say about policies. The local school-board soon became his private preserve. The wandering cony-catchers of the tin-pot fraternal orders found him a useful man. He was, by now, a specialist in all forms of public rectitude, from teetotalism to patriotism. He was put up on days of ceremony to sob for the flag, vice the county judge, retired. When the Klan burst upon the peasants all of his new duties were synthetized. He was obviously the chief local repository of its sublime principles, theological, social, ethnological and patriotic.   In every country town in America to-day, wherever the Klan continues to rowel the hinds, its chief engine is a clerk in holy orders.   If the Baptists are strong, their pastor is that engine.   Failing Baptists, the heroic work is assumed by the Methodist parson, or the Presbyterian, or the Campbellite. Without these sacerdotal props the Invisible Empire would have faded long ago.

What one mainly notices about these ambassadors of Christ, observing them in the mass, is their vast lack of sound information and sound sense.   They constitute, perhaps, the most ignorant class of teachers ever set up to lead a civilized people; they are even more ignorant than the county superintendents of schools.   Learning, indeed, is not esteemed in the evangelical denominations, and any literate plowhand, if the Holy Spirit inflames him, is thought to be fit to preach.   Is he commonly sent, as a preliminary, to a training camp, to college?   But what a college!   You will find one in every mountain valley of the land, with its single building in its bare pasture lot, and its faculty of half-idiot pedagogues and broken-down preachers.   One man, in such a college, teaches oratory, ancient history, arithmetic and Old Testament exegesis.   The aspirant comes in from the barnyard, and goes back in a year or two to the village. His body of knowledge is that of a street-car motorman or a vaudeville actor. But he has learned the clichés of his craft, and he has got him a long-tailed coat, and so he has made his escape from the harsh labors of his ancestors, and is set up as a fountain of light and learning.

It is from such ignoramuses that the lower half of American Protestantdom gets its view of the cosmos. Certainly Fundamentalism should not be hard to understand when its sources are inspected. How can the teacher teach when his own head is empty? Of all that constitutes the sum of human knowledge he is as innocent as an Eskimo. Of the arts he knows absolutely nothing; of the sciences he has never so much as heard. No good book ever penetrates to those remote "colleges," nor does any graduate ever take away a desire to read one. He has been warned, indeed, against their blandishments; what is not addressed solely to the paramount business of saving souls is of the devil. So when he hears by chance of the battle of ideas beyond the sky-rim, he quite naturally puts it down to Beezlebub. What comes to him, vaguely and distorted, is unintelligible to him. He is suspicious of it, afraid of it—and he quickly communicates his fears to his dupes. The common man, in many ways, is hard to arouse; it is a terrific job to ram even the most elemental ideas into him. But it is always easy to scare him.

That is the daily business of the evangelical pastors of the Republic. They are specialists in alarms and bugaboos. The rum demon, atheists, Bolsheviki, the Pope, bootleggers, the Jews,—all these have served them in turn, and in the demonology of the Ku Klux Klan all have been conveniently brought together. The old stock company of devils has been retired, and with it the old repertoire of private sins. The American peasant of to-day finds it vastly easier to claw into heaven than he used to. Personal holiness has now been handed over to the Holy Rollers and other such survivors from a harsher day. It is sufficient now to hate the Pope, to hate the Jews, to hate the scientists, to hate all foreigners, to hate whatever the cities yield to. These hatreds have been spread in the land by rev. pastors, chiefly Baptists and Methodists. They constitute, with their attendant fears, the basic religion of the American clod-hopper to-day. They are the essence of the new Protestantism, second division, American style.

Their public effects are constantly underestimated until it is too late. I ask no indulgence for calling attention to the case of Prohibition. Fundamentalism, it may be, is sneaking upon the nation in the same disarming way. The cities laugh at the yokels, but meanwhile the politicians take careful notice; such mountebanks as Peay of Tennessee and Blease of South Carolina have already issued their preliminary whoops. As the tide rolls up the pastors will attain to greater and greater consequence. Already, indeed, they swell visibly in power and pretension. The Klan, in its earlier days, kept them discreetly under cover; they labored valiantly in the hold, but only lay go-getters were seen upon the bridge. But now they are everywhere on public display, leading the anthropoid host. The curious thing is that their activity gets little if any attention from the established publicists. Let a lone Red arise to annoy a bar-room full of Michigan lumber-jacks, and at once the fire-alarm sounds and the full military and naval power of the nation is summoned to put down the outrage. But how many Americans would the Reds convert to their rubbish, even supposing them free to spout it on every street-corner? Probably not enough, all told, to make a day's hunting for a regiment of militia. The American moron's mind simply does not run in that direction; he wants to keep his Ford, even at the cost of losing the Bill of Rights. But the stuff that the Baptist and Methodist dervishes have on tap is very much to his taste; he gulps it eagerly and rubs his tummy. I suggest that it might be well to make a scientific inquiry into the nature of it. The existing agencies of sociological snooting seem to be busy in other directions. There are elaborate surveys of some of the large cities, showing how much it costs to teach a child the principles

of Americanism, how often the average citizen falls
into the hands of the cops, how many detective stories
are taken out of the city library daily, and how many
children a normal Polish woman has every year.
Why not a survey of the rustic areas, where men are
he and God still reigns?   Why not an attempt to find
out just what the Baptist dominies have drilled into
the heads of the Tennesseeans, Arkansans and Nebras-
kans?   It would be amusing, and it would be instructive.   And useful.   For it is well, in such matters, to see clearly what is ahead.   The United States
grows increasingly urban, but its ideas are still
hatched in the little towns.   What the swineherds
credit to-day is whooped to-morrow by their agents
and attorneys in Congress, and then comes upon the
cities suddenly, with all the force of law.   Where do
the swineherds get it?   Mainly from the only publicists and metaphysicians they know: the gentlemen of
the sacred faculty.   It was not the bawling of the
mountebank Bryan, but the sermon of a mountain
Bossuet that laid the train of the Scopes case and
made a whole State forever ridiculous.   I suggest
looking more carefully into the notions that such ignoramuses spout.

Meanwhile, what is the effect of all this upon the
Protestant who retains some measure of sanity, the
moderate and peaceable fellow—him called by William Graham Sumner the Forgotten Man?   He is

silent white the bombs burst and the stink bombs go off, but what is he thinking? I believe that he is thinking strange and dreadful thoughts—thoughts that would have frozen his own spine a dozen years ago. He is thinking, *imprimis*, that there must be something in this evolution heresy after all, else Methodist bishops and other such bristling foes to sense would not be so frantically against it. And he is thinking, secondly, that perhaps a civilized man, in the last analysis, would not be worse off if Sherman's march were repeated by the Papal Guard. Between these two thoughts American Protestantism is being squeezed, so to speak, to death.

VIII. FROM THE FILES OF A BOOK REVIEWER

1

Counter-Offensive

IS IT GOD'S WORD? by Joseph Wheless. New York: *Alfred A. Knopf*. [The American Mercury, May, 1926.]

THE author of this book, who is an associate editor of the *American Bar Association Journal*, was trained as a lawyer, but that training, somewhat surprisingly, seems to have left his logical powers unimpaired, and with them his capacity for differentiating between facts and mere appearances. There is no hint of the usual evasions and obfuscations of the advocate in his pages. His business is to examine calmly the authority and plausibility of Holy Writ, both as history and as revelation of the Omnipotent Will, and to that business he brings an immense and meticulous knowledge, an exact and unfailing judicial sense, and a skill at orderly exposition which is quite extraordinary. There is no vaporing of the orthodox exegetes that he is not familiar with, and none that he fails to refute, simply and devastatingly. Nine-tenths of his evidence he takes out of the mouths of his opponents. Patiently, mercilessly, irresistibly, he subjects it to logical analysis, and when he is done at last—his book runs to 494 pages of fine print—there is little left of the two Testaments save a farrago of palpable nonsense, swathed, to be sure, in very lovely poetry. He exposes all their gross and preposterous contradictions, their violations of common sense and common decency, their grotesque collisions with the known and indubitable facts, their petty tergiversations and fraudulences. He goes behind the mellifluous rhetoric of the King James Version to the harsh balderdash of the originals, and brings it out into the horrible light of day. He exposes the prophecies that have failed to come off. He exhibits the conflicts of romantic and unreliable witnesses, most of them with something to sell. He tracks down ideas to their barbaric sources. He concocts an almost endless series of logical dilemmas. And he does it all with good manners, never pausing to rant and nowhere going beyond the strict letter of the record.

Obviously, there is room and need for such a book, and it deserves to be widely read. For in the America of to-day, after a time of quiescence, the old conflict between religion and science has been resumed with great ferocity, and the partisans of the former, not content with denouncing all free inquiry as evil, have now undertaken to make it downright unlawful.

Worse, they show signs of succeeding. And why? Chiefly, it seems to me, because the cause of their opponents has been badly handled—above all, because it has lacked vigorous *offensive* leadership. Even the defense is largely an abject running away. We are assured with pious snuffling that there is actually no conflict, that the domains of science and religion do not overlap, that it is quite possible for a man to be a scientist (even a biologist!) and yet believe that Jonah swallowed the whale. No wonder the whoopers for Genesis take courage, and lay on with glad, *sforzando* shouts. At one stroke they are lifted to parity with their opponents, nay, to superiority. The bilge they believe in becomes something sacrosanct; its manifest absurdities are not mentioned, and hence tend to pass unnoticed. But meanwhile they are quite free to belabor science with their whole armamentarium of imbecilities. Every cross-roads Baptist preacher becomes an authority upon its errors, and is heard gravely. In brief, science exposes itself to be shot at, but agrees not to shoot back. It would be difficult to imagine any strategy more idiotic.

Or to imagine a Huxley adopting it. Huxley, in his day, followed a far different plan. When the Gladstones, Bishop Wilberforces and other such obscurantists denounced the new biology, he did not waste any time upon conciliatory politeness. In-

stead, he made a bold and headlong attack upon
Christian theology—an attack so vigorous and so
skillful that the enemy was soon in ignominious
flight. Huxley knew the first principle of war: he
knew that a hearty offensive is worth a hundred de-
fensives. How well he succeeded is shown by the
fact that even to-day, with theology once more on the
prowl and the very elements of science under heavy
attack, some of the gaudiest of the ancient theological
notions are not heard of. Huxley disposed of them
completely; even in Darkest Tennessee the yokels no
longer give them credit. But if the Robert Andrews
Millikans and other such amiable bunglers continue
to boss the scientific camp you may be sure that all
these exploded myths and superstitions will be re-
vived, and that the mob will once more embrace them.
For it is the natural tendency of the ignorant to
believe what is not true. In order to overcome that
tendency it is not sufficient to exhibit the true; it is
also necessary to expose and denounce the false. To
admit that the false has any standing in court, that
it ought to be handled gently because millions of
morons cherish it and thousands of quacks make
their livings propagating it—to admit this, as the
more fatuous of the reconcilers of science and religion inevitably do, is to abandon a just cause to its
enemies, cravenly and without excuse.

It is, of course, quite true that there is a region

in which science and religion do not conflict. That is the region of the unknowable. No one knows Who created the visible universe, and it is infinitely improbable that anything properly describable as evidence on the point will ever be discovered. No one knows what motives or intentions, if any, lie behind what we call natural laws. No one knows why man has his present form. No one knows why sin and suffering were sent into this world—that is, why the fashioning of man was so badly botched. Naturally enough, all these problems have engaged the interest of humanity since the remotest days, and in every age, with every sort of evidence completely lacking, men of speculative mind have sought to frame plausible solutions. Some of them, more bold than the rest, have pretended that their solutions were revealed to them by God, and multitudes have believed them. But no man of science believes them. He doesn't say positively that they are wrong; he simply says that there is no proof that they are right. If he admitted, without proof, that they are right, he would not be a man of science. In his view all such theories and speculations stand upon a common level. In the most ambitious soarings of a Christian theologian he can find nothing that differs in any essential way from the obvious hocus-pocus of a medicine man in the jungle. Superficially, of course, the two stand far apart. The Christian theologian, confined like all the rest to the unknowable, has to be more careful than the medicine man, for in Christendom the unknowable covers a far less extensive field than in the jungle. Christian theology is thus, in a sense, more reasonable than voodooism. But it is not more reasonable because its professors know more than the voodoo-man about the unknowable; it is more reasonable simply because they are under a far more rigorous and enlightened scrutiny, and run a risk of being hauled up sharply every time they venture too near the borders of the known.

This business of hauling them up is one of the principal functions of science. Its prompt execution is the gauge of a high and progressive civilization. So long as theologians keep within their proper bounds, science has no quarrel with them, for it is no more able to prove that they are wrong than they themselves are able to prove that they are right. But human experience shows that they never keep within their proper bounds voluntarily; they are always bulging over the line, and making a great uproar over things that they know nothing about. Such an uproar is going on in the United States at the present moment. Hordes of theologians come marching down from the Southern mountains, declaring raucously that God created the universe during a certain single week of the year 4004 B. C., and demanding that all persons who presume to doubt it be handed over to the secular arm. Here, obviously, science cannot suffer them gladly, nor even patiently. Their proposition is a statement of scientific fact; it may be examined and tested like any other statement of scientific fact. So examined and tested, it turns out to be wholly without evidential support. All the known evidence, indeed, is against it, and overwhelmingly. No man who knows the facts—that is, no man with any claim to scientific equipment—is in any doubt about that. He disbelieves it as thoroughly as he believes that the earth moves 'round the sun. Disbelieving it, it is his professional duty, his first obligation of professional honor, to attack and refute those who uphold it. Above all, it is his duty to attack the false evidence upon which they base their case.

Thus an actual conflict is joined, and it is the height of absurdity for the Millikans and other such compromisers to seek to evade it with soft words. That conflict was not begun by science. It did not start with an invasion of the proper field of theological speculation by scientific raiders. It started with an invasion of the field of science by theological raiders. Now that it is on, it must be pressed vigorously from the scientific side, and without any flabby tenderness for theological susceptibilities. A defensive war is not enough; there must be a forthright onslaught upon the theological citadel, and every effort must be made to knock it down. For so long as it remains a stronghold, there will be no security for sound sense among us, and little for common decency. So long as it may be used as a recruiting-station and rallying-point for the rabble, science will have to submit to incessant forays, and the same forays will be directed against every sort of rational religion. The latter danger is not unobserved by the more enlightened theologians. They are well aware that, facing the Fundamentalists, they must either destroy or be destroyed. It is to be hoped that the men of science will perceive the same plain fact, and so give over their vain effort to stay the enemy with weasel words.

2

Heretics

ALTGELD OF ILLINOIS, by Waldo R. Browne, New York: *B. W. Huebsch.* THE LAST OF THE HERETICS, by Algernon Sidney Crapsey. New York: *Alfred A. Knopf.* [The American Mercury, October, 1924.]

When I was a boy, in the early nineties of the last century, the reigning hobgoblin of the United States was John P. Altgeld, Governor of Illinois. From this distance the ill-fame that played about him seems almost fabulous. He was a sort of horrendous combination of Trotsky and Raisuli, Darwin and the German Crown Prince, Jesse James and Oscar Wilde, with overtones of Wayne B. Wheeler and the

McNamara brothers. We have had, in these later years, no such communal devil. The La Follette of 1917 was a popular favorite compared to him; the Debs of the same time was a spoiled darling. What I gathered from my elders, in the awful years of adolescence, when my voice began to break and vibrissæ sprouted on my lip, was that Altgeld was a shameless advocate of rapine and assassination, an enemy alike to the Constitution and the Ten Commandments—in short, a bloody and insatiable anarchist. I was thus bred to fear him even more than I feared the anonymous scoundrels who had stolen Charlie Ross. When I dreamed, it was of catching him in some public place and cutting off his head, to the applause of the multitude.

The elders that I have mentioned were mainly business men, with a few *Gelehrte* thrown in. I learned later on, by hard experience, that the opinions of such gentlemen, particularly of public matters and public men, were not always sound. Nevertheless, I continued to have a bilious suspicion of the Hon. Mr. Altgeld, and it survived even the discovery, made much later, that men who had actually known him— for example, Theodore Dreiser—regarded him very highly. I remember very well how shocked I was when Dreiser made me privy to this fact. It made a dent, I suppose, in my old view, but it surely did not dispose of it altogether. I continued to believe that Altgeld, though perhaps not an anarchist, as alleged, was at least a blathering Socialist, and hence deserving of a few prophylactic kicks in the pantaloons. I was far gone in my forties before ever I got at the truth. Then I found it in this modest book of Mr. Browne's—a volume that is dreadfully written, but extremely illuminating. That truth may be put very simply. Altgeld was not an anarchist, nor was he a Socialist: he was simply a sentimentalist. His error consisted in taking the college yells of democracy seriously.

I do not go into the evidence, but refer you to the book. It is very completely documented, and it leaves little room for doubt, despite Mr. Browne's obvious prejudice in favor of some of Altgeld's more dubious ideas, especially the idea of government ownership. On the main points his argument is quite beyond cavil. Did Altgeld pardon the Chicago anarchists? Then it was simply because they had been railroaded to jail on evidence that should have made the very judge on the bench guffaw—as men are still railroaded in California to-day. Did he protest against Cleveland's invasion of Chicago with Federal troops at the time of the Pullman strike? Then it was because he knew only too well how little they were needed—and what sinister influences had cajoled poor old Grover into sending them. In brief, Altgeld was one of the first public men in America to

protest by word and act against government by usurers and their bashi-bazouks—the first open and
avowed advocate of the Bill of Rights since Jackson's
time.   A romantic fellow, and a firm believer in the
virtues of the common people, he couldn't rid himself
of the delusion that they would follow him here—
that after the yell of rage there would come a resounding cheer.   That belief gradually degenerated into
a hope, but I doubt that it ever disappeared altogether.
The common people met it by turning Altgeld out of
office, swiftly and ignominiously.   After they had got
rid of him as Governor of Illinois, they even rejected
him as mayor of Chicago.   His experience taught
him a lesson, but like that of the Aframerican on the
gallows, it came too late.

What lesson is in his career for the rest of us?
The lesson, it seems to me, that any man who devotes
himself to justice and common decency, under
democracy, is a very foolish fellow—that the gen-
erality of men have no genuine respect for these
things, and are always suspicious of the man who
upholds them.   Their public relations, like their
private relations, are marked by the qualities that
mark the inferior man at all times and everywhere:
cowardice, stupidity and cruelty.   They are in favor
of whoever is wielding the whip, even when their own
hides must bear the blows.   How easy it was to turn
the morons of the American Legion upon their fellow-

slaves! How heroically they voted for Harding, and then for Coolidge after him—and so helped to put down the Reds! Dog eats dog, world without end. In the Pullman strike at least half the labor unions of the United States were against the strikers, as they were against the more recent steel strikers, and helped to beat them. Altgeld battled for the under dog all his life—and the under dog bit him in the end. A pathetic career, but not without its touches of sardonic comedy. Altgeld, in error at bottom, was often also in error on the surface, and not infrequently somewhat grotesquely. He succumbed to the free silver mania. He supported Bryan—nay more, he may be said to have discovered and made Bryan. It is fortunate for him that he was dead and in hell by 1902, and so not forced to contemplate the later states of his handiwork. He was excessively romantic, but certainly no ignoramus. Imagine him listening to one of good Jennings' harangues against the elements of biology! Such men, indeed, are always happier dead. This world, and especially this Republic, is no place for idealists.

Another proof of it is offered by the career of Dr. Crapsey, whose trial for heresy entertained the damned in 1906. He is still alive as I write, and still full of steam. But I doubt that he is as sure as he used to be that common sense and common honesty pay. Many of the frauds who drove him out of the church, though they knew that he was right, are bishops to-day, and licensed to bind and loose. Others have been called by God, and sit upon His right hand. The church itself, as it has grown more sordid and swinish, has only grown more prosperous. In New York City its income approaches that of the bootleggers and it is almost as well regarded. Every new profiteer, even before he tries to horn into the Piping Rock Club, subscribes to its articles. It is robbing the Church of Christ Scientist of all the rich Jews; they are having their sons baptized in its fonts and christened Llewellyn, Seymour and Murray. Certainly it would be difficult to imagine a more gloriously going concern. The rising spires of its steel and concrete cathedrals begin to bulge the floor of heaven; its clergy are sleek, fat and well-oiled; its bishops come next in precedence after movie stars and members of the firm of J. P. Morgan & Company. Lately it threw out another heretic—like Dr. Crapsey, one accused of putting the Sermon on the Mount above the conflicting genealogies of the Preacher. As for Crapsey himself, he has naught to console him in his old age save the thought that hell will at least be warm.

His book is extremely amusing and instructive. Like Altgeld, he confesses to foreign and poisonous blood. The *Stammvater* of the American Crapseii was a fellow named Kropps, apparently a Hessian.

But his great-great grandson, the father of the heretic, married the daughter of a United States Senator, and so there is some amelioration of the horror. Like Altgeld again, Crapsey went to the Civil War as a boy scarcely out of knee breeches. Altgeld was so poor that he gladly took the $100 offered by a patriot who had been drafted and wanted a substitute; Crapsey volunteered. Both succumbed to camp fevers and were discharged. Both then took to Service among the downtrodden, Altgeld in politics and the law, and Crapsey in one of the outlying hereditaments of Trinity parish. Both were safe so long as they appeared to be fraudulent; the moment they began to show genuine belief in their doctrines they found themselves in difficulties. So Altgeld became the favorite hobgoblin of the Republic and Crapsey became its blackest heretic.

3

The Grove of Academe

THE GOOSE-STEP, by Upton Sinclair, Pasadena, Calif.: *Published by the Author.* [The Smart Set, May, 1923.]

The doctrine preached in this fat volume—to wit, that the American colleges and universities, with precious few exceptions, are run by stock-jobbers and manned by intellectual prostitutes—this doctrine will certainly give no fillip of surprise to steady readers of my critical compositions. I have, in fact, maintained it steadily since the earliest dawn of the present marvelous century, and to the support of it I have brought forward an immense mass of glittering and irrefragable facts and a powerful stream of eloquence. Nor have I engaged in this moral enterprise *a cappella*. A great many other practitioners have devoted themselves to it with equal assiduity, including not a few reformed and conscience-stricken professors, and the net result of that united effort is that the old assumption of the pedagogue's *bona fides* is now in decay throughout the Republic. In whole departments of human knowledge he has become suspect, as it were, *ex officio*. I nominate, for example, the departments of history and of what is commonly called English language and literature. If a professor in the first field shows ordinary honesty, or, in the second field, ordinary sense, it is now regarded as a sort of marvel, and with sound reason. Barring a scant dozen extraordinary men, no American professor of history has written anything worth reading since the year 1917; nearly all the genuine history published in the United States since then has come from laymen, or from professors who have ceased to profess. And so in the domain of the national letters. The professors, with a few exceptions, mainly belated rice-converts, are unanimously and furiously consecrated to vain attacks upon the literature that is in being. Either, like the paleozoic Beers, of Yale, they refuse to read it and deny that it exists, or, like the patriotic Matthews, of Columbia, they seek to put it down by launching Ku Klux anathemas against it. The net result is that the professorial caste, as a whole, loses all its old dignity and influence. In universities large and small, East, West, North and South, the very sophomores rise in rebellion against the incompetence and imbecility of their preceptors, and in the newspapers the professor slides down gradually to the level of a chiropractor, a press-agent or a Congressman.

Thus there is nothing novel in the thesis of Dr. Sinclair's book, which deals, in brief, with the internal organization of the American universities, and their abject subjection to the Money Power, which is to say, to Chamber of Commerce and Rotary Club concepts of truth, liberty and honor. But there is something new, and very refreshing, in the manner of it, for the learned author, for the first time, manages to tell a long and dramatic story without intruding his private grievances into it. Sinclair's worst weakness, next to his vociferous appetite for Remedies that never cure, is his naïve and almost actorial vanity. As everyone knows, it botched "The Brass Check." So much of that book was given over to a humorless account of his own combats with yellow journals—which, in the main, did nothing worse to him than

laugh at him when he was foolish—that he left untold
a great deal that might have been said, and with perfect justice and accuracy, about the venality and swinishness of American newspapers.   In "The Profits of
Religion" he wobbled almost as badly; the subject,
no doubt, was much too vast for a single volume; the
Methodists and Baptists alone, to say nothing of Holy
Church, deserved a whole shelf.   But in "The Goose-
Step" he tells a straightforward story in a straightforward manner—simply, good-humoredly and con-
vincingly.   When he comes into the narrative himself,
which is not often, he leaves off his customary martyr's chemise.   There is no complaining, no pathos,
no mouthing of platitude; it is a plain record of plain
facts, with names and dates—a plain record of truly
appalling cowardice, disingenuousness, abjectness,
and degradation.   Out of it two brilliant figures
emerge: first the typical American university president, a jenkins to wealth, an ignominious waiter in
antechambers and puller of wires, a politician, a
fraud and a cad; and secondly, the typical American
professor, a puerile and pitiable slave.

Such are the common and customary bearers of
the torch in the Republic.   Such is the usual machin-
ery and inner nature of the higher learning among
us.   Its aim, briefly stated, is almost indistinguishable from the aim of the Ku Klux Klan, the American
Legion, and Kiwanis.   The thing it combats most ar-

dently is not ignorance, but free inquiry; it is devoted to forcing the whole youth of the land into one rigid mold. Its ideal product is a young man who is absolutely correct in all his ideas—a perfect reader for the *Literary Digest,* the *American Magazine,* and the editorial page of the New York *Times.* To achieve this end Big Business has endowed it with unprecedented liberality; there are single American universities with more invested wealth and more in-income than all the universities of Germany, France or England taken together. But in order to get that ocean of money, and to pay for the piles of pseudo-Gothic that now arise all over the land, scholarship in America has had to sacrifice free inquiry to the prejudices and private interests of its masters—the search for the truth has had to be subordinated to the safeguarding of railway bonds and electric light stocks. As Sinclair shows, there is scarcely a university in the United States, whether maintained out of the public funds or privately endowed, that is not run absolutely, in all departments, by precisely the same men who run the street railways, the banks, the rolling mills, the coal mines and the factories of the country—in brief, by men who have no more respect for scholarship than an ice-wagon driver has for beautiful letters. There is scarcely an American university or college in which the scholars who constitute it have any effective control over its general policies and enterprises, or even over the conduct of their own departments. In almost every one there is some unspeakable stock-broker, or bank director, or railway looter who, if the spirit moved him, would be perfectly free to hound a Huxley, a Karl Ludwig or a Jowett from the faculty, and even to prevent him getting a seemly berth elsewhere. It is not only possible; it has been done, and not once, but scores and hundreds of times.

Sinclair is content to set forth the basic facts; his book, as it is, is very long; he neglects laboring all of the deductions and implications that flow from his thesis, some of them obvious enough. One of them is this: that the control of the universities by Mr. Babbitt is making it increasingly difficult to induce intelligent and self-respecting young men to embrace the birchman's career, and that the personnel of the teaching staffs thus tends to decline in competence, steadily and sharply. This accounts, in large measure, for the collapse of the old public influence of the scholar in America; he begins to be derided simply because he is no longer the dignified man that he once was. In certain departments, of no immediate interest to trustees and contributors, a certain show of freedom, of course, still prevails. What is taught in astronomy, or paleontology, or Greek cannot menace the nail manufacturer on the board, and so he does not issue any orders about it, nor does his agent, the university president. But what is taught in economics, or modern history, or "education," or sociology, or even literature, involves a dealing with ideas that are apt to hit him where he lives, and so he keeps a wary eye upon those departments, and at the slightest show of heresy he takes measures to protect himself. It is in these regions, consequently, that conformity is most comfortable, and that professional character is most lamentably in decay. Even here, to be sure, a few stout-hearted survivors of an earlier day hold out, but they are surely not many, and they will have no successors. The professor of to-morrow, in all departments that have to do with life as men are now living it in the world, will either be a scholastic goose-stepper or he will be out of a job. The screws are tightening every year. In the past the Babbitts have contented themselves with farming out the management of their intellectual brothels to extra-plaint professors, but now they begin to turn to yet more reliable men: army officers, lame-duck politicians, and engineers. The time will come, no doubt, when the president of Columbia will be just as frankly a partner in J. P. Morgan & Company as the head of the Red Cross or the chief vestryman of Trinity Church.

How far will this debauching of education go? Will the universities sink eventually to the level of the public-schools of such barbarous States as Texas,

Arkansas and Mississippi?   Here education has been reduced to a bald device for multiplying Shriners, Knights of Pythias and Rotarians—in brief, ignoramuses.   In the institutions of higher learning one may reasonably look for some resistance to the process, soon or late.   I doubt, however, that it will come from the professors; they are already too much cowed and demoralized, as Sinclair shows abundantly.   The American Association of University Professors, an organization formed to protect pedagogues against wanton attack by the Babbitts, numbers but 5000 members; the remaining 195,000 American professors are either afraid to join, or already too much battered to want to.   How far their degradation has gone was made visible during the late war, when all save an infinitesimal minority of them yielded to the most extravagant manias of the time and thousands gave astounding exhibitions of moronic sadism.   The Neandertal qualities thus awakened are still visible in many directions; in the Southern States, I am informed by an exceptional professor, fully five-sixths of his colleagues became charter members of the Ku Klux Klan.   It is hopeless to look for a *Freiheitskrieg* among such poor serfs.   But the students remain, and in them lies some promise for the future. The American university student, in the past, has been a victim of the same process of leveling that destroyed his teacher.   He has been taught conformity, obedience, the social and intellectual goose-step; the ideal held before him has been the ideal of correctness. But that ideal, it must be plain, is not natural to youth. Youth is aspiring, rebellious, inquisitive, iconoclastic, a bit romantic. All over the country the fact is bursting through the chains of repression. In scores of far-flung colleges the students have begun to challenge their professors, often very harshly. After a while, they may begin to challenge the masters of their professors. Not all of them will do it, and not most of them. But it doesn't take a majority to make a rebellion; it takes only a few determined leaders and a sound cause.

4

The Schoolma'm's Goal

THE SOCIAL OBJECTIVES OF SCHOOL ENGLISH, by Charles S. Pendleton. Nashville, Tenn.: *Published by the Author.* [The American Mercury, March, 1925.]

Here, in the form of a large flat book, eight and a half inches wide and eleven inches tall, is a sightseeing bus touring the slums of pedagogy. The author, Dr. Pendleton, professes the teaching of English (not English, remember, but the teaching of English) at the George Peabody College for Teachers, an eminent seminary at Nashville, in the Baptist Holy Land, and his object in the investigation he describes was, in brief, to find out what the teachers who teach English hope to accomplish by teaching it.   In other words, what, precisely, is the improvement that they propose to achieve in the pupils exposed to their art and mystery?   Do they believe that the aim of teaching English is to increase the exact and beautiful use of the language?   Or that it is to inculcate and augment patriotism?   Or that it is to diminish sorrow in the home?   Or that it has some other end, cultural, economic or military?

In order to find out, Prof. Pendleton, with true pedagogical diligence, proceeded to list all the reasons for teaching English that he could find. Some he got by cross-examining teachers.   Others came from educators of a higher degree and puissance.   Yet others he dug out of the text-books of pedagogy in common use, and the dreadful professional journals ordinarily read by teachers.   Finally, he threw in some from miscellaneous sources, including his own inner consciousness.   In all, he accumulated 1581 such reasons, or, as he calls them, objectives, and then he sat down and laboriously copied them upon 1581 very thin 3x5 cards, one to a card. Some of these cards were buff in color, some were blue, some were yellow, some were pink, and some were green.   On the blue cards he copied all the objectives relating to the employment of English in conversation, on the yellow cards all those dealing with its use in literary composition, on the green cards all those having to do with speech-making, and so on. Then he shook up the cards, summoned eighty professional teachers of English, and asked them to sort out the objectives in the order of appositeness and merit. The results of this laborious sorting he now sets before the learned.

Don't be impatient! I won't keep you waiting. Here is the objective that got the most votes—the champion of the whole 1581:

The ability to spell correctly without hesitation all the ordinary words of one's writing vocabulary.

Here is the runner-up:

The ability to speak, in conversation, in complete sentences, not in broken phrases.

And here is No. 7:

The ability to capitalize speedily and accurately in one's writing.

And here is No. 9:

The ability to think quickly in an emergency.

And here are some more, all within the first hundred:

The ability to refrain from marking or marring in any way a borrowed book.

An attitude of democracy rather than snobbishness within a conversation.

Familiarity with the essential stories and persons of the Bible.

And some from the second hundred:

The ability to sing through—words and music—the national anthem.

The ability courteously and effectively to receive orders from a superior.

The avoidance of vulgarity and profanity in one's public speaking.

The ability to read silently without lip movements.

The habit of placing the page one is reading so that there will not be shadows upon it.

The ability to refrain from conversation under conditions where it is annoying or disagreeable to others.

The ability to converse intelligently about municipal and district civic matters.

The ability to comprehend accurately the meaning of all common abbreviations and signs one meets with in reading.

The ability, during one's reading, to distinguish between an author's central theme and his incidental remarks.

I refrain from any more: all these got enough votes to put them among the first 200 objectives—200 out of 1581.   Nor do I choose them unfairly; most of those that I have not listed were quite as bad as those I have.   But, you may protest, the good professor handed his cards to a jury of little girls of eight or nine years, or to the inmates of a home for the feeble-minded! He did, in fact, nothing of the kind. His jury was very carefully selected. It consisted of eighty teachers of such professional keenness that they were assembled at the University of Chicago for post-graduate study. Every one of them had been through either a college or a normal school; forty-seven of them held learned degrees; all of them had been engaged professionally in teaching English, some for years. They came from Michigan, Nebraska, Iowa, Missouri, Wisconsin, Toronto, Leland Stanford, Chicago and Northwestern Universities; from Oberlin, De Pauw, Goucher, Beloit and Drake Colleges; from a dozen lesser seminaries of the higher learning. They represented, not the lowest level of teachers of English in the Republic, but the highest level. And yet it was their verdict by a solemn referendum that the principal objective in teaching English was to make good spellers, and that after that came the breeding of good capitalizers!

I present Dr. Pendleton's laborious work as overwhelming proof of a thesis that I have maintained for years, perhaps sometimes with undue heat: that pedagogy in the United States is fast descending to the estate of a childish necromancy, and that the worst idiots, even among pedagogues, are the teachers of English. It is positively dreadful to think that the young American species are exposed day in and day out to the contamination of such dark minds. What can be expected of education that is carried on in the very sewers of the intellect? How can morons teach anything that is worth knowing? Here and there, true enough, a competent teacher of English is encountered. I could name at least twenty in the whole country. But it does not appear that Dr. Pendleton, among his eighty, found even one. There is not the lightest glimmer of intelligence in all the appalling tables of statistics and black, zig-zag graphs that he has so painfully amassed. Nor any apparent capacity for learning. The sound thing, the sane thing and the humane thing to do with his pathetic herd of A. B.'s would be to take them out in the alley and knock them in the head.

5

The Heroic Age

JEFFERSON AND HAMILTON, by Claude G. Bowers. Boston: *The Houghton Mifflin Company*. JEFFERSON AND MONTI-CELLO, by Paul Wilstach. Garden City, L. I. : *Doubleday, Page & Company*. CORRESPONDENCE OF JOHN ADAMS AND THOMAS JEFFERSON, 1812–1826, selected by Paul Wilstach. Indianapolis: *The Bobbs-Merrill Company*. [The American Mercury, March, 1926.]

Jefferson, in one of his last letters to Adams, dated March 25, 1826, spoke of the time when both came into fame as the heroic age. The phrase was certainly not mere rhetoric. The two men differed enormously, both in their personalities and in their ideas —perhaps quite as much as Jefferson differed from Hamilton or Adams from his cousin Sam—but in one thing at least they were exactly alike: they were men of complete integrity. As Frederick the Great said of the Prussian *Junker,* one could not buy them, and they would not lie. The fact, at times, made them bitter enemies, and the virtues of the one were cancelled by the virtues of the other, to the damage of their common country. But when they stood together, they were irresistible, for complete integrity, when it does not spend itself against itself, is always irresistible—one of the few facts, to me known, that is creditable to the human race. The masses of men, like children, are easily deceived, but in the long run, like children again, they show a tendency to yield to character. Bit by bit it conquers them. They see in it all the high values that they are incapable of reaching themselves. They see the courage that they lack, and the honesty that they lack, and the resolution that they lack. All these things were in both Adams and Jefferson. They fell, in their day, into follies, but I don't think that anyone believes they were ever *pushed* into them. Adams, no doubt, could be bamboozled, but neither he nor Jefferson could be scared.

I fear that the gallant iconoclasts who revise our history-books sometimes forget all this. Engaged upon the destruction of legends, all of them maudlin and many of them downright insane, they also, at times, do damage to facts. One of these facts, it seems to me, ought not to be forgotten, to wit, that it took a great deal of courage, in the Summer of 1776, to sign Jefferson's celebrated exercise in colonial Johnsonese. There were ropes dangling in the air, and they were uncomfortably near. There were wives and children to be considered, and very agreeable estates. However dubious their primary motives, the men who signed took a long chance, quietly, simply, and with their faces to the front. How many of their successors in our own time have ever followed their example? I find it hard to think of one. The politician of to-day lacks their courage altogether; he lacks their incorruptible integrity. He is a complete coward. The whip of the Anti-Saloon League is enough to make him leap and tremble; the shadow of the rope would paralyze him with terror. He is for sale to anyone who has anything valuable to offer him, and the day after he has sold out to A he is ready to sell out to A's enemy, B. His honor is that of a street-walker.

So far we have progressed along the highroad of democracy. The gentleman survives in our politics only as an anachronism; his day is done. Mr. Bowers, in "Hamilton and Jefferson," traces the beginning of the decline; Mr. Wilstach, in the volume of Adams-Jefferson letters, shows it in full tide. Both authors are partial to Jefferson, and present charming portraits of him, especially Mr. Wilstach, in his other book, "Jefferson at Monticello." It seems to me that they often confuse the man and his ideas, especially Mr. Bowers. Jefferson was unquestionably one of our giants. There was more in his head than there has been in the heads of all the Presidents in office since he went out. He was a man of immense intellectual curiosity, profound originality, and great daring. His integrity was of Doric massiveness. But was he always right? I don't think many reflective Americans of to-day would argue that he was. Confronting enemies of great resourcefulness and resolute determination, he was forced, bit by bit, into giving his democratic doctrine a sweep and scope that took it far beyond the solid facts. It became a religious dogma rather than a political theory. Once he was gone, it fell into the hands of vastly inferior men, and soon it had reached its *reductio ad absurdum.* Jefferson died in 1826. By 1829, when Jackson came in, it was a nuisance; by 1837, when he went out, it was a joke.

Jefferson's enthusiasm blinded him to the fact that the liberty to which he had consecrated the high days of his early manhood was a two-headed boon. There was, first, the liberty of the people as a whole to determine the forms of their own government, levy their own taxes, and make their own laws—in brief, freedom from the despotism of the King.   There was, second, the liberty of the individual man to live his own life, within the limits of decency and decorum, as he pleased—in brief, freedom from the despotism of the majority.   Hamilton was as much in favor of the first kind of liberty as Jefferson: he made, in fact, even greater sacrifices for it.   But he saw that it was worth nothing without the second kind—that it might easily become worth less than nothing, for the King, whatever his oppressions *en gros*, at least gave some protection to the isolated subject.   Monarchy might be the protector of liberty as well as the foe of liberty. It had been so, in fact, in the Prussia of Frederick. And democracy might be far more the foe than the protector.   It was obviously so in the France of the Reign of Terror.   Hamilton, a hard-headed man, given to figures rather than to theories, saw all this; Jefferson, a doctrinaire, even in his best moments, saw only half of it.   That failure to see together was at the bottom of their difference—and their difference came very near wrecking the United States. Burr's bullet probably prevented a colossal disaster. But it also opened the way for troubles in the years to come.   We are in the midst of them yet, and we are by no means near the end of them.

The shadow of Jeffersonism, indeed, is still over us.   We are still bound idiotically by the battle-cries of a struggle that was over more than a century ago. We have got the half of liberty, but the other half is yet to be wrested from the implacable fates, and there seems little likelihood that it will be wrested soon. All the fears of Hamilton have come to realization—and some of the fears of Jefferson to fill the measure. Minorities among us have no rights that the majority is bound to respect; they are dragooned and oppressed in a way that would make an oriental despot blush. Yet behind the majority, often defectively concealed, there is always a sinister minority, eager only for its own advantage and willing to adopt any device, however outrageous, to get what it wants. We have a puppet in the White House, pulled by wires, but with dangerous weapons in its hands. Law Enforcement becomes the new state religion. A law is something that A wants and can hornswoggle B, C, D, E and F into giving him—by bribery, by lying, by bluff and bluster, by making faces. G and H are therefore bound to yield it respect—nay, to worship it. It is something sacred. To question it is to sin against the Holy Ghost.

I wonder what Jefferson would think if he could come out of his tomb and examine the Republic that he helped to fashion. He was a man of towering enthusiasms, but he was also sharply intelligent: he knew an accomplished fact when he saw one. My guess is that, at the first Jefferson Day dinner follow-

ing his emergence, he would make a startling and
scandalous speech.

6

The Woes of a 100% American

THE NEW BARBARIANS, by Wilbur C. Abbott. Boston:
Little, Brown & Company. [The American Mercury, May, 1925.]

It would be easy to poke fun at this disorderly and
indignant tract; even, perhaps, to denounce the
learned author, in a lofty manner, as a mere jackass.
His argument, at more than one place, is so shaky
that it tempts ribaldry with a powerful lure, almost a
suction.   His premises are often gratuitous and absurd; his conclusions are often fantastic.   Worse, he
argues in circles, and it is frequently hard to make
out what he is advocating, and why.   Worst of all,
the urbanity suitable to a learned gentleman resident
in Sparks street, Cambridge, Mass., sometimes yields
to a libido far more suitable to an auctioneer, a
Federal district attorney or a Methodist bishop, and
he rants dreadfully.   But against all this there is
yet something to be said, and that something, I think,
is sufficient to stay the impulse to have at him
brutally, either with cackles or with invective.   It is,
in brief, this: that what he inveighs against, given
his natural and laudable prejudices, is plentifully
sufficient to excuse all his indignation, and all his in-

coherence, and even his occasional departures from the strict letter of the record—that it is a merit in any man, facing what he deems to be incubi and succubi, to belabor them in a hearty and vociferous manner, and without too pedantic a respect for the rules of evidence. That merit has nothing to do, at bottom, with his rightness or wrongness; it lies in his mere sincerity. Dr. Abbott is obviously full of sincerity; no fair reader can doubt it for an instant. But he has something more: he has under him a respectable body of facts, sound ones as well as shaky ones. The deductions he draws from them are often extravagant, and now and then he mingles them with assumptions that seems to me to do violence to the most elemental common sense. Nevertheless, his basic facts remain, and if I were an Anglo-Saxon as he is I suspect that they would fever me as they fever him.

What he complains of, in a few words, is the assault that has been made of late upon the old American tradition and the fundamental canons of American idealism, *i. e.*, upon the body of ideas that Americans cherish as peculiarly their own, and believe in with a romantic devotion. What he complains of, especially, is that this assault has been made, in the main, by men who are not "Anglo-Saxons" (the professor himself quotes the term: a touching concession to ethnological exactness)—that it has been largely led by men whose very Americanism, when they claim to be Americans at all, is open to question. When I say open to question, I mean, of course, by "Anglo-Saxon" Americans. Dr. Abbott seems to be firmly convinced that these are the only ones entitled to the name. They are the pure stock; their ancestors conquered the continent unaided. They alone partake of the true national spirit, and may be trusted to guard the national hearth. All other Americans are in the position of visitors, interlopers, relatives-in-law. They may become in time, if they are good, creditable assistant Americans, but they can no more enter into the full national heritage, as free equals, than they can lift themselves by their boot-straps. The American tradition, it appears, must forever remain a bit strange to them; they are the children, not of heroes, but of serfs. Thus it is no wonder that their political notions, when they make bold to state them, are exotic and subversive. They can imagine government only as a power above and beyond the citizen. If they are not in favor of kaiserism, then they are in favor of communism, which is simply kaiserism imposed from below. Their politics is essentially a slave politics. They stand opposed eternally to that self-reliant and somewhat pugnacious individualism which is the mark of the true "Anglo-Saxon." If they ever come into power the Constitution will be destroyed and freedom will perish.

Dr. Abbott's book, as I have said, is somewhat

difficult; perhaps I misrepresent him in a few details. But in the main, I believe, I gather his doctrine correctly; it is, indeed, a doctrine that has grown very familiar. The Klu Klux has carried it into every hamlet in the land, and bolstered it with the authority of Holy Writ. I could, if I would, amuse myself by exhibiting the holes in it. Is it a fact, then, that the "Anglo-Saxons" conquered the continent unaided? What of the Spaniards and French? What of the Dutch and Germans? What of the Scotch-Irish? Is it a fact that they invented the American scheme of government? What of Rousseau? Is it a fact that all assaults upon that scheme have been made by assistant Americans? What of Jefferson, Jackson, Robert E. Lee, Jeff Davis, Bryan? Is it a fact that all the enemies of the Constitution came from below the salt? What of the Eighteenth Amendment: does it damage the Bill of Rights more or less than the late Dr. La Follette's vaporous schemes? Such questions suggest themselves in great variety. I could roll them off until you stood agape. But I have no desire to press a professor of history unduly; his authority, in the last analysis, cannot be upset by facts. And in the present case, whatever his errors in detail, it seems to me to be quite clear that the fundamental facts are on his side. There *is* unquestionably a difference between the "Anglo-Saxon" American and the non-"Anglo-Saxon"—a difference in their primary instincts, in their reactions to common stimuli, in their ways of looking at the world. And that difference, of late years, *has* come to the estate of a conflict, with the "Anglo-Saxon" striving to keep what he has—his point of view, his cultural leadership, his political hegemony—and the non-"Anglo-Saxon" trying to take it away from him.   To deny that conflict is to fall into an absurdity far worse than any Dr. Abbott is guilty of.   To admit it is to admit his clear right, nay, his bounden duty, to do battle for his side, passionately, desperately, and with any weapon at hand.

This he does in his book, and up to the limit of his forensic skill, which, I regret to have to add, is not noticeably great.   If, at times, he grows a bit muddled, and even maudlin, then let us not hold the fact against him, for a man performing a *pas seul* upon a red-hot stove cannot be expected to achieve an impeccable step.   It seems to me that this red-hot stove, at the moment, is under every conscious "Anglo-Saxon" in our great Republic—that he must be an insensate clod, indeed, if he does not feel the heat. The cultural leadership of the country is passing out of his hands, and he is beginning to lose even his political hegemony.   I sat in the Democratic National Convention in 1924 as the Hon. Al Smith rolled up his votes, and watched the Ku Kluxers on the floor. They were transfixed with horror: if it was a comedy,

then pulling tonsils is also a comedy. Dr. Abbott
mentions Dreiser. The influence of Dreiser upon the
literature of to-morrow in this land—upon all the
youngsters who are now coming to maturity in the
universities, and turning away from their ordained
professors—will be a hundred times as potent as that
of any New Englander now alive. Who is Dreiser?
When the grandfathers of the Republic were hanging
witches at Salem his forbears were raising grapes on
the Rhine. Dr. Abbott professes history at Harvard.
During the past ten years but one professor at that
great university has materially colored the stream of
ideas in America. He has since escaped abroad—
and is a Spaniard. Every day a new Catholic church
goes up; every day another Methodist or Presbyterian
church is turned into a garage. But there is no need
to labor the point. The fact is too obvious that the
old easy dominance of the "Anglo-Saxon" is passing,
that he must be up and doing if he would fasten his
notions upon the generations to come. And the fact
is equally obvious that his success in that emprise, so
far, has been extremely indifferent—that, despite the
great advantages that he enjoys, of position, of authority, of ancient right, he is making very heavy
weather of it, and not even holding his own. I am
frankly against him, and believe, as I have often
made known, that he is doomed—that his opponents
will turn out, in the long run, to be better men than

he is.   But I confess that I'd enjoy the combat more
if he showed less indignation and more skill.

Dr. Abbott himself reveals many characteristic
"Anglo-Saxon" weaknesses.   His incoherence I have
mentioned.   There is also a downright inconsistency,
often glaring.   On one page he denounces all non-
"Anglo-Saxons" as opponents of democracy; on another (for example, page 242) he denounces the
fundamental tenets of democracy himself.   This inconsistency is visible in nine "Anglo-Saxon" gladia-
tors out of ten.   What ails them all is that they have
to defend democracy, and yet do not believe in it.
Has any good "Anglo-Saxon" ever believed in it?
I sometimes doubt it.   Did Washington?   Did John
Adams?   Jefferson did, but wasn't there a Celtic
strain in him—wasn't he, after all, somewhat dubious,
a sort of assistant American?   In any case, the surviving Fathers were all apparently against him.   In
our own time how many "Anglo-Saxons" of the
educated class actually believe in democracy?   I
know of none, and have heard of none.   The late
war revealed their true faith very brilliantly and even
humorously.   It was a crusade for democracy, and
yet one of the shining partners was the late Czar of
Russia!   The assault upon the Kaiser was led by
Roosevelt!   The chief official enemy of absolutism
was Wilson!   No wonder the whole thing collapsed
into absurdity.   Dr. Abbott falls into a similar ab-

surdity more than once. His book would be vastly
more effective if he took all the idle prattle about democracy out of it, and grounded it upon the forthright doctrine that the "Anglo-Saxons," having got
here first, own the country, and have a clear right
to impose political disabilities upon later comers—
in other words, if he advocated the setting up of an
"Anglo-Saxon" aristocracy, with high privileges and
prerogatives, eternally beyond the reach of the mon-
grel commonalty. This, in point of fact, is what he
advocates, however much he may cloud his advocacy
in democratic terms. I call upon him with all
solemnity to throw off his false-face and come out
with the bald, harsh doctrine. There is more logic
in it than in his present nonsense; he could preach it
more powerfully and beautifully. More, he would
get help from unexpected quarters. I can speak, of
course, only for one spear. I might quibble and protest, but I'd certainly be sorely tempted.

7

Yazoo's Favorite

AN OLD-FASHIONED SENATOR, by Harris Dickson. New York:
The Frederick A. Stokes Company. [The Nation, October 14,
1925.]

Some time ago, essaying a literary survey of the
Republic, I animadverted sadly upon the dreadful

barrenness of the great State of Mississippi.   Speaking as a magazine editor, I said that I had never heard of a printable manuscript coming out of it. Speaking as a frequenter of the Athenian grove, I said that I had never heard of it hatching an idea. Instantly there was an uproar from Iuka to Pascagoula.   The vernacular press had at me with appalling yells; there were demands from the Ku Klux that I come down to Jackson and say it again; Kiwanis joined the Baptist Young People's Society in denouncing me as one debauched by Russian gold.   Worse, the Mississippi intelligentsia also had at me.   Emerging heroically from the crypts and spring-houses where they were fugitive from Rotary, they bawled me out as ignorant and infamous.   Had I never heard, they demanded, of Harris Dickson, the Mississippi Balzac?   Had I never heard of John Sharp Williams, the Mississippi Gladstone?

I had, but remained unmoved.   I now continue unmoved after reading Balzac's tome on Gladstone.   It is, in its small way, a tragic book.   Here, obviously, is the best that Mississippi can do, in theme and treatment—and it is such puerile, blowsy stuff that reviewing it realistically would be too cruel.   Here the premier literary artist of Mississippi devotes himself *con amore* to the life and times of the premier Mississippi statesman—and the result is a volume so maudlin and nonsensical that it would disgrace a schoolboy. The book is simply mush—and out of the mush there emerges only a third-rate politician, professionally bucolic and as hollow as a jug.

Yet this Williams, during his long years in Congress, passed in Washington as an intellectual. Cloak-room and barroom gossip credited him with a profound education and very subtle parts. Such ideas, when they prevail in Washington, perhaps need and deserve no investigation; the same astute correspondents who propagated this one later coupled the preposterous Coolidge with Pericles. But maybe there was some logic in it, after all; Williams, at some time in the past, had been to Heidelberg and knew more or less German and French. That accomplishment, in a Southern politician, was sufficient to set the capital by the ears. So the Williams legend grew, and toward the end it rose to the dignity of a myth, like that of Dr. Taft's eminence as a constitutional lawyer. Even the learned hero's daily speeches on Teutonic mythology during the war did not drag him out of Valhalla himself. The press-gallery gaped and huzzahed.

But the Heidelberg chapter in Mr. Dickson's book leaves the myth rather sick. It starts off, indeed, with a disconcerting couplet:

> In Germany 'twas very clear
> He'd leave the rapiers for beer.

And what follows is distressingly silent about cultural accretions. Young Williams' main business at Heidelberg, it appears, was putting the abominable Prussian *Junker* in their place. They naturally assumed that their American fellow-student could be thrown about with impunity. Encountering him on the sidewalk, they tried, in the manner made historic by the Creel Press Bureau, to shove him off. Presently one of these fiends in human form came melodramatically to grief. Williams challenged him, and "according to Prussian ethics," named the weapons—pistols. A shock, indeed! The monster expected sabers, at which he was diabolically expert, but Williams didn't intend "to go home with his face all slashed, and have folks jeer at him for getting his jaw cut on a beer glass." Facing cold lead, the Prussian was so scared that he fired prematurely. Worse, he so lost his wits that he addressed his antagonist as Freiherr Williams. That antagonist fired into a snowbank. Some time later, having thus got all that was of worth out of Heidelberg, he came sailing home, "full even then of his ultimate intention: he'd go in for politics, he'd become a professional politician."

A professional politician he remained for thirty years, always in office, first in the House and then in the Senate. His start was slow—he practiced law for a time—, but once he was on the payroll he stayed there until old age was upon him. For a number of years he was Democratic leader in the House; twice he got the party vote for the Speakership. In the Senate he was technically in the ranks, but on great occasions he stepped forward. His specialties, toward the end, were the divine inspiration of Woodrow Wilson, the incomparable valor of the American soldier, the crimes of the Kaiser, the superiority of the "Anglo-Saxon," the godlike bellicosity of the Confederate gentry, and the nature and functions of a gentleman. On these themes he discoursed almost every afternoon. The boys in the press-gallery liked him, and he got plenty of space. Always his rodomontades brought forth dark hints about his esoteric learning, and the news that, next after Henry Cabot Lodge, he was the most cultivated man in the Senate.

Mr. Dickson prints extracts from some of his speeches. Criticism, obviously, is an art not yet in practice in Mississippi, even among the literati. I used to read him in the *Congressional Record;* he was really not so bad as Dickson makes him out. His career, seen in retrospect, seems to have been mainly a vacuum. Once or twice he showed a certain fine dignity, strange in a Southern politician. He opposed the Prohibition frenzy. He voted against the bonus. But usually, despite his constant talk of independence, he ran with the party pack. For years a professional Jeffersonian, he brought his career to a climax by giving lyrical support to the Emperor Woodrow, who heaved the Jeffersonian heritage into the ash-can.   During the La Follette uproar he was one of the most vociferous of the witch-burners.   He passed out in silence, regretted for his rustic charm, but not much missed.

I commend "An Old-Fashioned Senator" to all persons who are interested in the struggle of the South to throw off its cobwebs.   Both as document and as work of art the book makes it very plain why Mississippi's place in that struggle is in the last rank.

8

The Father of Service

THE LIFE STORY OF ORISON SWETT MARDEN, by Margaret Connolly. New York: *The Thomas Y. Crowell Company.* [The American Mercury, February, 1926.]

If Dr. Martin had not written his first book, said Frank A. Munsey one day, he would have been a millionaire.   By Munseyan standards, praise could go no higher—and Munsey knew his man, for they were fellow-waiters in a Summer hotel back in the '70's and kept up friendly exchange until Marden's death in 1924.   Both sprang from the hard, inhospitable soil of Northern New England, both knew dire poverty in youth, both got somewhere a yearning for literary exercises, and both cherished an immense respect for the dollar. But though fate brought them together when they were young, they chose different paths later on. Munsey, with "Afloat in a Great City," "The Boy Broker," and other inspirational master-works behind him, abandoned beautiful letters for the stock market, and eventually gathered in so much money that he could afford to butcher great newspapers in sheer excess of animal spirits, as lesser men butcher clay pigeons. Marden, going the other way, abandoned the hotel business, for which he seemed to have had genius, for the pen, and devoted the last thirty years of his life to composition.

His bibliography runs to a hundred or more volumes—a colossal, relentless, overwhelming deluge of bilge. All his books have the same subject: getting on in the world. That was, to him, the only conceivable goal of human aspiration. Day in and day out, for three decades, he preached his simple gospel to all mankind, not only in his books, but also in countless pamphlets, in lectures, and in the pages of his magazine, *Success*. Its success was instantaneous and durable. His first book, "Pushing to the Front," rapidly went through a dozen editions, and was presently translated into a dozen foreign languages. It remained, to the end, his best-seller, but it had many formidable rivals. Altogether, his writings in book-form must have reached a total of 20,000,000 copies, including 3,000,000 in twenty-five tongues other than

English. In Germany alone he sold more than 500,000 copies of thirty volumes. He remains to-day the most popular of American authors in Europe, and by immense odds. I have encountered transla-tions of his books on the news-stands of remote towns in Spain, Poland and Czecho-Slovakia. In places where even Mark Twain is unknown—nay, even Jack London, Upton Sinclair and James Oliver Curwood— he holds aloft the banner of American literature.

I lack the stomach for the job myself, but I think a lot could be learned about the psychology of *Homo boobiens* through an intensive study of Marden's vast shelf of books. The few I have read seem to be ex-actly alike; no doubt all the rest resemble them very closely. What they preach, in brief, is the high value of hopefulness, hard work, high purpose and unflagging resolution. The appeal is to the natural discontent and vague aspiration of the common man. The remedy offered is partly practical and partly mystical—practical in its insistence upon the sound utility of the lowly virtues, mystical in its constant implication that matter will always yield to mind, that high thinking has a cash value. An evil philos-ophy? Surely not. A valid one? There it is not so easy to answer. Marden is full of proofs that what he preaches works—but only too often those proofs show the incredible appositeness and impeccability of patent-medicine testimonials. How many false hopes he must have raised in his day! One imagines humble hearts leaping to the gaudy tales of Judge Elbert Gary, Beethoven and Edison in the darkest reaches of Montenegro, Norway and Tennessee. Down went the dose, but was the patient actually cured? Well, perhaps, he at least *felt* better—and that was something. Marden was not to be pinned down to clinical records; he was, in his way, a poet, and even more a prophet. A religious exaltation was in him; he knew how to roll his eyes. The first article of his creed was that it was a sin to despair— that realism was a black crime against the Holy Ghost. He reduced the Beatitudes to one: Blessed are they that believe in their stars, and are up and doing.

His influence was immense, and perhaps mainly for the good. He soothed his customers with his optimistic taffy, and made them happier. It is, indeed, small wonder that eminent figures in finance and industry admired him greatly, and gave his books to their slaves. He turned the discontents of those slaves inward; instead of going on strike and breaking windows they sat up nights trying to generate inspiration and practicing hope and patience. He was thus a useful citizen in a democratic state, and comparable to the Rev. Dr. Billy Sunday. He preached a Direct Action of a benign and laudable sort, with Service running through it. His mark shines brilliantly from the forehead of every Y. M. C. A. secretary in the land, and from the foreheads, too, of most of the editorial writers. Many lesser platitudinarians followed him—for example, Dr. Frank Crane and the Rev. Dr. Henry van Dyke—, but he kept ahead of all of them. None other could put the obvious into such mellow and caressing terms. None other could so completely cast off all doubts and misgivings. When he spit on his hands and let himself out, the whole world began to sparkle like a Christmas tree. He was Kiwanis incarnate, with whispers of the Salvation Army. In early manhood he had cast off the demoniacal theology of his native hills, but one treasure of his Puritan heritage he retained to the end: he knew precisely and certainly what God wanted His children to be and do. God wanted them to be happy, and He wanted them to attain to happiness by working hard, saving money, obeying the boss, and keeping on the lookout for better jobs. Thus, after a hiatus of 137 years, Marden took up the torch of Poor Richard. He was, in his way, the American St. Paul. He was the pa of Kiwanis. He carried the gospel of American optimism to all the four quarters of the world.

9

A Modern Masterpiece

THE POET ASSASSINATED, by Guillaume Apollinaire, translated from the French by Matthew Josephson. New York: *The Broom Publishing Company.* [The American Mercury, March, 1924.]

Whatever may be said against the young literary lions of the Foetal School, whether by such hoary iconoclasts as Ernest Boyd or by such virginal presbyters as John S. Sumner, the saving fact remains that the boys and girls have, beneath their false faces, a sense of humor, and are not shy about playing it upon one another. Such passionate pioneers of the movement as *Broom* and the *Little Review* printed, in their day, capital parodies in every issue, many of them, I believe, deliberate and malicious—parodies of Ezra Pound by the Baroness Elsa von Freytag-Loringhoven, and of the Baroness Elsa Freytag-Loringhoven by E. E. Cummings, and of E. E. Cummings by young Roosevelt J. Yahwitz, Harvard '27. And the thing goes on to this day. Ah, that the rev. seniors of the Hypoendocrinal School were as gay and goatish! Ah, specifically, that Dr. Paul Elmer More would occasionally do a salacious burlesque of Dr. Brander Matthews, and that Dr.

Matthews would exercise his forecastle wit upon the Pennsylvania Silurian, Prof. Fred Lewis Pattee!

In the present work, beautifully printed by the *Broom* Press, there is jocosity in the grand manner. For a long while past, as time goes among such neologomaniacs, the youths of the movement have been whooping up one Guillaume Apollinaire. When this Apollinaire died in 1918, so they lamented, there passed out the greatest creative mind that France had seen since the Middle Ages. He was to Jean Cocteau, even, as Cocteau was to Eugène Sue. His books were uncompromising and revolutionary; had he lived he would have done to the banal prose of the Babbitts of letters what Eric Satie has done to the art of the fugue. Such news was not only printed in the *Tendenz* magazines that come and go; it was transmitted by word of mouth from end to end of Greenwich Village. More, it percolated to graver quarters. The estimable *Dial* let it be known that Apollinaire was a profound influence on the literature and perhaps still more on the art and spirit of this modern period. Once, when Dr. Canby was off lecturing in Lancaster, Pa., his name even got into the *Literary Review*.

This electric rumor of him was helped to prosperity by the fact that specific data about him were extremely hard to come by. His books seemed to be rare—some of them, indeed, unprocurable—, and even when one of them was obtained and examined it turned out to be largely unintelligible. He wrote, it appeared, in an occult dialect, partly made up of fantastic slang from the French army. He gave to old words new and mysterious meanings. He kept wholly outside the vocabulary at the back of "College French." Even returning exiles from La Rotonde were baffled by some of his phrases; all that they could venture was that they were unprecedented and probably obscene. But the Village, as everyone knows, does not spurn the cabalistic; on the contrary, it embraces and venerates the cabalistic. Apollinaire grew in fame as he became unscrutable. Displacing Cocteau, Paul Morand, Harry Kemp, T. S. Eliot, André Salmon, Paul Valéry, Maxwell Bodenheim, Jean Giraudoux and all the other gods of that checkered dynasty, he was lifted to the first place in the Valhalla of the Advanced Thinkers. It was Apollinaire's year. . . .

The work before us is the pricking of the bladder —a jest highly effective, but somewhat barbarous. M. Josephson simply translates Apollinaire's masterpiece, adds an *apparatus criticus* in the manner of T. S. Eliot, and then retires discreetly to wait for the yells. They will make a dreadful din, or I am no literary pathologist! For what does "The Poet Assassinated" turn out to be? It turns out to be a dull pasquinade in the manner of a rather atheistic sophomore, with a few dirty words thrown in to shock the *booboisie*.   From end to end there is not as much wit in it as you will hear in a genealogical exchange between two taxicab drivers.   It is flat, flabby and idiotic.   It is as profound as an editorial in the Washington *Star* and as revolutionary as Ayer's Almanac.   It is the best joke pulled off on the Young Forward-Lookers since Eliot floored them with the notes to "The Waste Land."

M. Josephson rather spoils its effect, I believe, by rubbing it in—that is, by hinting that Apollinaire was of romantic and mysterious origin—that his mother was a Polish lady of noble name and his father a high prelate of the Catholic Church—that he himself was born at Monte Carlo and baptized in Santa Maria Maggiore at Rome.   This is too much.   Apollinaire was, like all Frenchmen of humor, a German Jew. His father was a respectable waiter at Appenrodt's, by name Max Spritzwasser: hence the *nom de plume*. His mother was a Mlle. Kunigunda Luise Schmidt, of Holzkirchen, Oberbayern.

10

Sweet Stuff

SIX DAYS OF THE WEEK: A BOOK OF THOUGHTS ABOUT LIFE AND RELIGION, by Henry van Dyke. New York: *Charles Scribner's Sons*. [The American Mercury, March, 1925.]

I offer a specimen:

As living beings we are part of a universe of life.

A second:

Unless we men resolve to be good, the world will never be better.

A third:

Behind Christianity there is Christ.

A fourth:

If Washington had not liberated the American Republic, Lincoln would have had no Union to save.

A fifth:

Some people say that a revolution is coming on in our own age and country. It is possible.

A sixth:

God made us all.

A seventh:

It is a well-known fact that men can lie, and that very frequently they do.

An eighth:

To be foolish is an infirmity. To fool others is a trick.

A ninth:

The Bible was not given to teach science, but religion.

A tenth:

A whole life spent with God is better than half a life.

An eleventh:

Drunkenness ruins more homes and wrecks more lives than war.

A twelfth:

Anything out of the ordinary line will attract notice.

Tupper *est mort! Hoch* Tupper! *Hoch, hoch! Dreimal hoch!*

IX. THE FRINGES OF LOVELY LETTERS

1

Authorship as a Trade

I T is my observation as an editor that most beginning authors are attracted to the trade of letters, not because they have anything apposite and exigent to say, but simply because it seems easy. Let us imagine an ambitious and somewhat gassy young gal, turned out of the public highschool down the street with good marks in English—that is, in the sort of literary composition practiced by schoolma'ms. Having read "Ulysses," "Jurgen" and "Babbitt," she is disinclined to follow her mother too precipitately into the jaws of holy monogamy—or, at all events, she shrinks from marrying such a clod as her father is, and as her brothers and male classmates will be to-morrow. What to do? The professions demand technical equipment. Commerce is sordid. The secretary, even of a rich and handsome man, must get up at 7.30 A. M. Most of the fine arts are regarded, by her family, as immoral. So she pays $3 down on a second-hand typewriter, lays in a stock of copy paper, and proceeds to enrich the national literature.

It is such aspirants, I suppose, who keep the pot boiling for the schools of short-story writing and scenario writing that now swarm in the land. Certainly these schools, in so far as I have any acquaintance with them, offer nothing of value to the beginner of genuine talent. They seem to be run, in the main, by persons as completely devoid of critical sense as so many Congressmen, street railway curve-greasers or Methodist revivalists. Their text-books are masses of unmitigated rubbish. But no doubt that rubbish seems impressive enough to the customers I have mentioned, for it is both very vague and very cocksure—an almost irresistible combination. So a hundred thousand second-hand Coronas rattle and jingle in ten thousand remote and lonely towns, and the mail of every magazine editor in America is as heavy as the mail of a get-rich-quick stock-broker.

Unluckily, there is seldom anything in this mail to bulge his eyes and make his heart go pitter-pat. What he finds in it, day in and day out, is simply the same dull, obvious, shoddy stuff—the same banal and threadbare ideas set forth in the same flabby and unbeautiful words. They all seem to write alike, as, indeed, they all seem to think alike. They react to stimuli with the machine-like uniformity and precision of soldiers in a file. The spectacle of life

is to all of them exactly the same spectacle. They
bring no more to it, of private, singular vision, than
so many photographic lenses. In brief, they are
unanimously commonplace, unanimously stupid.
Free education has cursed them with aspirations beyond their congenital capacities, and they offer the
art of letters only the gifts suitable to the lowly crafts
of the jazz-baby and the schoolma'm. They come
from an intellectual level where conformity seems the
highest of goods, and so they lack the primary requis-
ite of the imaginative author: the capacity to see the
human comedy afresh, to discover new relations
between things, to discover new significances in man's
eternal struggle with his fate. What they have to
say is simply what any moderately intelligent suburban pastor or country editor would have to say, and
so it is not worth hearing.

This disparity between aspiration and equipment
runs through the whole of American life; material
prosperity and popular education have made it a sort
of national disease. Two-thirds of the professors in
our colleges are simply cans full of undigested knowledge, mechanically acquired; they cannot utilize it;
they cannot think. We are cursed likewise with
hordes of lawyers who would be happier and more
useful driving trucks, and hordes of doctors who
would be strained even as druggists. So in the realm
of beautiful letters. Poetry has become a recrea-

tion among us for the intellectually unemployed and
unemployable: persons who, a few generations ago,
would have taken it out on china-painting.   The writing of novels is undertaken by thousands who lack
the skill to describe a dog-fight.   The result is a
colossal waste of paper, ink and postage—worse, of
binding cloth and gold foil.   For a great deal of
this drivel, by one dodge or another, gets into print.
Many of the correspondence-school students, after
hard diligence, learn how to write for the cheap magazines; not a few of them eventually appear between
covers, and are solemnly reviewed.

Does such stuff sell?   Apparently it does, else
the publishers would not print so much of it.   Its
effect upon those who read it must be even worse
than that of the newspapers and popular magazines.
They come to it with confident expectations.   It is
pretentiously bound; *ergo,* there must be something
in it.   That something is simply platitude.   What
has been said a thousand times is said all over again.
This time it must be true!   Thus the standardization
of the American mind goes on, and against ideas
that are genuinely novel there are higher and higher
battlements erected.   Meanwhile, on the lower levels,
where the latest recruits to letters sweat and hope, this
rubbish is laboriously imitated.   Turn to any of the
cheap fiction magazines, and you will find out how
bad it can be at its worst.   No, not quite at its worst,

for the contributors to the cheap fiction magazines have at least broken into print—they have as they say, made the grade. Below them are thousands of aspirants of even slenderer talents—customers of the correspondence schools, patrons of lectures by itinerant literary pedagogues, patient manufacturers of the dreadful stuff that clogs every magazine editor's mail. Here is the ultimate reservoir of the national literature—and here, unless I err, is only bilge.

The remedy? I know of none. Moreover, I do not believe in remedies. So long as the prevailing pedagogues are not found out, and the absurd effort to cram every moron with book-learning goes on in the Republic, that long there will be too much reading, and too much writing. But let us get out of the fact whatever consolation is in it: too much writing, at worst, is at least a bearable evil. Certainly it is vastly less dangerous than too much religion, and less a nuisance than too much politics, The floggers of Coronas, if they were halted by law, might take to the uplift—as, indeed, many corn-fed pedagogues are already doing, driven out of their jobs by the murrain of Fundamentalism. If I yell against them it is because, on days when the rain keeps me indoors, I am a critic. Perhaps other folks suffer less. Nevertheless, I often wonder what the genuinely competent novelists of the nation think of it—how the invasion of their craft by so many bunglers and numskulls appears to them, and affects them. Surely it must tend to narrow the audience they appeal to, and so do them damage. Who was it who said that, in order that there may be great poets, there must be great audiences too? I believe it was old Walt. He knew. Facing an audience deluged with molasses by Whittier, Felicia Hemans and Fanny Fern, he found the assumptions all against him. He was different, and hence suspicious: it took him two generations to make his way. The competent novelist, setting up shop in America to-day, is confronted by the same flood. If he is pertinacious, he may win in the end, but certainly it takes endurance. Hergesheimer, in his first book, unquestionably had something to say. Its point of view was new; there was a fine plausibility in it; it was worth attending to. But Hergesheimer drove along for eight or ten years, almost in a vacuum. I could add others: Anderson, Cabell, even Dreiser. Cabell became known to the women's clubs with his twelfth book. Meanwhile, a dozen cheesemongers had been adored, and a thousand had made good livings with their sets of rubber-stamps.

2

Authors as Persons

My trade forces me into constant association with persons of literary skill and aspiration, good and bad,

male and female, foreign and domestic. I can only
report, after a quarter of a century of commerce with
them, that I find them, with a few brilliant exceptions, very dull, and that I greatly prefer the society
of Babbitts. Is this heresy? If so, I can only offer
my sincere regrets. The words are wrung from me,
not by any desire to be unpleasant, but simply by a
lifelong and incurable affection for what, for want
of a better name, is called the truth. Nine-tenths
of the literary gents that I know, indeed, are hotter
for the dollar than any Babbitt ever heard of. Their
talk is not about what they write, but about what they
get for it. Not infrequently they get a great deal.
I know a number who make more annually than honest
bank presidents, even than Christian bank presidents. A few probably top the incomes of railroad
purchasing-agents and nose-and-throat specialists, and
come close to the incomes of realtors, lawyers and
bootleggers. They practice a very profitable trade.

And no wonder, for they pursue it in the most
assiduously literate country in Christendom. Our
people, perhaps, seldom read anything that is good,
but they at least read—day and night, weekdays and
Sundays. We have so many magazines of more than
500,000 circulation that a list of them would fill
this page. We have at least a dozen above 1,000,000.
These magazines have immense advertising revenues,
and are thus very prosperous. They can therefore

pay high prices for manuscripts. The business of supplying such manuscripts has made a whole herd of authors rich. I do not object to their wealth; I simply report its lamentable effects upon them, and upon the aspirants who strive to imitate them. For those effects go down to the lowest levels. The neophyte, as I have said, seldom shows any yearning to discharge ideas, to express himself, to tackle and master a difficult enterprise; he shows only a desire to get money in what seems to him to be an easy way. Short cuts, quick sales, easy profits—it is all very American. Do we gabble about efficiency? Then the explanation is to be sought in the backwashes of Freudism. Nowhere else on earth is genuine competence so rare. The average American plumber cannot plumb; the average American cook cannot cook; the average American literary gent has nothing to say, and says it with rubber-stamps.

But I was speaking of the literati as persons. They suffer, I believe from two things. The first is what I have just described: their general fraudulence. The second springs out of the fact that their position, in the Republic, is very insecure—that they have no public dignity. It is no longer honorable *per se* to be engaged in travails of the spirit, as it used to be in the New England of the *Aufklärung;* it is honorable only if it pays. I believe that the fact discourages many aspirants who, if they went on, might come to something. They are blasted in their tender years, and so literature loses them. Too sensitive to sit below the salt, they join the hearty, red-blooded men who feast above it, admired by the national gallery. It is, indeed, not surprising that the majority of college graduates, once headed as a matter of course for the grove of Athene, now go into business—that Harvard now turns out ten times as many bond salesmen every year as metaphysicians and martyrs. Business, in America, offers higher rewards than any other human enterprise, not only in money but also in dignity. Thus it tends to attract the best brains of the country. Is Kiwanis idiotic? The answer is that Kiwanis no more represents business than Greenwich Village represents literature. On the higher levels its bilge does not flow—and on those higher levels, as I have hinted, there are shrewder fellows, and more amusing, than ever you will find in the Authors' Club. These fellows, by the strict canons of ethnology, are Babbitts, but it seems to me that they are responsible nevertheless for everything that makes life in the United States tolerable. One finds, in their company, excellent wines and liquors, and one seldom hears any cant.

I don't believe that this is a healthy state of affairs. I believe that business should be left to commonplace and insensitive minds, and that men of originality, and hence of genuine charm, should be sucked auto-

matically into enterprises of a greater complexity and
subtlety.   It is done in more ancient countries; it has
been done from remote antiquity under civilizations
that have aged in the wood, and are free from fusel
oil.   But it is not yet done in These States.   Only an
overwhelming natural impulse—perhaps complicated
by insanity—can urge an American into the writing
of fugues or epics.   The pull is toward the investment securities business.   That pull, yielded to,
leads to high rewards.   The successful business man
among us—and only the sheer imbecile, in such
gaudy times as these, is not successful—enjoys the
public respect and adulation that elsewhere bathe
only bishops and generals of artillery.   He is treated
with dignity in the newspapers, even when he appears
in combat with his wife's lover.   His opinion is
sought upon all public questions, including the
æsthetic.   In the stews and wine-shops he receives
the attention that, in old Vienna, used to be given to
Beethoven.   He enjoys an aristocratic immunity to
most forms of judicial process.   He wears the *legion
d'honneur*, is an LL. D. of Yale, and is received cor-
dially at the White House.

The literary gent, however worthy, scales no such
heights under our *Kultur*.   Only one President since
the birth of the Republic has ever welcomed men of
letters at the White House, and that one, the sainted
Roosevelt, judged them by their theological orthodoxy

and the hair upon their chests. A few colored poets were added to make the first pages; that was all. The literati thus wander about somewhat disconsolately among us, and tend to become morose and dull. If they enjoy the princely fees of the train-boy magazines, they are simply third-rate business men— successful, perhaps, but without the Larger Vision. If they happen to be genuine artists—and now and then it *does* happen—they are as lonely as life insurance solicitors at a convention of Seventh Day Adventists. Such sorrows do not make for *Gemütlichkeit.* There is much more of it in the pants business.

3

Birth Pangs

I have just said that the typical American author, when he talks intelligibly at all, talks of money. I have said also that his aim in writing is not to rid himself of ideas that bulge and fever his skull, but to get that money in an easy way. Both statements, though true, need a certain qualification. Writing looks easier to the neophyte than any other job open to him, but once he settles down to its practice he finds that it is full of unanticipated pains. So he tends, as he grows older, to talk of those pains almost as much as he talks of their rewards in cash. Here, indeed, all the authors that I know agree, if they agree on nothing else, and in their agreement they show the greatest heat and eloquence. And the beautiful ladies of the trade reënforce and ratify the plaint of the bucks. Writing, they all say, is the most dreadful chore ever inflicted upon human beings. It is not only exhausting mentally; it is also extremely fatiguing physically. The writer leaves his desk, his day's work done, with his mind empty and the muscles of his back and neck full of a crippling stiffness. He has suffered horribly that the babies may be fed and beauty may not die.

The worst of it is that he must always suffer alone. If authors could work in large, well-ventilated factories, like cigarmakers or garment-workers, with plenty of their mates about and a flow of lively professional gossip to entertain them, their labor would be immensely lighter. But it is essential to their craft that they perform its tedious and vexatious operations *a cappella*, and so the horrors of loneliness are added to its other unpleasantnesses. An author at work is continuously and inescapably in the presence of himself. There is nothing to divert and soothe him. So every time a vagrant regret or sorrow assails him, it has him instantly by the ear, and every time a wandering ache runs down his leg it shakes him like the bite of a tiger. I have yet to meet an author who was not a hypochondriac. Saving only physicians, who are always ill and in fear of death, the literati are perhaps the most lavish consumers of pills and philtres in this world, and the most willing customers of surgeons. I can scarcely think of one, known to me personally, who is not constantly dosing himself with medicines, or regularly resorting to the knife. At the head of the craft stand men who are even more celebrated as invalids than they are as authors. I know of one who——

But perhaps I had better avoid invading what, after all, may be private confidences, though they are certainly not imparted in confidential tones. The point is that an author, penned in a room during all his working hours with no company save his own, is bound to be more conscious than other men of the petty malaises that assail all of us. They tackle him, so to speak, in a vacuum; he can't seek diversion from them without at the same time suffering diversion from his work. And what they leave of him is tortured and demoralized by wayward and uncomfortable thoughts. It must be obvious that other men, even among the intelligentsia, are not beset so cruelly. A judge on the bench, entertaining a ringing in the ears, can do his work almost as well as if he heard only the voluptuous rhetoric of the lawyers. A clergyman, carrying on his degraded mummery, is not appreciably crippled by a sour stomach: what he says has been said before, and only scoundrels question it. And a surgeon, plying his exhilarating art and mystery, suffers no professional damage from the wild thought that the attending nurse is more sightly than his wife. But I defy anyone to write a competent sonnet with a ringing in his ears, or to compose sound criticism with a sour stomach, or to do a plausible love scene with a head free of private amorous fancies. These things are sheer impossibilities. The poor literatus encounters them and their like every time he enters his work-room and spits on his hands. The moment the door bangs he begins a depressing, losing struggle with his body and his mind.

Why then, do rational men and women engage in so barbarous and exhausting a vocation—for there are relatively intelligent and enlightened authors, remember, just as there are relatively honest politicians, and even bishops. What keeps them from deserting it for trades that are less onerous, and, in the eyes of their fellow creatures, more respectable? The first, and perhaps the foremost reason I have already exposed at length: the thing pays. But there is another, and it ought to be heard too. It lies, I believe, in the fact that an author, like any other so-called artist, is a man in whom the normal vanity of all men is so vastly exaggerated that he finds it a sheer impossibility to hold it in. His overpowering impulse is to gyrate before his fellow men, flapping his wings and emitting defiant yells. This being forbidden by the *Polizei* of all civilized countries, he takes it out by putting his yells on paper. Such is the thing called self-expression.

In the confidences of the literati, of course, it is always depicted as something much more mellow and virtuous. Either they argue that they are moved by a yearning to spread the enlightenment and save the world, or they allege that what steams them and makes them leap is a passion for beauty. Both theories are quickly disposed of by an appeal to the facts. The stuff written by nine authors out of ten, it must be plain at a glance, has as little to do with spreading the enlightenment as the state papers of the late Dr. Warren Gamaliel Harding. And there is no more beauty in it, and no more sign of a feeling of beauty, than you will find in a hotel dining-room or a college yell. The impulse to create beauty, indeed, is rather rare in literary men, and almost completely absent from the younger ones. If it shows itself at all, it comes as a sort of after-thought. Far ahead of it comes the yearning to make money. And after the yearning to make money comes the yearning to make a noise. The impulse to create beauty lingers far behind; not infrequently there is a void where it ought to be. Authors, as a class, are extraordinarily insensitive to beauty, and the fact reveals itself in their customary (and often incredibly extensive) ignorance of the other arts.

I'd have a hard job naming six American novelists who could be depended upon to recognize a fugue without prompting, or six poets who could give a rational account of the difference between a Gothic cathedral and a Standard Oil filling-station. The thing goes even further. Most novelists, in my experience, know nothing of poetry, and very few poets have any feeling for the beauties of prose. As for the dramatists, three-fourths of them are unaware that such things as prose and poetry exist at all. It pains me to set down such inconvenient and blushful facts. They will be seized upon, I daresay, by the evangelists of Kiwanis, and employed to support the doctrine that authors are public enemies, and ought to be deported to Russia. I do not go so far. I simply say that many who pursue the literary life are less romantic and high-toned than they might be—that communion with them is anything but the thrilling thing that provincial club ladies fancy. If the fact ought to be concealed, then blame my babbling upon scientific passion. That passion, to-day, has me by the ear.

4

Want Ad

The death of William Dean Howells in 1920 brought to an end a decorous and orderly era in American letters, and issued in a sort of anarchy.

One may best describe the change, perhaps, by throwing it into dramatic form. Suppose Joseph Conrad and Anatole France were still alive and on their way to the United States on a lecture tour, or to study Prohibition or sex hygiene, or to pay their respects to Henry Ford. Suppose they were to arrive in New York at 2 P. M. to-day. Who would go down the bay on a revenue-cutter to meet them—that is, who in addition to the newspaper reporters and baggage-searchers—who to represent American Literature? I can't think of a single fit candidate. So long as Howells kept to his legs he was chosen almost automatically for all such jobs, for he was the dean of the national letters, and acknowledged to be such by everyone. Moreover, he had experience at the work and a natural gift for it. He looked well in funeral garments. He had a noble and ancient head. He made a neat and caressing speech. He understood etiquette. And before he came to his growth, stretching back into the past, there was a long line precisely like him—Mark Twain, General Lew Wallace, James Russell Lowell, Edmund Clarence Stedman, Richard Watson Gilder, Bryant, Emerson, Irving, Cooper, and so on back to the dark abysm of time.

Such men performed a useful and highly onerous function. They represented letters in all public and official ways. When there was a grand celebration at one of the older universities they were present in their robes, freely visible to the lowliest sophomore. When there was a great banquet, they sat between generals in the Army and members of the firm of J. P. Morgan & Company. When there was a solemn petition or protest to sign—against fiat money, the massacres in Armenia, municipal corruption, or the lack of international copyright—they signed in fine round hands, not for themselves alone, but for the whole fraternity of American literati. Most important of all, when a literary whale from foreign parts was sighted off Fire Island, they jumped into their frock coats, clapped on their plug-hats and made the damp, windy trip through the Narrows on the revenue-cutter, to give the visitor welcome in the name of the eminent living and the illustrious dead. It was by such men that Dickens was greeted, and Thackeray, and Herbert Spencer, and Max O'Rell, and Blasco Ibáñez, and Matthew Arnold, and James M. Barrie, and Kipling, and (until they found his bootleg wife under his bed) Maxim Gorky. I name names at random. No worthy visitor was overlooked. Always there was the stately committee on the revenue-cutter, always there was the series of polite speeches, and always there was the general feeling that the right thing had been done in the right way—that American literature had been represented in a tasteful and resounding manner.

Who is to represent it to-day? I search the country

without finding a single suitable candidate, to say nothing of a whole posse. Turn, for example, to the mystic nobles of the American Academy of Arts and Letters. I pick out five at random: William C. Brownell, Augustus Thomas, Hamlin Garland, Owen Wister and Henry van Dyke. What is wrong with them? The plain but dreadful fact that no literary foreigner has even heard of them—that their appearance on the deck of his incoming barge would puzzle and alarm him, and probably cause him to call for the police. These men do not lack the homely virtues. They all spell correctly, write neatly, and print nothing that is not constructive. In the five of them there is not enough sin to raise a Congressman's temperature one-hundredth of a degree. But they are completely devoid of what is absolutely essential to the official life: they have, so to speak, no stage presence. There is nothing rotund and gaudy about them. No public and unanimous reverence bathes them. What they write or say never causes any talk. To be welcomed by them, jointly or severally, would appear to Thomas Hardy or Gabriel D'Annunzio as equal to being welcomed by representatives of the St. Joe, Mo., Rotary Club. Nor do I find any better stock among their heirs and apprentices in the National Institute. Put Henry Sydnor Harrison, say, against Howells: it it a wart succeeding Ossa. Match Clayton Hamilton with Edmund Clarence Stedman: Broadway against

Wall Street.   Shove Robert W. Chambers or Herman Hagedorn into the coat of Lowell: he would rattle in one of its pockets.

Worse, there are no better candidates outside the academic cloister.   I daresay that most literate foreigners, asked to name the principal American novelist in practice to-day, would nominate Theodore Dreiser.   He would get probably seventy-five per cent of the votes, with the rest scattered among Upton Sinclair, Sinclair Lewis, Cabell, Hergesheimer and Sherwood Anderson.   But try to imagine any of these gentlemen togged out in a long-tailed coat, shivering on the deck of a revenue-cutter while Gerhart Hauptman got a grip on himself aboard the *Majestic!*   Try to imagine Cabell presiding at a banquet to Knut Hamsun, with Dr. A. Lawrence Lowell to one side of him and Otto Kahn to the other!   Try to picture Sinclair handing James Joyce a wreath to put upon the grave of James Whitcomb Riley!   The vision, indeed, is more dismal than ludicrous.   Howells, the last of his lordly line, is missed tremendously; there is something grievously lacking in the official hospitality of the country.   The lack showed itself the instant he was called away.   A few weeks later Columbia University gave a soirée in honor of the centenary of Lowell.   The president of Columbia, Dr. Nicholas Murray Butler, is a realist.   Moreover, he is a member of the American Academy himself, elected as a wet to succeed Edgar Allan Poe. He was thus privy to the deficiencies of his colleagues. To conceal the flabbiness of the evening he shoved them into back seats—and invited John D. Rockefeller, Jr., Tex Rickard, General Pershing and the board of governors of the New York Stock Exchange to the platform!

I believe that, of living masters of letters, H. G. Wells was the first to feel the new chill. When he last visited the Republic he was made welcome by a committee of ship-news reporters. It was as if one of the justices of the King's Bench, landing in America, had been received by a committee of police-court lawyers from Gary, Ind. Later on American literature bestirred itself and gave Wells a banquet in New York. I was present at this feast, and a singular one it was. Not a single author read in Iowa or taught at Harvard was present. The principal literatus at the board was the late Frank A. Munsey, author of "Derringforth" and "The Boy Broker," and the principal address was made by Max Eastman, formerly editor of the *Masses!* . . .

I come to a constructive suggestion. Let the literati of America meet in their respective places of social relaxation, each gang determining the credentials of its own members, and elect delegates to a national convention. Then let the national convention, by open ballot, choose ten spokesmen and ten alter-

nates to represent the national letters on all formal
occasions—not only when an eminent foreigner is
to be made welcome, but also when Columbia University holds memorial services, when a President is
inaugurated, when Harvard meets Yale, when monuments are unveiled—in brief at all times of solemn
public ceremonial. Let these representatives practice deportment and elocution. Let them employ
good tailors and trustworthy bootleggers. I have,
alas, no candidates for the committee. As I have
said, there is a dreadful dearth of them. Does
Dr. Frank Crane wear whiskers? If so, I nominate
him.

5

Literature and the Schoolma'm

With precious few exceptions, all the books on style
in English are by writers quite unable to write. The
subject, indeed, seems to exercise a special and dreadful fascination over schoolma'ms, bucolic college professors, and other such pseudo-literates. One never
hears of treatises on it by George Moore or James
Branch Cabell, but the pedagogues, male and female,
are at it all the time. In a thousand texts they set
forth their depressing ideas about it, and millions of
suffering high-school pupils have to study what they
say. Their central aim, of course, is to reduce the

whole thing to a series of simple rules—the overmastering passion of their melancholy order, at all times and everywhere. They aspire to teach it as bridge whist, the American Legion flag-drill and double-entry bookkeeping are taught. They fail as ignominiously as that Athenian of legend who essayed to train a regiment of grasshoppers in the goose-step.

For the essence of a sound style is that it cannot be reduced to rules—that it is a living and breathing thing, with something of the devilish in it—that it fits its proprietor tightly and yet ever so loosely, as his skin fits him. It is, in fact, quite as securely an integral part of him as that skin is. It hardens as his arteries harden. It has *Katzenjammer* on the days succeeding his indiscretions. It is gaudy when he is young and gathers decorum when he grows old. On the day after he makes a mash on a new girl it glows and glitters. If he has fed well, it is mellow. If he has gastritis it is bitter. In brief, a style is always the outward and visible symbol of a man, and it cannot be anything else. To attempt to teach it is as silly as to set up courses in making love. The man who makes love out of a book is not making love at all; he is simply imitating someone else making love. God help him if, in love or literary composition, his preceptor be a pedagogue!

The schoolma'm theory that the writing of English may be taught is based upon a faulty inference from a sound observation. The sound observation is that the great majority of American high-school pupils, when they attempt to put their thoughts upon paper, produce only a mass of confused and puerile nonsense—that they express themselves so clumsily that it is often quite impossible to understand them at all. The faulty inference is to the effect that what ails them is a defective technical equipment—that they can be trained to write clearly as a dog may be trained to walk on its hind legs. This is all wrong. What ails them is not a defective technical equipment but a defective natural equipment. They write badly simply because they cannot think clearly. They cannot think clearly because they lack the brains. Trying to teach them is as hopeless as trying to teach a dog with only one hind leg. Any human being who can speak English understandably has all the materials necessary to write English clearly, and even beautifully. There is nothing mysterious about the written language; it is precisely the same, in essence, as the spoken language. If a man can think in English at all, he can find words enough to express his ideas. The fact is proved abundantly by the excellent writing that often comes from so-called ignorant men. It is proved anew by the even better writing that is done on higher levels by persons of great simplicity, for example, Abraham Lincoln. Such writing commonly arouses little enthusiasm among pedagogues.

Its transparency excites their professional disdain, and they are offended by its use of homely words and phrases. They prefer something more ornate and complex—something, as they would probably put it, demanding more thought. But the thought they yearn for is the kind, alas, that they secrete themselves—the muddled, highfalutin, vapid thought that one finds in their own text-books.

I do not denounce them because they write so badly; I merely record the fact in a sad, scientific spirit. Even in such twilight regions of the intellect the style remains the man. What is in the head infallibly oozes out of the nub of the pen. If it is sparkling Burgundy the writing is full of life and charm. If it is mush the writing is mush too. The late Dr. Harding, twenty-ninth President of the Federal Union, was a highly self-conscious stylist. He practiced prose composition assiduously, and was regarded by the pedagogues of Marion, Ohio, and vicinity as a very talented fellow. But when he sent a message to Congress it was so muddled in style that even the late Henry Cabot Lodge, a professional literary man, could not understand it. Why? Simply because Dr. Harding's thoughts, on the high and grave subjects he discussed, were so muddled that he couldn't understand them himself. But on matters within his range of customary meditation he was clear and even charming, as all of us are. I once heard him deliver a brief address upon the ideals of the Elks. It was a topic close to his heart, and he had thought about it at length and *con amore*. The result was an excellent speech—clear, logical, forceful, and with a touch of wild, romantic beauty. His sentences hung together. He employed simple words, and put them together with skill. But when, at a public meeting in Washington, he essayed to deliver an oration on the subject of the late Dante Alighieri, he quickly became so obscure and absurd that even the Diplomatic Corps began to snicker. The cause was plain: he knew no more about Dante than a Tennessee county judge knows about the Institutes of Justinian. Trying to formulate ideas upon the topic, he could get together only a few disjected fragments and ghosts of ideas—here an ear, there a section of tibia, beyond a puff of soul substance or other gas. The resultant speech was thus enigmatical, cacophonous and awful stuff. It sounded precisely like a lecture by a college professor on style.

A pedagogue, confronted by Dr. Harding in class, would have set him to the business of what is called improving his vocabulary—that is, to the business of making his writing even worse than it was. Dr. Harding, in point of fact, had all the vocabulary that he needed, and a great deal more. Any idea that he could formulate clearly he could convey clearly. Any idea that genuinely moved him he could invest with charm—which is to say, with what the peda-gogues call style.   I believe that this capacity is pos-sessed by all literate persons above the age of four-teen.   It is not acquired by studying text-books; it is acquired by learning how to think.   Children even younger often show it.   I have a niece, now eleven years old, who already has an excellent style.   When she writes to me about things that interest her—in other words, about the things she is capable of think-ing about—she puts her thoughts into clear, dignified and admirable English.   Her vocabulary, so far, is unspoiled by schoolma'ms.   She doesn't try to knock me out by bombarding me with hard words, and phrases filched from Addison.   She is unaffected, and hence her writing is charming.   But if she es-sayed to send me a communication on the subject, say, of Balkan politics or government ownership, her style would descend instantly to the level of that of Dr. Harding's state papers.

To sum up, style cannot go beyond the ideas which lie at the heart of it.   If they are clear, it too will be clear.   If they are held passionately, it will be elo-quent.   Trying to teach it to persons who cannot think, especially when the business is attempted by persons who also cannot think, is a great waste of time, and an immoral imposition upon the taxpayers of the nation.   It would be far more logical to de-vote all the energy to teaching, not writing, but logic

—and probably just as useless. For I doubt that the art of thinking can be taught at all—at any rate, by school-teachers. It is not acquired, but congenital. Some persons are born with it. Their ideas flow in straight channels; they are capable of lucid reasoning; when they say anything it is instantly understandable; when they write anything it is clear and persuasive. They constitute, I should say, about one-eighth of one per cent. of the human race. The rest of God's children are just as incapable of logical thought as they are incapable of jumping over the moon. Trying to teach them to think is as vain an enterprise as trying to teach a streptococcus the principles of Americanism. The only thing to do with them is to make Ph.D.'s of them, and set them to writing handbooks on style.

6

The Critic and his Job

The assumption that it may be scientific is the worst curse that lies upon criticism. It is responsible for all the dull, blowsy, "definitive" stuff that literary pedagogues write, and it is responsible, too, for the heavy posturing that so often goes on among critics less learned. Both groups proceed upon the theory that there are exact facts to be ascertained, and that it is their business to ascertain and proclaim them.

That theory is nonsense. There is, in truth, no such thing as an exact fact in the whole realm of the beautiful arts. What is true therein to-day may be false to-morrow, or vice versa, and only too often the shift is brought about by something that, properly speaking, is not an æsthetic consideration at all.

The case of Whitman comes to mind at once. Orthodox criticism, in his own time, was almost unanimously against him. At his first appearance, true enough, a few critics were a bit dazzled by him, notably Emerson, but they quickly got control of their faculties and took to cover. Down to the time of his death the prevailing doctrine was that he was a third-rate poet and a dirty fellow. Any young professor who, in the seventies or even in the early eighties, had presumed to whoop for him in class would have been cashiered at once, as both incompetent and immoral. If there was anything definitively established in those days, it was that old Walt was below the salt. To-day he is taught to sophomores everywhere, perhaps even in Tennessee, and one of the most unctuously respectable of American publishing houses brings out "Leaves of Grass" unexpurgated, and everyone agrees that he is one of the glories of the national letters. Has that change been brought about by a purely critical process? Does it represent a triumph of criticism over darkness? It does not. It represents, rather, a triumph of external forces over criticism.   Whitman's first partisans were not interested in poetry; they were interested in sex. They were presently reënforced by persons interested in politics.   They were finally converted into a majority by a tatterdemalion horde of persons interested mainly, and perhaps only, in making a noise.

Literary criticism, properly so-called, had little if anything to do with this transformation.   Scarcely a critic of any recognized authority had a hand in it. What started it off, after the first furtive, gingery snuffling over "A Woman Waits for Me" and the "Calamus" cycle, was the rise of political radicalism in the early eighties, in reaction against the swinish materialism that followed the Civil War.   I am tempted to say that Terence V. Powderly had more to do with the rehabilitation of Whitman than any American critic, or, indeed, than any American poet. And if you object to Powderly, then I offer you Karl Marx, with William Jennings Bryan—no less!— peeping out of his coat-pocket.   The radicals made heavy weather of it at the start.   To the average respectable citizen they seemed to be mere criminals. Like the Bolsheviki of a later era, they were represented by their opponents as the enemies of all mankind.   What they needed, obviously, was some means of stilling the popular fear of them—some way of tapping the national sentimentality.   There stood Whitman, conveniently to hand.   In his sonorous strophes to an imaginary and preposterous democracy there was an eloquent statement of their own vague and windy yearnings, and, what is more, a certificate to their virtue as sound Americans. So they adopted him with loud hosannas, and presently he was both their poet and their philosopher. Long before any professor at Harvard dared to mention him (save, perhaps, with lascivious winks), he was being read to tatters by thousands of lonely Socialists in the mining-towns. As radicalism froze into Liberalism, and so began to influence the intelligentsia, his vogue rose, and by the end of the century even school-teachers had begun to hear of him. There followed the free verse poets, *i. e.*, a vast herd of emerging barbarians with an itch to make an uproar in the world, and no capacity for mastering the orthodox rules of prosody. Thus Whitman came to Valhalla, pushed by political propagandists and pulled by literary mountebanks. The native Taines and Matthew Arnolds made a gallant defense, but in vain. In the remoter denominational colleges some of them still hold out. But Whitman is now just as respectable at Yale as Martin Tupper or Edmund Clarence Stedman.

The point is that his new respectability is just as insecure as his old infamy—that he may be heaved out, on some bright to-morrow, just as he was heaved in, and by a similar combination of purely non-literary forces. Already I hear rumors of a plan to make

Dr. Coolidge King.   If his conscience stays him, then the throne may go to William Wrigley, Jr., or Judge Elbert H. Gary, LL.D.   Democracy, indeed, begins to sicken among us.   The doctors at its bedside dose it out of a black bottle, and make sinister signals to the coroner.   If it dies, then Whitman will probably die with it.   Criticism, of course, will labor desperately to save him, as it once labored to dispose of him, but such struggles are nearly always futile. The most they ever accomplish is to convert the author defended into a sort of fossil, preserved in a showcase to plague and puzzle schoolboys.   The orthodox literature books, used in all schools, are simply such showcases.   They represent the final effort of pedants to capture zephyrs and chain torrents.   They are monuments to the delusion that criticism may be definitive—that appeals to the emotions, which shift and change with every wind, may be appraised and sorted out by appeals to the mind, which is theoretically unchangeable.   Certainly every reflective student of any of the fine arts should know that this is not so.   There is no such thing as a literary immortality.   We remember Homer, but we forget the poets that the Greeks, too, forgot.   You may be sure that there were Shakespeares in Carthage, and more of them at the court of Amenophis IV, but their very names are lost.   Our own Shakespeare, as year chases year, may go the same way; in fact, his going the same way is quite as certain as anything we can imagine. A thousand years hence, even five hundred years hence, he may be, like Beowulf, only a name in a literature book, to be remembered against examination day and then forgotten.

Criticism is thus anything but scientific, for it cannot reach judgments that are surely and permanently valid. The most it can do, at its best, is to pronounce verdicts that are valid here and now, in the light of living knowledge and prejudice. As the background shifts the verdict changes. The best critic is not that fool who tries to resist the process—by setting up artificial standards, by prattling of laws and principles that do not exist, by going into the dead past for criteria of the present—, but that more prudent fellow who submits himself frankly to the flow of his time, and rejoices in its aliveness. Charles Augustin Sainte-Beuve was a good critic, for he saw everything as a Frenchman of the Second Empire, and if his judgments must be revised to-day it still remains true that they were honest and intelligent when he formulated them. Professor Balderdash is a bad critic, for he judges what is done in the American Empire of 1926 in the light of what was held to be gospel in the pastoral Republic of a century ago. For the rest, the critic survives, when he survives at all, mainly as artist. His judgments, in the long run, become archaic, and may be disregarded. But if,

in stating them, he has incidentally produced a work
of art on his own account, then he is read long after
they are rejected, and it may be plausibly argued that
he has contributed something to the glory of letters.
No one takes much stock in Macaulay's notions to-
day.   He is, in fact, fair game for any college tutor
who has majored in what is called history.   He fell
into many gross errors, and sometimes, it is probable,
he fell into them more or less deliberately.   But his
criticism is still read—that is, as much as any criticism is read.   It holds all its old charm and address.
For Macaulay, when he sat himself down to be critical, did not try fatuously to produce a scientific
treatise.   What he tried to do was to produce a work
of art.

7

Painting and its Critics

Having emerged lately from a diligent course of
reading in so-called art criticism, and especially in
that variety of it which is concerned with the painters
since Cézanne, I can only report that I find it windy
stuff, and sadly lacking in clarity and sense.   The
new critics, indeed, seem to me to be quite as vague
and absurd as some of the new painters they celebrate.
The more they explain and expound the thing they
profess to admire, the more unintelligible it becomes.

Criticism, in their hands, turns into a sort of cabbalism. One must prepare for it, as one prepares for the literature of Service or of the New Thought, by acquiring a wholly new vocabulary, and a new system of logic.

I do not argue here that the new painting, in itself, is always absurd. On the contrary, it must be manifest to anyone with eyes that some of its inventions are bold and interesting, and that now and then it achieves a sort of beauty. What I argue is simply that the criticism it has bred does not adequately account for it—that no man of ordinary sense, seeking to find out just what it is about, will get any light from what is currently written about it. All he will get will be a bath of metaphysics, heated with indignation. Polemics take the place of exposition. One comes away with a guilty feeling that one is somehow grossly ignorant and bounderish, but unable to make out why. The same phenomenon is occasionally witnessed in other fields. I have mentioned the cases of Service and the New Thought. There was, a generation ago, the case of Ibsen and the symbolists. These imbeciles read such extravagant meanings into the old man's plays that he was moved, finally, to violent protests. He was not trying to compose cryptograms, he said; he was simply trying to write stage plays. In much the same way Cézanne protested against the balderdash of his earliest disciples and interpreters. He was no messiah, he said; he was only a painter who tried to reduce what he saw in the world to canvas. The Ibsen symbolists eventually subsided into Freudism and other such rubbish, but the Cézannists continue to spoil paper with their highfalutin and occult tosh. I have read nearly all of them, and I denounce all that I have read as quacks.

This tendency to degenerate into a mere mouthing of meaningless words seems to be peculiar to so-called art criticism. There has never been, so far as I know, a critic of painting who wrote about it simply and clearly, as Sainte-Beuve, say, wrote about books, or Schumann and Berlioz about music. Even the most orthodox of the brethren, when he finds himself before a canvas that genuinely moves him, takes refuge in esoteric winks and grimaces and mysterious gurgles and belches. He can never put his feelings into plain English. Always, before he is done, he is sweating metaphysics, which is to say, nonsense. Painters themselves, when they discuss their art, commonly go the same route. Every time a new revolutionist gives a show he issues a manifesto explaining his aims and achievements, and in every such manifesto there is the same blowsy rodomontadizing that one finds in the texts of the critics. The thing, it appears, is very profound. Something new has been discovered. Rembrandt, poor old boy, lived and

died in ignorance of it. Turner, had he heard of
it, would have yelled for the police. Even Gaugin
barely glimpsed it. One can't make out what this
new arcanum is, but one takes it on faith and goes
to the show. What one finds there is a series of can-
vases that appear to have been painted with asphalt
and mayonnaise, and by a man afflicted with bin-
ocular diplopic strabismus. Is this sound drawing?
Is this a new vision of color? Then so is your grand-
mother left-fielder of the Giants. The exceptions are
very few. I have read, I suppose, at least two hundred such manifestos during the past twenty years;
at one time I even started out to collect them, as odd
literary delicatessen. I can't recall a single one that
embodied a plain statement of an intelligible idea—
that is, intelligible to a man of ordinary information
and sanity. It always took a special talent to comprehend them, as it took a special talent to paint the
fantastic pictures they discussed.

Two reasons, I believe, combine to make the pro-
nunciamentos of painters so bombastic and flatulent.
One lies in the plain fact that painting is a relatively simple and transparent art, and that nothing
much of consequence is thus to be said about it.
All that is remarkable in even the most profound
painting may be grasped by an educated spectator
in a few minutes. If he lingers longer he is simply
seeing again what he has seen before. His essential

experience, in other words, is short-lived. It is not like getting shaved, coming down with the cholera morbus, or going to the wars; it is like jumping out of the way of a taxicab or getting kissed. Consider, now, the position of a critic condemned to stretch this experience into material for a column article or for a whole chapter in a book. Obviously, he soon finds it insufficient for this purpose. What, then, is he to do? Tell the truth, and then shut up? This, alas, is not the way of critics. When their objective facts run out they always turn to subjective facts, of which the supply is unlimited. Thus the art critic begins to roll his eyes inward. He begins to poetize and philosophize his experience. He indulges himself in dark hints and innuendos. Putting words together aimlessly, he presently hits upon a combination that tickles him. He has invented a new cliché. He is a made man. The painter, expounding his work, falls into the same bog. The plain fact, nine times out of ten, is that he painted his picture without any rational plan whatever. Like any other artist, he simply experimented with his materials, trying this combination and then that. Finally he struck something that pleased him. Now he faces the dreadful job of telling why. He simply doesn't know. So he conceals his ignorance behind recondite and enigmatical phrases. He soars, insinuates, sputters, coughs behind his hand. If he is lucky, he, too, invents a cliché. Three clichés in a row, and he is a temporary immortal.

Behind what is written about painting there is always, of course, the immense amount of drivel that is talked about it. No other art is so copiously discussed by its practitioners, or encrusted with so much hollow theorizing. The reason therefor—the second of the two I mentioned above—lies in the obvious fact that painters can talk while they work, and are debarred from working at least half of their waking hours. A poet, when his hormones begin to ferment, not infrequently labors all night; when there is a fog, a thunder-storm or a torch-light parade he is specially inspired. So with a musical composer. But a painter can work only while the light is good, and in the north temperate zone that is not often. So he has much time on his hands, and inasmuch as he seldom has money enough to venture into general society and is usually too ignorant to enjoy reading, he puts in that time talking. Nowhere else on this earth is there so much gabbling as you will find in painters' studios, save it be in the pubs and more or less public bed-rooms that they frequent. It begins as soon as the sun goes down, and it keeps on all night. And it is always about painting, painting, painting. No other class of artists is so self-centered. Once a youth gets a brush into his hand and turpentine in his hair, he appears to join a race apart, and is interested no longer in the general concerns of the world. Even the other arts do not commonly engage any of his attention. If he ventures into music, it is into the banal music of college boys and colored stevedores. If he reads it is only the colicky nonsense that I have been describing. Even his amours are but incidents of his trade. Now put this immense leisure and this great professional keenness against the plain fact that the problems of painting, in the main, are very simple—that very little that is new is to be said about any of them. The result is a vast dilution of ideas, a stormy battle of mere words, an infinite logomachy. And on its higher levels, embellished with all the arts of the auctioneer, it is art criticism.

8

Greenwich Village

The whole saga of Greenwich Village is in Alfred Kreymborg's autobiography, which he calls, very appropriately, "Troubadour." The story begins with an earnest and insolvent young man in a garret, fighting cockroaches and writing free verse. It ends with a respectable gentleman of passing forty, legally married to one very charming wife, and in receipt of a comfortable income in royalties from the 6000 Little Theatres which now freckle and adorn our eminent Republic, distracting the males of the Younger Married Set from the Red Peril and Service, and their wives from millinery and birth control.

Of all the motley revolutionaries who flourished in the Village in its heyday, say fifteen years ago, Kreymborg was surely one of the most engaging, as he was one of the most honest. Most of the others, for all their heroic renunciation of commercialism, were quite as hot for the *mazuma* as other literary artists. With one breath they pledged themselves to poverty—though not, surely, to chastity or obedience!—and denounced such well-heeled poets as Kipling and Shakespeare as base harlots of the marts. With the next they bargained with such editors as ventured to buy their wares like Potash tackling One-Eye Feigenbaum. From this lamentable trafficking Kreymborg held aloof, a genuine Parnassian. He composed his bad poetry and his worse novels on a diet of *Schnecken* and synthetic coffee, and paid for that meager fare by teaching Babbitts the elements of chess.

Gradually the tumult died, and Greenwich Village fell into decay. The poets moved out, and Philistines moved in; it was all over. But Kreymborg kept the faith—at all events, longer than most. He continued to write poems like a series of college yells, plays unearthly and impossible, novels that brought the Comstocks sliding down their poles like firemen.

But gradually he, too, began to show change. His hair grew thin on top; his blood grew sluggish. Presently some of his plays were produced; he had at last squeezed through the proscenium arch. Then he began to accept calls to read his dithyrambs before provincial Poetry Societies. Then he became an editor and an anthologist—ten paces behind his ancient enemy, Louis Untermeyer. Then he went through two divorces, one of them legal, and married an estimable lady of Brooklyn. Now he is past forty, has an agent, and pays income-tax. *Schön ist die Jugendzeit; sie kommt nicht mehr!* As I have hinted, there was always something charming about Kreymborg, even in the days of his most raucous verse. He threw up a good job with the Aeolian Company, demonstrating mechanical-piano records, in order to become a poet, and he stuck to his dream through many a long year. The waspishness of the other Villagers was not in him, and he was happily free of their worst imbecilities. Between cantos of free verse, I suspect, he often read Swinburne and even Tennyson; in his mandolute he concealed Howells and Mark Twain.

As one who poked many heavy jocosities at it while it lasted, I hope I may now say with good grace that I believe Greenwich Village did a good service to all the fine arts in this great land, and left a valuable legacy behind it. True enough, its own heroes were nearly all duds, and most of them have been forgotten, but it at least broke ground, it at least stirred up the animals. When it began to issue smoke and flame, the youth of the country were still under the hoof of the schoolma'm; when it blew up at last they were in full revolt. Was it Greenwich Village or Yale University that cleared the way for Cabell? Was it the Village or the Philharmonic Society that made a place for Stravinsky? Was it the Village or the trustees of the Metropolitan Museum that first whooped for Cézanne? That whooping, of course, did not stop with Cézanne, or Stravinsky, or Cabell. There were whoops almost as loud for Sascha Gilhooly, who painted sunsets with a shaving brush, and for Raoul Goetz, who wrote quartettes for automobile horns and dentist's drills, and for Bruce J. Katzenstein, whose poetry was all figures and exclamation points. But all that excess did no harm. The false prophets changed from day to day. The real ones remained.

X. ESSAY IN PEDAGOGY

1

ON the purely technical side the American novel has obviously made immense progress. As ordinarily encountered, it is very adeptly constructed, and not infrequently it is also well written. The old-time amorphous novel, rambling all over the place and ending with pious platitudes, has pretty well gone out. The American novelists of to-day, and especially the younger ones, have given earnest study to form—perhaps, indeed, too much. For in concentrating their powerful intellects upon it they have lost sight of something that is far more important. I allude, of course, to the observation of character. Thus the average contemporary American novel, though it is workmanlike and well-mannered, fails to achieve its first business. It does not evoke memorable images of human beings. One enjoys reading it, perhaps, but one seldom remembers it. And when it gets beyond the estate of a mere technical exercise, it only too often descends to the even worse estate of a treatise. It attempts to prove something—usually the simple fact that its author is a clever fellow, or a saucy gal. But all a novel of genuine bulk and beam ever proves is that the proper study of mankind is man—the proper study and the most engrossing.

In brief, a first-rate novel is always a character sketch. It may be more than that, but at bottom it is always a character sketch, or, if the author is genuinely of the imperial line, a whole series of them. More, it is a character sketch of an individual not far removed from the norm of the race. He may have his flavor of oddity, but he is never fantastic; he never violates the common rules of human action; he never shows emotions that are impossible to the rest of us. If Thackeray had made Becky Sharp seven feet tall, and given her a bass voice, nine husbands and the rank of lieutenant-general in the British Army, she would have been forgotten long ago, along with all the rest of "Vanity Fair." And if Robinson Crusoe had been an Edison instead of a normal sailorman, he would have gone the same way.

The moral of all this is not lost upon the more competent minority of novelists in practice among us. It was not necessary to preach it to Miss Cather when she set out to write "My Antonía," nor to Abraham Cahan when he tackled "The Rise of David Levinsky," nor to Sinclair Lewis when he was at work on "Babbitt." All such novelists see the character first and the story afterward. What is the story of "Babbitt"? Who remembers? Who, indeed, remembers the story of "The Three Musketeers"? But D'Artagnan and his friends live brilliantly, and so, too, I believe, will George F. Babbitt live brilliantly—at all events, until Kiwanis ceases to trouble, and his type ceases to be real. Most of the younger American novelists, alas, seem to draw no profit from such examples. It is their aim, apparently, to shock mankind with the vivacity of their virtuosity and the heterodoxy of their ideas, and so they fill their novels with gaudy writing and banal propaganda, and convert their characters into sticks. I read novel after novel without getting any sense of contact with actual human beings. I am, at times, immensely amused and sometimes I am instructed, but I seldom carry away anything to remember. When I do so, it is not an idea, but a person. Like everyone else, I have a long memory for persons. But ideas come and go.

All this becomes the more remarkable when one considers the peculiar richness of the American scene in sharply-outlined and racy characters. Our national ideas, indeed, are mainly third-rate, and some of them are almost idiotic, but taking one year with another we probably produce more lively and diverting people than all the rest of the world taken together. More, these lively and diverting people tend to cluster into types. Mark Twain put half a dozen of them into "Hucklebery Finn" and as many more into "Roughing It," a novel disguised as history. Montague Glass collared a whole flock for his Potash and Perlmutter stories, and Ring Lardner has got another flock into his studies of the American bounder. But the younger novelists, or at least the overwhelming majority of them, stick to their sticks. Thus even the most salient and arresting of American types still lack historians, and seem doomed to perish and be forgotten with the Bill of Rights. Babbitt stood around for a dozen years, waiting for Lewis; the rest of the novelists of the land gaped at him without seeing him. How long will they gape at the American politician? At the American university president? At the American policeman? At the American lawyer? At the American insurance man? At the Prohibition fanatic? At the revival evangelist? At the bootlegger? At the Y. M. C. A. secretary? At the butter-and-egg man? At the journalist?

2

I have put the politician at the top of my list. He probably embodies more typical American traits than any other; he is, within his limits, the arch-Americano. Yet how seldom he gets into a novel!

And how seldom, having got there, is he real! I can recall, indeed, but one American political novel of any value whatever as a study of character, and that is Harvey Fergusson's story of Washington, "Capitol Hill"—a series of casual sketches, but all of them vivid and true. Fergusson really understands the American politician. There is, in "Capitol Hill," no division of the *dramatis personæ* between Democrats and Republicans, progressives and reactionaries, materialists and idealists, patriots and traitors; the only division is between men and women who have something, and men and women who want it. In that simple fact lies most of the book's curious reality. For the truth about Washington is that it is not a town of politics, in the conventional and romantic sense; it is, if anything, a town almost devoid of politics. The people in the industrial cities and out on the farms take political ideas seriously; what they cherish in that department they refuse passionately to surrender. But so far as I know there are not a dozen professional politicians in Washington, high or low, who would not throw overboard, instantly and gladly, every political idea they are assumed to be devoted to, including especially every political idea that has helped them into public office, if throwing it overboard would help them to higher and gaudier and more lucrative office. I say high or low, and I mean it literally. There has not been a President of the United States for half a century who did not, at some time or other in his career, perform a complete *volte face* in order to further his career. There is scarcely a United States Senator who does not flop at least three times within the limits of a single session.

The novelists who write about Washington are partly recruited from the ranks of the Washington newspaper correspondents, perhaps the most naïve and unreflective body of literate men in Christendom, and for the rest from the ranks of those who read the dispatches of such correspondents, and take them seriously. The result is a grossly distorted and absurd picture of life in the capital city. One carries off the notion that the essential Washington drama is based on a struggle between a powerful and corrupt Senator and a sterling young uplifter. The Senator is about to sell out the Republic to the Steel Trust, J. P. Morgan or the Japs. The uplifter detects him, exposes him, drives him from public life, and inherits his job. The love interest is supplied by a fair stenographer who steals the damning papers from the Senator's safe, or by an Ambassador's wife who goes to the White House at 3 A. M., and, at the peril of her virtue, arouses the President and tells him what is afoot. All this is poppycock. There are no Senators in Washington powerful enough to carry on any such operations single-handed, and very few of them are corrupt: it is too easy to bamboozle them to go to the expense of buying them. The most formidable bribe that the average Senator receives from year's end to year's end is a bottle or two of very dubious Scotch, and that is just as likely to come from the agent of the South Central Watermelon Growers' Association as from John D. Rockefeller or the Mikado of Japan. Nor are there any sterling young uplifters in the town. The last was chased out before the Mexican War. There are today only gentlemen looking for something for themselves—publicity, eminence, puissance, jobs—especially jobs. Some take one line and some another. Further than that the difference between them is no greater than the difference between a Prohibition agent and a bootlegger, or tweedledum and tweedledee.

Ideas count for nothing in Washington, whether they be political, economic or moral. The question isn't what a man thinks, but what he has to give away that is worth having. Ten years ago a professional Prohibitionist had no more standing in the town than a professional astrologer, Assyriologist or wartremover; five years ago, having proved that his gang could make or break Congressmen, he got all the deference that belonged to the Chief Justice; now, with the wet wolves chasing him, he is once more in eclipse. If William Z. Foster were elected President

to-morrow, the most fanatical Coolidge men of to-day
would flock to the White House the day after, and try
to catch his eye.   Coolidge, while Harding was living, was an obscure and impotent fellow, viewed with
contempt by everyone.   The instant he mounted the
throne he became a Master Mind.   Fergusson got all
of this into "Capitol Hill," which is not the story
of a combat between the True and the False in politics, but the simple tale of a typical Washingtonian's
struggle to the front—a tale that should be an inspiration to every Rotarian in the land.   He begins as a
petty job-holder in the Capitol itself, mailing congressional speeches to constituents on the steppes;
he ends at the head of a glittering banquet table, with
a Senator to one side of him and a member of the
Cabinet to the other—a man who has somehow got
power into his hands, and can dispense jobs, and is
thus an indubitable somebody.   Everybody in Washington who has jobs to dispense is somebody.

This eternal struggle is sordid, but, as Fergusson
has shown, it is also extremely amusing.   It brings
out, as the moralists say, the worst that is in human
nature, which is always the most charming.   It re-
duces all men to one common level of ignominy, and
so rids them of their customary false-faces.   They
take on a new humanity.   Ceasing to be Guardians
of the Constitution, Foes to the Interests, Apostles of
Economy, Prophets of World Peace, and such-like

banshees, they become ordinary men, like John Doe
and Richard Roe.   One beholds them sweating, not
liquid idealism, but genuine sweat.   They hope,
fear, aspire, suffer.   They are preyed upon, not by
J. P. Morgan, but by designing cuties.   They go
to the White House, not to argue for the World
Court, but to hog patronage.   From end to end
of Fergusson's chronicle there is absolutely no
mention of the tariff, or of the farmer and his
woes, or of the budget system, or of the Far Eastern
question.   I marvel that more American novelists
have not gone to this lush and delightful material.
The supply is endless and lies wide open.   Six
months in Washington is enough to load an ambitious
novelist for all eternity.   (Think of what George
Moore has made of his one love-affair, back in
1877!)   The Washington correspondents, of course,
look at it without seeing it, and so do all the Washington novelists save Fergusson.   But that is saying
nothing.   A Washington correspondent is one with
a special talent for failing to see what is before his
eyes.   I have beheld a whole herd of them sit through
a national convention without once laughing.

Fergusson, in "Capitol Hill," keeps mainly to that
end of Pennsylvania avenue which gives his book
its name.   I believe that the makings of a far better
novel of Washington life are to be found at the other
end, to wit, in and about the alabaster cage which

houses the heir of Washington, Lincoln and Chester A. Arthur. Why, indeed, has no one ever put *kaiserliche Majestät* into fiction—save, of course, as a disembodied spirit, vaguely radiating idealism? The revelations in the Daugherty inquiry gave a hint of unworked riches—but there is enough dramatic and even melodramatic material without descending to scandal. A President is a man like the rest of us. He can laugh and he can groan. There are days when his breakfast agrees with him, and days when it doesn't. His eyes have the common optical properties: they can see a sweet one as far as they can see a member of the Interstate Commerce Commission. All the funnels of intrigue are aimed at him. He is the common butt of every loud-speaker. No other man in this sad vale has so many jobs to give out, or one-half so many. Try to imagine a day in his life, from dawn to midnight. Do it, and you will have the best American novel ever heard of.

3

But I am forgetting my other candidates—for example, the American university president. I mean, of course, the university president of the new six-cylinder, air-cooled, four-wheel-brake model —half the quack, half the visionary, and wholly the go-getter—the brisk, business-like, confidential, but-ton-holing, regular fellow who harangues Rotary and Kiwanis, extracts millions from usurers by alarming them about Bolshevism, and so builds his colossal pedagogical slaughter-house, with its tens of thousands of students, its professors of cheese-making, investment securities and cheer-leading, its galaxy of football stars, and its general air of Barnum's circus. Why has this astounding mountebank not got into a book? He fairly yells for loving embalming *à la* Babbitt. He is not only stupendously picaresque and amusing in himself—the final heir, at once, of Abelard, Cagliostro, Increase Mather, the Fox sisters, Pestalozzi, Dr. Munyon, Godey of the *Ladies' Book,* and Daniel Drew—; he is also thoroughly and magnificently characteristic of the great land we live in. No other country has ever produced anything quite like him. No other country, I suspect, would tolerate him. But here he lives and flourishes, a superb and perfect American—and yet our novelists all neglect him.

Worse and more incredible still, they neglect the most American of all Americans, the very *Ur-Amerikaner*—to wit, the malignant moralist, the Christian turned cannibal, the snouting and preposterous Puritan. Where is there the American novel in which he is even half limned? There are, to be sure, glimpses of him in "The Song of the Lark," by Willa Cather, and in "Babbitt," and there is a more

elaborate but still incomplete sketch in E. W. Howe's
"The Story of a Country Town." But Howe,
unfortunately, had other fish to fry: he slapped
in his bucolic wowser brilliantly, and then passed
on to melodrama and the agonies of young
love. So, too, with Lewis and Miss Cather. Thus,
though the Puritan Father lies embalmed magnificently in the pages of Hawthorne, his heir and assign
of the present day, the high-powered uplifter, the
prophet of harsh and unenforceable laws, the incurable reformer and nuisance—this sweet fellow yet
awaits his anatomist.

What a novel is in him! Indeed, what a shelf of
novels! For he has as many forms as there are
varieties of human delusion. Sometimes he is a
tin-pot evangelist, sweating to transform Oklahoma
City or Altoona, Pa., into the New Jerusalem. Sometimes he is a hireling of the Anti-Saloon League,
sworn to Law Enforcemnt. Sometimes he is a strict
Sabbatarian, bawling for the police whenever he
detects his neighbor washing bottles or varnishing the
Ford on Sunday morning. Again he is a vice-
crusader, chasing the scarlet lady with fierce Christian shouts. Yet again he is a comstock, wearing out
his eyes in the quest for smut. He may even be
female—a lady Ph.D. in a linoleum hat, patrolling
the cow towns and the city slums, handing out edifying literature, teaching poor Polish women how to

have babies. Whatever his form, he is tremendously grotesque and tremendously amusing—and always he drips with national juices, always he is as thoroughly American as a bootlegger or a college yell. If he exists at all in other lands, it is only in rudimentary and aberrant forms. Try to imagine a French Wayne B. Wheeler, or a Spanish Billy Sunday, or a German William Jennings Bryan. It is as impossible as imagining a Coolidge in the Rome of Julius.

Since the earliest days, as everyone knows, American jurisprudence has been founded upon the axiom that it is the first duty of every citizen to police his neighbors, and especially those he envies, or otherwise dislikes. There is no such thing, in this grand and puissant nation, as privacy. The yokels out in Iowa, neglecting their horned cattle, have a right, it appears—nay, a sacred duty!—to peek into my home in Baltimore, and tell me what I may and may not drink with my meals. An out-at-elbow Methodist preacher in Boston sets himself up to decide what I may read. An obscure and unintelligent job-holder in Washington, inspired by God, determines what I may receive in the mails. I must not buy lottery tickets because it offends the moral sentiment of Kansas. I must keep Sunday as the Sabbath, which is in conflict with Genesis, because it is ordered by persons who believe that Genesis can't be wrong.

Such are the laws of the greatest free nation ever seen on earth. We are all governed by them. But a government of laws, of course, is a mere phantasm of political theorists: the thing is always found, on inspection, to be really a government of men. In the United States, it seems to me, the tendency is for such men to come increasingly from the class of professional uplifters. It is not the bankers who run the ostensible heads of the state, as the Liberals believe, nor the so-called bosses, as the bosses themselves believe, but the wowsers. And what is a wowser? What does the word mean? It means precisely what you think of inevitably when you hear it. A wowser is a wowser. He bears a divine commission to regulate and improve the rest of us. He knows exactly what is best for us. He is what Howe calls a Good Man. So long as you and I are sinful, he can't sleep. So long as we are happy, he is after us.

I throw off the guess that there are at least forty novels in the wowser—that is, forty good ones. He has, as I have said, as many forms as the demons who ride him, and every one of them should make a competent novelist, authentically called to the vocation, leap in air with loud hosannas, and spit upon his hands. His psychology remains mysterious. The Freudians, I believe, have misunderstood him, and the psychiatrists have avoided him. What are the springs of his peculiar frenzy to harass and punish his fellow men? By what process of malign eugenics is he hatched? And what is his typical life history? Here is work for the novelist, which is to say, for the professional anatomist of character. I believe that Frank Norris, had he lived, would have tackled it with enthusiasm, and made a great success of its execution. Norris, like Dreiser after him, had a romantic and even a mystical inclination, but at bottom he was a satirist—and the American Puritan was made for satirists as catnip was made for cats. It is easy to laugh at him, but it is hard to hate him. He is eternally in the position of a man trying to empty the ocean with a tin-dipper. He will be mauled, and the chance he offers thrown away, if the novelist who attempts him in the end forgets the tragedy under his comedy. I have known many American wowsers in my time, some of them intimately. They were all intensely unhappy men. They suffered as vastly as Prometheus chained to his rock, with the buzzards exploring his liver. A novelist blind to that capital fact will never comprehend the type. It needs irony—but above all it needs pity.

4

So does another type that also awaits its Thackeray: to wit, the American journalist. Most American novelists, before they challenge Dostoevski, put

in an apprenticeship on the public prints, and thus
have a chance to study and grasp the peculiarities of
the journalistic mind; nevertheless, the fact remains
that there is not a single genuine newspaper man, done
in the grand manner, in the whole range of American
fiction. As in the case of the wowser, there are some
excellent brief sketches, but there is no adequate portrait of the journalist as a whole, from his beginnings
as a romantic young reporter to his finish as a Babbitt, correct in every idea and as hollow as a jug.
Here, I believe, is genuine tragedy. Here is the matter that enters into all fiction of the first class. Here
is human character in disintegration—the primary
theme of every sound novelist ever heard of, from
Fielding to Zola and from Turgeniev to Joseph Conrad. I know of no American who starts from a
higher level of aspiration than the journalist. He
is, in his first phase, genuinely romantic. He plans
to be both an artist and a moralist—a master of lovely
words and a merchant of sound ideas. He ends,
commonly, as the most depressing jackass in his community—that is, if his career goes on to what is
called success. He becomes the repository of all its
worst delusions and superstitions. He becomes the
darling of all its frauds and idiots, and the despair of
all its honest men. He belongs to a good club, and
the initiation fee was his soul.

Here I speak by the book, for I have been in active

practice as a journalist for more than a quarter of a century, and have an immense acquaintance in the craft.   I could name a man who fits my specifications exactly in every American city east of the Mississippi, and refrain only on the advice of counsel. I do not say that all journalists go that route.   Far from it!   Many escape by failing; some even escape by succeeding.   But the majority succumb.   They begin with high hopes.   They end with safe jobs. In the career of any such man, it seems to me, there are materials for fiction of the highest order.   He is interesting intrinsically, for his early ambition is at least not ignoble—he is not born an earthworm.   And he is interesting as a figure in drama, for he falls gradually, resisting all the while, to forces that are beyond his strength.   If he can't make the grade, it is not because he is unwilling or weak, but because the grade itself is too steep.   Here is tragedy—and here is America.   For the curse of this country, as of all democracies, is precisely the fact that it treats its best men as enemies.   The aim of our society, if it may be said to have an aim, is to iron them out. The ideal American, in the public sense, is a respectable vacuum.

I heave this typical American journalist to the massed novelists of the Federal Union, and invite them to lay on.   There is a capital novel in him— a capital character sketch and a capital picture of

the American scene.   He is representative and yet he
is not commonplace.   People will recognize him, and
yet they are not familiar with him.   Let the fic-
tioneers have at him!   But let them bear in mind that,
like the wowser, he is not to be done to the tune of
superior sneers.   He is a wreck, but he has not succumbed to the gales without resistence.   Let him be
done ironically, as Lewis did Babbitt, but let him be
done also with pity.   He is not a comedian, but a
tragedian.   Above all, let him be done without any
mouthing of theories.   His simple story is poignant
enough.

Is he too difficult?   Then I offer a substitute: the
American policeman.   Certainly it is high time for
him to get into a book.   I dedicate him to the novelists of the nation at once, and provide them simultaneously with all the plot they will need.   A moron with
an IQ of 53, despairing of ever getting a better job,
goes on the force and begins pounding a beat.   A
chance favor to a saloonkeeper makes a sergeant of
him, and thereafter he slowly mounts the ladder.   At
the end he is an inspector, and in charge of operations against a fabulous crime wave, imagined by the
city editor of a tabloid newspaper.   Isn't that enough?
What a vivid and exhilarating picture of American
life could be got out of it!   What humors are there,
and what genuine drama!   Nor are the materials
esoteric.   Every newspaper reporter's head is stuffed

with them. I myself could do such a work in ten volumes folio. Nine young journalists out of ten, I believe, aspire to the novel. Well, here is a chance to write a novel as good as "Babbitt."

XI. ON LIVING IN BALTIMORE

SOME time ago, writing in an eminent Baltimore newspaper upon the Baltimore of my boyhood, I permitted myself an eloquent passage upon its charm, and let fall the doctrine that nearly all of that charm had vanished. Mere rhetoric, I greatly fear. The old charm, in truth, still survives in the town, despite the frantic efforts of the boosters and boomers who, in late years, have replaced all its ancient cobblestones with asphalt, and bedizened it with Great White Ways and suburban boulevards, and surrounded it with stinking steel plants and oil refineries, and increased its population from 400,000 to 800,-000. I am never more conscious of the fact than when I return to it from New York. Behind me lies the greatest city of the modern world, with more money in it than all Europe and more clowns and harlots than all Asia, and yet it has no more charm than a circus lot or a second-rate hotel. It can't show a single genuinely distinguished street. It hasn't a single park that is more lovely than a cemetery lot. It is without manner as it is without manners. Escaping from it to so ancient and solid a town as Baltimore is like coming out of a football crowd into quiet communion with a fair one who is also amiable, and has the gift of consolation for hard-beset and despairing men.

I have confessed to rhetoric, but I surely do not indulge in it here. For twenty-five years I have resisted a constant temptation to move to New York, and I resist it more easily to-day than I did when it began. I am, perhaps, the most arduous commuter ever heard of, even in that Babylon of commuters. My office is on Manhattan Island and has been there since 1914; yet I live, vote and have my being in Baltimore, and go back there the instant my job allows. If my desk bangs at 3 P. M. I leap for the 3.25 train. Four long hours in the Pullman follow, but the first is the worst. My back, at all events, is toward New York! Behind lies a place fit only for the gross business of getting money; ahead is a place made for enjoying it.

What makes New York so dreadful, I believe, is mainly the fact that the vast majority of its people have been forced to rid themselves of one of the oldest and most powerful of human instincts—the instinct to make a permanent home. Crowded, shoved about and exploited without mercy, they have lost the feeling that any part of the earth belongs to them, and so they simply camp out like tramps, waiting for the constables to rush in and chase them away. I am not speaking here of the poor (God knows how they exist in New York at all!) ; I am speaking of the well-to-do, even of the rich. The very richest man, in New York, is never quite sure that the house he lives in now will be his next year—that he will be able to resist the constant pressure of business expansion and rising land values. I have known actual millionaires to be chased out of their homes in this way, and forced into apartments. In Baltimore too, the same pressure exists, to be sure, but it is not oppressive, for the householder can meet it by yielding to it half way. It may force him into the suburbs, even into the adjacent country, but he is still in direct contact with the city, sharing in its life, and wherever he lands he may make a stand. But on Manhattan Island he is quickly brought up by the rivers, and once he has crossed them he may as well move to Syracuse or Trenton.

Nine times out of ten he tries to avoid crossing them. That is, he moves into meaner quarters on the island itself, and pays more for them. His house gives way to a flat—one offering perhaps half the room for his goods and chattels that his house offered. Next year he is in a smaller flat, and three-fourths of his goods and chattels have vanished. A few years more, and he is in two or three rooms. Finally, he lands in an hotel. At this point he ceases to exist as the head of a house. His quarters are pre-

cisely like the quarters of 50,000 other men. The
front he presents to the world is simply an anonymous
door on a gloomy corridor.   Inside, he lives like a
sardine in a can.   Such a habitation, it must be plain,
cannot be called a home.   A home is not a mere transient shelter: its essence lies in its permanence, in its
capacity for accretion and solidification, in its quality of representing, in all its details, the personalities
of the people who live in it.   In the course of years
it becomes a sort of museum of these people; they
give it its indefinable air, separating it from all other
homes, as one human face is separated from all
others.   It is at once a refuge from the world, a
treasure-house, a castle, and the shrine of a whole hierarchy of peculiarly private and potent gods.

This concept of the home cannot survive the mode
of life that prevails in New York.   I have seen it
go to pieces under my eyes in the houses of my own
friends.   The intense crowding in the town, and the
restlessness and unhappiness that go with it, make it
almost impossible for anyone to accumulate the
materials of a home—the trivial, fortuitous and often
grotesque things that gather around a family, as
glories and debts gather around a state.   The New
Yorker lacks the room to house them; he thus learns
to live without them.   In the end he is a stranger in
the house he lives in.   More and more, it tends to be
no more than Job No. 16432b from this or that

decorator's studio. I know one New Yorker, a man of considerable means, who moves every three years. Every time he moves his wife sells the entire contents of the apartment she is leaving, and employs a decorator to outfit the new one. To me, at all events, such a mode of living would be unendurable. The charm of getting home, as I see it, is the charm of getting back to what is inextricably my own—to things familiar and long loved, to things that belong to me alone and none other. I have lived in one house in Baltimore for nearly forty-five years. It has changed in that time, as I have—but somehow it still remains the same. No conceivable decorator's masterpiece could give me the same ease. It is as much a part of me as my two hands. If I had to leave it I'd be as certainly crippled as if I lost a leg.

I believe that this feeling for the hearth, for the immemorial lares and penates, is infinitely stronger in Baltimore than in New York—that it has better survived there, indeed, than in any other large city of America—and that its persistence accounts for the superior charm of the town. There are, of course, thousands of Baltimoreans in flats—but I know of none to whom a flat seems more than a makeshift, a substitute, a necessary and temporary evil. They are all planning to get out, to find house-room in one of the new suburbs, to resume living in a home. What they see about them is too painfully not theirs.

The New Yorker has simply lost that discontent. He is a vagabond. His notions of the agreeable become those of a vaudeville actor. He takes on the shallowness and unpleasantness of any other homeless man. He is highly sophisticated, and inordinately trashy. The fact no doubt explains the lack of charm that one finds in his town; the fact that the normal man of Baltimore is almost his exact antithesis explains the charm that is there. Human relations, in such a place, tend to assume a solid permanence. A man's circle of friends becomes a sort of extension of his family circle. His contacts are with men and women who are rooted as he is. They are not moving all the time, and so they are not changing their friends all the time. Thus abiding relationships tend to be built up, and when fortune brings unexpected changes, they survive those changes. The men I know and esteem in Baltimore are, on the whole, men I have known and esteemed a long while; even those who have come into my ken relatively lately seem likely to last. But of the men I knew best when I first began going to New York, twenty-five years ago, not one is a friend to-day. Of those I knew best ten years ago, not six are friends. The rest have got lost in the riot, and the friends of to-day, I sometimes fear, will get lost in the same way.

In human relationships that are so casual there is seldom any satisfaction. It is our fellows who make life endurable to us, and give it a purpose and a meaning; if our contacts with them are light and frivolous there is something lacking, and it is something of the very first importance. What I contend is that in Baltimore, under a slow-moving and cautious social organization, touched by the Southern sun, such contacts are more enduring than elsewhere, and that life in consequence is more agreeable. Of the external embellishments of life there is a plenty there—as great a supply, indeed, to any rational taste, as in New York itself. But there is also something much better: a tradition of sound and comfortable living. A Baltimorean is not merely John Doe, an isolated individual of *Homo sapiens*, exactly like every other John Doe. He is John Doe *of* a certain place—of Baltimore, of a definite *house* in Baltimore. It is not by accident that all the peoples of Europe, very early in their history, distinguished their best men by adding *of* this or that place to their names.

XII. THE LAST NEW ENGLANDER

THE late Prof. Barrett Wendell, of Harvard, whose letters have been done into a stately volume by M. A. DeWolfe Howe, will probably go down into history as the last flower of the Puritan *Kultur*. Himself by no means a pure New Englander, for his surname was obviously Dutch, he yet had enough New England blood in him to feel himself wholly of that forlorn region, and he was accepted as a fit representative of it by all its tribal headmen. He was steeped in its tradition, and venerated its heroes. What came out of New England seemed to him to be virtuous and lovely, or, as he might have said, gentlemanly; what came out of the rest of the country was simply barbarous.

Nevertheless, Wendell was himself a walking proof that all he admired was passing into the shadows, for, try as he would, he could not, as a contemporary man, squeeze himself into the old Puritan mold. Over and over again he would make an effort to do so, but always, as he struggled with the lid, a diabolical, iconoclastic mood would overcome him, and he would leap up and emit a ribald yell. Harvard, startled and uneasy, never knew what to make of him. His principles were apparently impeccable; he was, in the current phrase, a consistent booster for the lost Golden Age, its glories and high deeds. And yet, whenever the answering cheer came back, he would make a mocking face and say something awful. The Cambridge campus is still warmed by these mockings. What saved him from downright infamy was the fact that, whenever they were actually in contempt of the Puritan mores and gnosiology, they were safely superficial —that is, they never questioned fundamentals. Wendell had a lot to say about the transient excesses and imbecilities of democracy, visible in his time, but he nevertheless believed in all the primary democratic fallacies, and even defended them eloquently. He was a tart critic of the whole educational process, and went to the length, in his own department of English, of denying it any value whatever; nevertheless, he remained a romantic Harvard man to the end of his days, and venerated *alma mater* with the best of them. He must have seen clearly that there was little that was sound and solid left in the New England culture, that the rest of the country had little need of it and would quickly surpass it; all the same, he clung to the superstition that the preposterous theologians of its early days constituted an intellectual aristocracy, and even wrote a book eulogizing the most absurd of them, Cotton Mather.

Wendell, in fact, was two men, separate and distinct, and they were often at war.   One of these men was highly intelligent (though surely not very learned); the other was a romantic under the spell of a disintegrating tradition. The latter was the more charming, but often a prey to mere lyrical fancy. The picture of the American character that Wendell presented to gaping throngs in his Sorbonne lectures was a sort of fantastic chromo of the primeval New England character, seen through nine thicknesses of amber gelatine—in brief, a thing as bizarre as the accounts of the Revolution that used to be in school-books. Fundamentally, he once said somewhere else, we believe in fair play.   It would be hard to imagine a more inaccurate saying. If any single quality, indeed, has marked off the Americano from all other civilized men since the start, it is his incapacity to purge combat of passion, his strong disinclination to allow any merit whatever to the other fellow;—in brief, his bad sportsmanship. Our history is a history of minorities put down with clubs. Even the duel, during the few years it flourished in America, took on a ferocity unheard of elsewhere. Gentlemen, going out at daybreak, shot to kill. Aaron Burr was a thorough American; Hamilton was an Englishman. In other fields, Wendell indulged himself in similar setimentalities. He reacted to the shock of the late war in the correct manner of a

State Street banker. He succumbed to the Coolidge buncombe far back in 1920. Yet always the sharply intelligent Wendell hauled up and stayed the orthodox romantic. The tribute to him by Prof. Kuno Francke, quoted by Mr. Howe, is a tribute not only to a gentleman, but also to a man of sense. And even in the midst of his banal speculation whether Coolidge, after all, would not turn out to be a Yankee Lincoln, he saw clearly the "small, hatchet-faced, colorless man, with a tight-shut, thin-lipped mouth"—in other words, the third-rate, small-town attorney, stuffed with copybook platitudes and quite without imagination. He saw, too, the truth about Wilson, and stated it blisteringly in a letter to his friend R. W. Curtis.

Wendell's actual books, I believe, are now all dead, even his arbitrary and ignorant but highly amusing "Literary History of America." His volume on Shakespeare, published in 1894, is admired by Sir Arthur Quiller-Couch and Mrs. Edith Wharton, but no one else seems to remember it. His novels and dramas are long forgotten. His "English Composition" was and is a school-book; he himself, in his old age, had doubts that it had accomplished even its pedagogic purpose. His political essays, once so salacious, now read like the heresies of the Jefferson era. What remains, then, of Prof. Barrett Wendell, A.B., Litt.D.? A great deal more, I believe, than a mere ghost. When, indeed, the roll of American literati is drawn up at last, and the high deeds of each are set down, it will be found that Wendell, too, did something, and that what he did was of considerable importance.   In a few words, he helped to divert criticism from books to life itself—he was one of the first to see that mere literature is, after all, mere literature—that it cannot be understood without knowing something about the society which produced it.   Even Poe, masterly critic that he was, overlooked this obvious and all-important fact.   His discussion of books went on in a sort of vacuum.   He had brilliant (and often sound) opinions about every technical problem imaginable, and about every question of taste, but only too often he overlooked the fact that his author was also a man, and that what the author wrote the man had first to think, feel and endure.   Wendell got rid of that narrow bookishness, still lingering in Lowell.   He was primarily a critic, not of literary manners and postures, but of human existence under the Republic.   There was no scholarly affectation about him, for all his superficial playacting, his delight in impressing sophomores.   He did not bury his nose in books; he went out and looked at the world, and what he saw there amused him immensely and filled him with ideas.   In Mr. Howe's index the name of Longfellow appears but once, and that of Gilder but once, and that of Aldrich not at all, but that of Blaine is there six times, and after Democracy there are twenty-two entries.

It seems to me that this break with the old American tradition had its high uses, and has left its mark upon American letters. Criticism among us is vastly less cloistered than it once was. Even professors of the loftiest tone, if they would have themselves attended to, must descend from their ivory towers and show themselves at the sea-level. The aloof and austere spirit is now viewed with suspicion. There are, I daresay, ancients who deplore the change. A natural regret, for it has made criticism vastly more difficult. But few deplore it, I believe, who know what literature really is—few, that is, who know the difference between mere intellectual prettiness and a body of living ideas.

As for Wendell's amazing contradictions and inconsistencies, his endless flounderings between orthodoxy and heresy, I believe that an adequate explanation of them is to be found in the compositions of Prof. Dr. Sigmund Freud, the Viennese necromancer. Freud, himself a Jew, discusses in one of his books the curious fact that jokes at the expense of the Jews are chiefly circulated by Jews themselves, and especially by the younger ones. Two Jewish drummers in a Pullman smoking-room fall into an exchange of such jocosities almost automatically. Why? Be-

cause, says Freud, they attain thereby to an escape
from their Jewishness, which often irks them. It is
not they are ashamed of being Jews; it is that
the Jewish practices of their elders are burdensome.
They dare not revolt openly, for their sense of filial
piety is strong, so they take it out by making jokes.
By much the same psychological process, I believe,
Wendell arrived at his curious mixture of contra-
rieties. Sentimentally and emotionally, he was
moved powerfully by the New England tradition, and
felt a strong impulse to defend it against the world.
Intellectually, he saw clearly that it was in collapse
around him—worse, that it had been full of defects
and weaknesses even when, by his own doctrine, it had
been strong. The result was his endless shuttling between worship and ribaldry. The last of the New
Englanders, he clung pathetically to a faith which
gradually succumbed to doubts. In his later years he
thus stood upon a burning deck, whence all but him
had fled.

Two things, for all his skepticism, he could never
bring himself to admit formally, both obvious: first,
that the so-called culture of Puritan New England was
largely imaginary, that civilization was actually introduced into the region by anti-Puritans, and second,
that when Transcendentalism came in, the leadership
of Puritanism passed from New England and went
to the South and Middle West. To admit the truth

of either proposition was psychically impossible to a man of his romantic feelings. Each, baldly stated, seemed to flout the local Holy Ghost. And yet both were true, and their proofs were visible at a glance. The first, I daresay, will never be granted formally, or even heard patiently, by any genuine New Englander. Only a short while ago Walter Prichard Eaton, a very able Puritan, was arguing eloquently that his blue-nosed ancestors were really lovers of beauty, nay, downright artists—and offering the charming old houses on Nantucket Island as exhibits. Unfortunate examples, alas, alas! The houses on Nantucket were not built until the Puritan theocracy was completely demoralized and impotent—until Boston had a theatre, and was already two-thirds of the way to hell. And if they were actually built by Puritans at all, then it was by Puritans who had gone out into the wide, wide word and savored its dreadful and voluptuous marvels—Puritans who had come back from the Eastern seas with gaudy silks in their sea-chests, and the perfume of strange gals upon their whiskers, and a new glitter to their eyes.

Orthodox history, at least as it appears in schoolbooks, assumes that the witch-burners and infant-damners had it all their own way in New England, even down to Revolutionary times. They actually met with sturdy oppositon from the start. All of their sea-ports gradually filled up with sailors who were anything but pious Christian men, and even the back-country had its heretics, as the incessant wars upon them demonstrate. The fact that only Puritans could vote in the towns has deceived the historians; they mistake what was the law for what was really said and done. We have had proofs in our own time that that error is easy. Made by students of early New England, it leads to multiple absurdities. The fact is that the civilization that grew up in the region, such as it was, owed very little to the actual Puritans; it was mainly the product of anti-Puritans, either home-bred or imported. Even the school system, so celebrated in legend, owed whatever value was in it to what were currently regarded as criminals. The Puritans did not found their schools for the purpose of propagating what is now known as learning; they found them simply as nurseries of orthodoxy. Beyond the barest rudiments nothing of any worldly value was taught in them. The principal subject of study, first and last, was theology, and it was theology of the most grotesque and insane sort ever cherished by man. Genuine education began in New England only when the rising minority of anti-Puritans, eventually to become a majority, rose against this theology, and tried to put it down. The revolt was first felt at Harvard; it gradually converted a seminary for the training of Puritan pastors

into a genuine educational institution. Harvard delivered New England, and made civilization possible
there. All the men who adorned that civilization in
the days of its glory—Emerson, Hawthorne and all
the rest of them—were essentially anti-Puritans.

To-day, save in its remoter villages, New England
is no more Puritan than, say, Maryland or Missouri.
There is scarcely a clergyman in the entire region
who, if the Mathers could come back to life, would
not be condemned by them instantly as a heretic, and
even as an atheist. The dominant theology is mild,
skeptical and wholly lacking in passion. The evangelical spirit has completely disappeared. Save in
a small minority of atavistic fanatics, there is a tolerance that is almost indistinguishable from indif-
ference. Roman Catholicism and Christian Science
are alike viewed amiably. The old heat is gone.
Where it lingers in America is in far places—on the
Methodist prairies of the Middle West, in the Baptist
back-waters of the South. There, I believe, it still
retains not a little of its old vitality. There Puritanism survives, not merely as a system of theology, but
also as a way of life. It colors every human activity.
Kiwanis mouths it; it is powerful in politics; learning wears its tinge. To charge a Harvard professor
of to-day with agnosticism would sound as banal as to
charge him with playing the violoncello. But his

colleague of Kansas, facing the same accusation, would go damp upon the forehead, and his colleague of Texas would leave town between days.

Wendell, a sentimentalist, tried to put these facts behind him, though he must have been well aware of them. There got into his work, in consequence, a sense of futility, even when he was discussing very real and important things. He opened paths that he was unable to traverse himself. Sturdier men, following him, were soon marching far ahead of him. He will live in the history of American criticism, but his own criticism is already dead.

XIII.   THE NATION

ONE often hears lamentation that the American weeklies of opinion are not as good as their English prototypes—that we have never produced anything in that line to equal, say, the *Athenæum* or the *Saturday Review*.   In the notion, it seems to me, there is nothing save that melancholy colonialism which is one of the curses of America.   The plain fact is that our weeklies, taking one with another, are quite as well turned out as anything that England has ever seen, and that at least two of them, the *Nation* and the *New Republic*, are a great deal better.   They are better because they are more hospitable to ideas, because they are served by a wider and more various range of writers, and because they show an occasional sense of humor.   Even the *New Republic* knows how to be waggish, though it also knows, especially when it is discussing religion, how to be cruelly dull.   Its Washington correspondence is better than any Parliamentary stuff in any English weekly ever heard of, if only because it is completely devoid of amateur statesmanship, the traditional defect of political correspondence at all times and everywhere. The editors of the English weeklies all ride political hobbies, and many of them are actively engaged in politics. Their American colleagues, I suspect, have been tempted in that direction more than once, but happily they have resisted, or maybe fate has resisted for them.

Of all the weeklies—and I go through at least twenty each week, American and English, including the Catholic *Commonweal* and a Negro journal—I like the *Nation* best. There is something charming about its format, and it never fails to print an interesting piece of news, missed by the daily newspapers. Moreover, there is always a burst of fury in it, and somewhere or other, often hidden in a letter from a subscriber, a flash of wit—two things that make for amusing reading. The *New Republic*, I suspect, is more authoritative in certain fields,—for example, the economic—but it is also more pontifical. The *Nation* gets the air of a lark into many of its most violent crusades against fraud and folly; one somehow gathers the notion that its editors really do not expect the millennium to come in to-morrow. Of late they have shown many signs of forsaking Liberalism for Libertarianism—a far sounder and more satisfying politics. A Liberal is committed to sure cures that always turn out to be swindles; a Libertarian throws the bottles out of the window, and asks only that the patient be let alone.

What the circulation of the *Nation* may be I don't know. In its sixtieth anniversary number, published in 1925, there was a hint that the number then sold each week ran far ahead of the 11,000 with which E. L. Godkin began in 1865. I have heard gabble in the saloons frequented by New York publishers that the present circulation is above 30,000. But no one, so far as I know, has ever suggested that it equals the circulation of even a third-rate daily paper. Such dull, preposterous sheets as the New York *Telegram*, the Washington *Star*, the Philadelphia *Public Ledger* and the Atlanta *Constitution* sell two or three times as many copies. Such magazines for the herd as *True Stories* and *Hot Dog* sell fifty times as many. Nevertheless, if I were a fellow of public spirit and eager to poison the Republic with my sagacity, I'd rather be editor of the *Nation* than editor of any of the other journals that I have mentioned—nay, I'd rather be editor of the *Nation* than editor of all of them together, with every other newspaper and magazine in America, save perhaps four or five, thrown in. For the *Nation* is unique in American journalism for one thing: it is read by its enemies. They may damn it, they may have it barred from libraries, they may even—as they did during the war—try to have it put down by the Postoffice, but all the while they read it. That is, the more intelligent of them— the least hopeless minority of them. It is to such minorities that the *Nation* addresses itself, on both sides of the fence. It has penetrated to the capital fact that they alone count—that the ideas sneaked into them to-day will begin to sweat out of the herd day after to-morrow.

Is the Creel Press Bureau theory of the late war abandoned? Is it impossible to find an educated man who is not ashamed that he succumbed to the Wilson buncombe? Then thank the *Nation* for that deliverance, for when it tackled Wilson it tackled him alone. Is the Coolidge Golden Age beginning to be sicklied o'er with a pale cast of green? Then prepare to thank the *Nation* again, for it began to tell the harsh, cold truth about good Cal at a time when all the daily journals of America, with not ten exceptions, were competing for the honor of shining his shoes. I often wonder, indeed, that the great success of the *Nation* under Villard has made such little impression upon American journalists—that they are so dead to the lessons that it roars into their ears. They all read it—that is, all who read anything at all. It prints news every week that they can't find in their own papers—sometimes news of the very first importance. It comments upon that news in a tart and well-informed fashion. It presents all the new ideas that rage in the world, always promptly and often pungently. To an editorial writer the *Nation* is indispensable. Either he reads it, or he is an idiot.

Yet its example is very seldom followed—that is, forthrightly and heartily. Editorial writers all over the land steal ideas from it daily; it supplies, indeed, all the ideas that most of them ever have. It lifts them an inch, two inches, three inches, above the sedimentary stratum of Rotarians, bankers and ice-wagon drivers; they are conscious of its pull even when they resist. Yet very few of them seem to make the inevitable deduction that the kind of journalism it practices is better and more effective than the common kind—that they, too, might amount to something in this world if they would imitate it.

In such matters, alas, change is very slow. The whole press of the United States, I believe, is moving in the direction of the *Nation*—that is, in the direction of independence and honesty. Even such papers as the New York *Herald-Tribune* are measurably less stupid and intransigeant than they used to be, in their news if not in their opinions. But the majority of active journalists in the higher ranks were bred on the old-time party organs, and it is very difficult for them to reform their ways. They still think, not as free men, but as party hacks. On the one side they put the truth; on the other side they put what they call policy. Thus there are thousands of them who still sit down nightly to praise Coolidge—though to the best of my knowledge and belief there is not a single journalist in the whole United States who ever speaks of Coolidge in private without sneering at him. This resistence to change grows all the more curious when one observes what happens to the occasional paper which abandons it. I offer the Baltimore *Sunpaper* as an example—an especially apposite one, for the influence of the *Nation* upon it must be apparent to everyone familiar with its recent history. It was, a dozen years ago, a respectable but immensely dull journal. It presented the day's news in a formal, unintelligent fashion. It was accurate in small things, and free from sensationalism, but it seldom if ever went beyond the overt event to the causes and motives behind it. Its editorial opinions were flabby, and without influence. To-day it is certainly something far different. It must still go a long, long way, I suspect, before it escapes its old self altogether, but that must be a dull reader, indeed, who cannot see how vastly it has improved. It no longer prints the news formally; it devotes immense energy to discovering and revealing what is behind the news. In opinion it has thrown off all chains of faction and party, and is sharply and often intelligently independent. Its reaction to a new public problem is not that of a party hack, but that of a free man. It is, perhaps, sometimes grossly wrong, but no sane person believes that it is ever deliberately disingenuous.

Well, the point is that this new scheme has been

tremendously successful—that it has paid in hard
cash as well as in the usufructs of the spirit.   There
is no sign that the readers of the *Sunpaper*—barring
a few quacks with something to sell—dislike its new
vigor, enterprise and independence.   On the contrary,
there is every evidence that they like it.   They have
increased greatly in numbers.   The paper itself rises
in dignity and influence.   And every other newspaper
in America that ventures upon the same innovations,
from the *World* in New York to the *Enquirer-Sun*
down in Columbus, Ga., rises in the same way.   It is
my contention that the *Nation* has led the way in this
reform of American journalism—that it will be followed by many papers to-morrow, as it is followed by
a few to-day.   Its politics are sometimes outrageous.
It frequently gets into lamentable snarls, battling for
liberty with one hand and more laws with the other.
It is doctrinaire, inconsistent, bellicose.   It whoops
for men one day, and damns them as frauds the next.
It has no sense of decorum.   It is sometimes a bit
rowdy.   But who will deny that it is honest?   And
who will deny that, taking one day with another, it
is generally right—that its enthusiasms, if they occasionally send it mooning after dreamers, at least
never send it cheering for rogues—that its wrongness, when it is wrong, is at all events not the dull,
simian wrongness of mere stupidity?   It is disliked
inordinately, but not, I believe, by honest men, even

among its enemies. It is disliked by demagogues and exploiters, by frauds great and small. They have all tasted its snickersnee, and they have all good reason to dislike it.

Personally, I do not subscribe to its politics, save when it advocates liberty openly and unashamed. I have no belief in politicians: the good ones and the bad ones seem to me to be unanimously thieves. Thus I hope I may whoop for it with some grace, despite the fact that my name appears on its flagstaff. How my name got there I don't know; I receive no emolument from its coffers, and write for it very seldom, and then only in contravention of its ideas. I even have to pay cash for my annual subscription—a strange and painful burden for a journalist to bear. But I know of no other expenditure (that is, of a secular character) that I make with more satisfaction, or that brings me a better return. Most of the papers that I am doomed to read are idiotic even when they are right. The *Nation* is intelligent and instructive even when it is wrong.

XIV. OFFICERS AND GENTLEMEN

HARD luck pursues the American Navy. It is the common butt, not only of political mountebanks, but also of all the brummagem uplifters and soul-snatchers who now sweat to save us. If a Mr. Secretary Denby is not permitting the Falls and Dohenys to raid its goods, a Mr. Secretary Wilbur or Josephus Daniels is trying to convert it into a Methodist Sunday-school. Worse, the Navy gets more than its fair share of the national dirty work. It is told off to put down free speech in the Virgin Islands, and it is delegated to flog, hang and butcher the poor Haitians, and so convert them into black Iowans, with money in the bank. Elsewhere in the world such disagreeable jobs are given to the Army. The British Army, for example, performs all the massacres that are necessary in India, and the French Army attends to whatever routine murders and mayhems are called for in Syria and Morocco. But the American custom puts all such Christian endeavor upon the Navy.

However, unless my agents lie, it is not the gore

that revolts the more high-toned naval officers, but the new rectitude that has been thrust upon them.   They are, as a class, excellent fellows, and full of pride in their uniform.   As officers, they are all theoretically gentlemen, and many of them are so in fact.   They have traveled widely, and are familiar with the usages of the civilized world.   They know what is decent and seemly.   Well, try to imagine how they must feel when they read the daily papers.   One day they read that the Secretary of the Navy has ordered a group of their colleagues to prosecute a woman nurse for bringing in a couple of jugs aboard a naval collier.   The next day they observe that a high officer in the Marines has filled the newspapers with a meticulous and indignant account of what went on at a table where he was a guest, in the house of one of his subordinates.   Explanations of this last episode have been offered, but they certainly do not explain it away.   The essential and immovable point is that one officer snitched on another, his host—that the immemorial and invariable obligations of a guest were sacrificed to Law Enforcement.   What would happen to an English naval officer who made any such assault upon the code?   What, indeed would happen to an honest Elk?

But I am not arguing here that any such things ought to happen; I am merely calling attention to the fact that, under democracy, it is becoming increasingly difficult for officers to be gentlemen, as the term is commonly understood in the world, and perhaps also increasingly improbable. We are, it would appear, passing through a time of changing values, and what was considered decent by our fathers will lose that quality to-morrow. The lower orders of men, having attained to political power, now proceed to force their ideas upon their betters, and some of those ideas naturally have to do with decorum. It is already unlawful in America to take a bottle of wine to a sick friend; in a few years it may also be indelicate. And simultaneously, it may become quite proper to go to the police with anything that is said or done in a friend's house. Personally, I am inclined to oppose such changes, if only in sheer hunkerousness, but I am surely under no illusion that opposing them will stop them. They flow naturally out of the character of the common man, now in the saddle, and are thus irresistible. He is extremely and even excessively moral, but the concept of what is called honor is beyond him. If, for example, he aspires to public office, he believes that it is entirely proper to abandon one conviction and take on its opposite in order to get votes. And, having got into office, he believes that it is entirely proper to hold on at any cost, even at the cost of common decency.

There is a familiar example. I allude to the Cathcart case. In that case a high officer of State found himself confronting an uncomfortable dilemma. On the one hand he was bound by an outrageous law to engage in a public and obscene chase of a woman taken in adultery. On the other hand he was bound by the code of all civilized men to refuse and refrain. What was the way out for him? The way out, obviously, was for him to resign his office —in other words, to decline flatly to perform any such ignoble and disgusting duty, and to spurn as insults the honors and emoluments offered for doing it. But, as far as I can make out, he never so much as thought of that. Instead he played the bounder —and kept his dirty job. His conduct, I believe, seemed quite proper to the overwhelming majority of his countrymen. The newspapers, in discussing it, never once suggested that a man of honor, in his boots, would resign forthwith. Instead, they simply denounced him for doing his plain duty under the law—that is, they proposed that he get out of his dilemma by violating his oath of office. The device is characteristically American. Anything is fair and decent that keeps a man his job. That has been the settled American doctrine since Jackson's time.

But it is only of late, I believe, that it has been defended openly, and its antithesis denounced as, in some mysterious fashion, inimical to democracy. We owe that change to the liberation of the lower orders which began with the Civil War. That liberation produced, on one side, an immense increase in political corruption, and, on the other, a rise in moral frenzy. All the characteristic ideas of the mob began to be reflected in public life and legislation. The typical American public officer, who had been a theorist willing to sacrifice anything, including his office, to his notions, became a realist willing to sacrifice anything, including his principles and his honor, to his job. We have him with us to-day, and he smells worse and worse as year chases year. Grover Cleveland was perhaps the last lonely survivor of the old days. He had his faults, God knows, but no one could have imagined him yielding to the mob in order to make votes. Right or wrong, he was his own man—and never more surely than when, by popular standards, he was wrong. In his successor, Dr. Coolidge, we have an almost perfect specimen of the new order. Coolidge is a professional trimmer, who has made his living at the art since his early manhood. It is impossible to imagine him sacrificing his political welfare to his convictions. He has vanity, but nothing properly describable as dignity or self-respect. One automatically pictures him doing, in the Cathcart case, precisely what his subordinate did. He performed many comparable acts during the stinking progress of the Fall case.

This general decay of honor is bound, plainly enough, to drive all the decenter sort of men out of public life among us.   The process, indeed, has already gone a long way.   I point to Congress.   I point to the Federal judiciary.   In both directions one observes an increase in trimmers and knee-benders and a decrease in independent and self-respecting men. The bench, in particular, has suffered.   The better sort of judges, torn between their lawyer-like respect for all law and their inescapable conviction that many of the new laws they are called upon to enforce are unjust and dishonest, tend to throw off the ermine and go back to practice.   And their places are filled by limber nonentities selected—and policed—by the Anti-Saloon League.

Until a few years ago the Army and the Navy escaped this general degradation.   Their officers stood apart from the main body of public job-holders. They held office for life, and they were assumed to be innocent of politics.   Having no need to curry favor with the mob, they could afford to disdain the common hypocrisies.   Inheriting an austere and exact tradition of professional honor, they were what is called gentlemen.   They did not blab upon one another.   They had the fine tolerance of civilized men. They had dignity.   It was as impossible to imagine a naval officer or an army officer playing the spy for the Anti-Saloon League as it was to imagine him using a table-napkin as a handkerchief or getting converted at a Methodist revival.   But I fear those days are past.   The pressure from outside, exerted through such mountebanks as Mr. Secretary Wilbur, becomes too heavy to be borne.   Worse, there is disintegration within, due in part, perhaps, to the packing of the two Services with civilians from the gutter, but in part also to changes in the method of selecting candidates for Annapolis and West Point.   Whatever the cause, the effects are already plain.   In a few short years, perhaps, we shall see a major-general in the Army preaching Fundamentalism in Tennessee, and an admiral in the Navy going to work for the Anti-Saloon League.

XV. GOLDEN AGE

THE rest of us, struggling onward painfully, must wait in patience for the boons and usufructs of Heaven; Judge Elbert Henry Gary, LL.D., chairman of the United States Steel Corporation, has them here and now. To few men in history, I believe, has it been given to live in a universe so nearly to their hearts' desire. Let the learned ex-jurist look East or West, he will find only scenes to content him. Let him look North or South, and his eye will be caressed and frankincense will spray his gills. The emperor and pope of all the Babbitts, he sits at the center of a Babbitts' paradise. For him and his like there dawns a Golden Age, and its hero is good Cal.

I hope I do not exaggerate. No doubt Judge Gary, in the privacy of his chamber, sweats and fumes against imperfections invisible to the rest of us. He is a man of imagination, and has, I daresay, a bold and soaring fancy. He can imagine a Republic even kinder and more osculatory than this one— that is, to Babbitts. He can even, perhaps, imagine a President more ineffable than Cal. But here we shoot into mere human weaknesses—the voluptuous, Freudian day-dreams of one who, like all of us, has his aberrant, goatish moods. Dr. John Roach Straton, I suppose, can imagine improvements in the Holy Scriptures—here a paragraph excised *pro bonos mores,* there a comma inserted to make sense. I myself have dreamed of a malt liquor better than Pilsner Bürgerbräu. But I do not sign my name to such inordinate speculations, and neither does Dr. Straton. Judge Gary, too, holds his tongue. The rest of us, contemplating him, can only envy him. A vast nation of 110,000,000 human beings, all of them alike, seems to be organized to the one end of making him happy. Whatever he wants it to do, it does. Its laws are framed to his precise taste; its public conscience approves his partisans and execrates his enemies; its high officers of state are his excellent friends, and humble and obedient servants. When he gives a feast, judges and ambassadors leap to grace it. When he would dine out, he is welcome at the White House. The newspapers fawn upon him. Labor licks his hand. His frown is dreaded in the Senate house and on the bench. Altogether, his life is happier than that of a Broadway actor, and if he is not content then it is only because contentment is physiologically impossible to *Homo sapiens.*

The United States, I believe, is the first great empire in the history of the world to ground its whole national philosophy upon business. There have been, of course, eminent trading nations in the past, but none ever went so far. Even in Carthage there was a *Junker* hierarchy that stood above the merchants; in Hannibal it actually had a Crown Prince. And even in England, the nation of shopkeepers of Napoleon's derision, there has always been an aristocracy (made up mainly of military freebooters, enterprising adulterers, the issue of the latter, and, in modern times, shyster lawyers, vaudeville magnates, and the proprietors of yellow newspapers) that has held its own against the men of trade, even at the cost of absorbing the more pugnacious of them. But here in this great Republic of the West the art of trafficking is king—and Judge Gary is its grand vizier, as Cal is its chief eunuch. No other human activity brings such great rewards in money and power, and none is more lavishly honored. The one aim of our jurisprudence is to safeguard business—to make its risks small and its profits sure. If the rights of the citizen get in the way, then the rights of the citizen must be sacrificed. Upon this point our higher courts have delivered themselves more than once, and in eloquent, ringing terms. Judge Gary and his friends prefer dry and dismal slaves to those who are stewed and happy. *Also*, to hell with the Bill of Rights! They prefer, when there is a strike, to win it rather than lose it. Out, then, with the pad of blank injunctions! They sweat under criticism, and shiver under attack. To the hoosegow, constable, with the Bolsheviks!

All this, of course, was not achieved without a struggle. For years the Constitution stood in the way—the Constitution and certain national superstitions—the latter sprung from the blather of the Revolutionary stump. But all those impediments are now surmounted. The bench gave Judge Gary to business, and business has reciprocated the favor by providing sound and sane men for the bench. To-day jurisprudence is unfettered. When, a year or so ago, the Supreme Court finally got rid of the Fourth Amendment, that delayed mopping up went almost unnoticed. As I say, Judge Gary, ought to be a happy man. The sun shines upon him from all four points of the compass. Congress, well rehearsed, plays soft jazz for him; bishops bring him his toddy; a straw issues from the White House and tickles him behind the ear. But never is his happiness greater, I believe, than when his thoughts turn idly upon the subject of labor, and he contemplates the state of the union movement in the Federal Union.

For this state, it is plain, he has the late Sam Gompers to thank—that great idealist and easy mark. If he sent less than ten hay-wagons of roses to Sam's funeral, then he is a niggard, indeed. For Sam got upon the back of the American labor movement when

it was beginning to be dangerous, and rode it so
magnificently that at the end of his life it was as tame
as a tabby cat.   It retains that character to-day, and
will continue to do so as long as the Gompersian hierarchy lasts,—that is, so long as Judge Gary and his
friends continue to appoint Sam's heirs and assigns
to high-sounding committees, and to invite them to
gaudy dinners.   A plate of puddle duck and a chance
to make a speech—that was always enough to fetch
Sam.   And when Sam was fetched, the 4,000,000
members of the American Federation of Labor were
also fetched.   Where else in the world is there a
great union organization that has so long and honorable a record as a strike-breaker?   Or that is so
diligently devoted to keeping the lower ranks of labor
in due subordination?   If it had been conceived and
hatched by Judge Gary himself, it could not have been
more nearly perfect.   Practically considered, it is
not a labor organization at all; it is simply a balloon
mattress interposed between capital and labor to
protect the former from the latter.   Gazing upon it,
I daresay, Judge Gary feels a glow flickering along
the periphery of his gizzard, and if he were not a
Christian he would permit himself a guffaw.

I leave the sweetest to the last.   The courts might
be docile, Congress might be consecrated to right
thought, labor might grovel and the bench of bishops
might applaud, but if there were an anarchist in

the White House it would all go for naught.
Imagine, then, Judge Gary's joy in contemplating the
incomparable Cal! It is almost as if, in New York,
a bootlegger were made king. The man's merits, in
the Babbitt view, are almost fabulous. He seems,
indeed, scarcely like a man at all, but more like
some miraculous visitation or act of God. He is
the ideal made visible, if not audible—perfection put
into a cutaway coat and trotted up and down like a
mannequin in a cloak and suit atelier. Nor was
there any long stress of training him—no season of
doubt and misgiving. Nature heaved him forth full-
blown, like a new star shot into the heavens. In him
the philosophy of Babbitt comes to its perfect and
transcendental form. Thrift, to him, is the queen of
all the virtues. He respects money in each and every
one of its beautiful forms—pennies, nickels, dimes,
dollars, five-dollar bills, and so on *ad infinitum*. He
venerates those who have it. He believes that they
have wisdom. He craves the loan and use of that
wisdom. He invites them to breakfast, and listens to
them. The things they revere, he reveres. The
things they long for, he longs to give them.

Judge Gary is an old man—just how old I do not
know, for he withholds the date of his birth from
"Who's Who in America," along with the principal
suffragettes. He remembers the dreadful days of
Roosevelt, with bombs going off every two hours.

He remembers the turmoils of the Taft administration. He remembers how *difficile* Woodrow was—how he had to be wooed, flattered, led by the nose, drenched with goose-grease. He remembers the crude carnival under the martyr Harding—Broadway sports, pug managers, small-town Elks at the trough. And then he thinks of Washington to-day, and sees it bathed in pink sunshine. There he is ever welcome. There he is *imperator in imperio*. There is good *Geschäft*. There is the Athens of the new Golden Age.

XVI. EDGAR SALTUS

FORTY years ago Edgar Saltus was a shining star in the national literature, leading the way out of the Egyptian night of Victorian sentimentality. To-day he survives only as the favorite anthor of the late Warren Gamaliel Harding. I can recall, in the circle of Athene, no more complete collapse. Saltus plunged from the top of the world to the bottom of the sea. His books, of late, have been reissued, and his surviving third wife has printed a biography of him. But all his old following, save for a few romantic die-hards, has vanished.

The causes of the débâcle are certainly not hard to determine. They were set forth twenty-five years ago by that ingenious man, the late Percival Pollard, and you will find them in his book, "Their Day in Court." Saltus was simply a bright young fellow who succumbed to his own cleverness. The gaudy glittering phrase enchanted him. He found early in life that he had a hand for shaping it; he found soon afterward that it had a high capacity for getting him notice. So he devoted himself to its concoction—and presently he was lost. His life after that was simply one long intoxication. He was drunk on words. Ideas gradually departed from him. Day and night, for years and years, he held his nozzle against the jug of nouns, adjectives, verbs, pronouns, prepositions and interjections. Some of his phrases, of course, were good ones. There were enough of that kind in "Imperial Purple," for example, to fascinate the sainted Harding, a voluptuary in all the arts. But the rest quickly wore out—and with them Saltus himself wore out. He passed into the shadows, and was forgotten. When he died, a few years ago, all that remained of him was a vague name.

His wife's biography is encased in an orange slipcover which announces melodramatically that it is "an extraordinary revealing life." It is, but I doubt that what it reveals will serve to recuscitate poor Saltus. The man who emerges from it is simply a silly and hollow trifler—a mass of puerile pretensions and affectations, vain of his unsound knowledge and full of sentimentalities. He began life by hawking the stale ribaldries of Arthur Schopenhauer, already dead twenty years; he departed to realms of bliss chattering the blowsy nonsense of theosophy. Mrs. Saltus, in the new and appalling fashion of literary wives, is extremely frank. Her Edgar was a handsome dog, but extremely foolish, and even childish. When he was engaged upon his rococo compositions he had to be protected like a queen bee in childbed.

The slightest sound dissipated his inspiration, and set him to yelling. If a fish-peddler stopped beneath his window he was done for the day. If a cat came in and brushed his leg he was thrown into hysterics, and had to go to bed. His love affairs were highly complex, and apparently took up a great deal of his time. Early in life, while he was a student at Heidelberg, he had an affair with a lady of noble birth, and even ran away with her. The business was quickly broken up, apparently by the allied sovereigns of Europe. The bride-elect was immured in a convent, and died there "the year following." Saltus then came back to the Republic and married the daughter of a partner in J. P. Morgan & Company. "She was no small catch," but the alliance was doomed. The man was too fascinating to women. His pulchritude charmed them, and his epigrams finished them. In a few years Mrs. Saltus was suing for divorce.

There followed a series of morganatic affairs, culminating in a second marriage. This one also blew up quickly; the bride denounced Saltus as a liar, and even hinted that he had induced her to marry him by fraud. But though she soon left his bed and board, she clung resolutely to her other rights as his wife, and thereafter, for many long years, he devoted all the time he could spare from his writing to efforts to get rid of her. He moved from New York to California, in fact, mainly because the divorce laws on the Coast were easier than in the East. But they were not easy enough to free him. Finally, after endless waiting, he got news one day that the party of the second part was dead. He displayed the correct regrets, but was obviously much relieved. Meanwhile, Wife No. 3 was at call in the anteroom. She had been there, in fact, for years. When Saltus first met her she was a school-girl with her hair down her back, and his attentions to her—he was then rising forty—naturally outraged her family. But her own heart was lost, and so the effort to warn him off failed. He followed her, after that, all over the civilized world. Did she go to London, he was at her heels on the next steamer. Did she move to Los Angeles, he arrived by the next train. In the end they were married in Montreal, on a very hot day and after a pretty lovers' quarrel.

This lady is the author of the biography with the orange slip-cover. Facing page 310 there is a portrait of her showing her "sitting at the table on which her husband wrote his books, burning incense before a Siamese Buddha, and meditating on a stanza from the Bhagavad-Gita." She denies, however, that Saltus took to theosophy under her tutelage. The actual recruiting officer was a certain Mr. Colville, of Pasadena, who combined the "enthusiasm of a scholar and the erudition of a sage." This Colville introduced

Saltus to the theosophical elements, and later guided his faltering steps. In the end poor old Schopenhauer lost a customer and the art of epigram a gifted and diligent practitioner. Saltus passed into senility with his thoughts concentrated powerfully upon Higher Things.

A grotesque and somewhat pathetic story. The man began life with everything in his favor. His family was well-to-do and of good social position in New York; he was sent to Eton and then to Heidelberg, and apparently made useful friends at both places; he plunged into writing at the precise moment when revolt against the New England Brahmins was rising; he attracted attention quickly, and was given a lavish welcome. No American author of 1885 was more talked about. When his first novel, "The Truth About Tristrem Varick," came out in 1888 it made a genuine sensation. But the stick came down almost as fast as the rocket had gone up. His books set the nation agog for a short while, and were then quietly forgotten. He began as the hope of American letters, and ended as a writer of yellow-backs and a special correspondent for the Hearst papers. What ailed him was simply lack of solid substance. He could be clever, as cleverness was understood during the first Cleveland administration, but he lacked dignity, information, sense. His books of "philosophy" were feeble and superficial, his novels were only facile improvisations, full of satanic melodrama and wooden marionettes.

Of late I have been re-reading them—a sad job, surely, for when I was a schoolboy they were nine-day wonders, barred from all the libraries but devoured eagerly by every aspiring youth. Now their epigrams are dulled, and there is nothing else left. "The Anatomy of Negation" and "The Philosophy of Disenchantment" have been superseded by far better books; "The Truth About Tristrem Varick" reads like one of the shockers of Gertrude Atherton; "Mary Magdalen" is a dead shell; the essays and articles republished as "Uplands of Dream" are simply ninth-rate journalism. Of them all only "Imperial Purple" holds up. A certain fine glow is still in it; it has gusto if not profundity; Saltus's worst faults do not damage it appreciably. I find myself, indeed, agreeing thoroughly with the literary judgment of Dr. Harding. "Imperial Purple" remains Saltus's best book. It remains also, alas, his only good one!

XVII. MISCELLANEOUS NOTES

1

Martyrs

TO die for an idea: it is unquestionably noble. But how much nobler it would be if men died for ideas that were true! Searching history, I can find no such case. All the great martyrs of the books died for sheer nonsense— often for trivial matters of doctrine and ceremonial, too absurd to be stated in plain terms. But what of the countless thousands who have perished in the wars, fighting magnificently for their country? Well, show me one who knew precisely what the war he died in was about, and could put it into a simple and plausible proposition.

2

The Ancients

The theory that the ancient Greeks and Romans were men of a vast and ineffable superiority runs aground on the fact that they were great admirers

of oratory.   No other art was so assiduously practiced among them.   To-day we venerate the archi-
tecture of Greece far more than we venerate its
orators, but the Greeks themselves put the orators
first, and so much better records of them are preserved to-day.   But oratory, as a matter of fact,
is the most primitive and hence the lowest of all the
arts.   Where is it most respected to-day?   Among
savages, in and out of civilization.   The yokels of
the open spaces flock by the thousand to hear imbeciles yawp and heave; the city proletariat glues
its ears to the radio every night.   But what genuinely
civilized man would turn out to hear even the champion orator of the country?   Dozens of the most eminent professors of the art show off their tricks every
day in the United States Senate.   Yet the galleries of
the Senate, save when news goes out that some Senator
is stewed and about to make an ass of himself, are
occupied only by Negroes who have come in to get
warm, and hand-holding bridal couples from rural
North Carolina and West Virginia.

3

Jack Ketch as Eugenist

Has any historian ever noticed the salubrious effect,
on the English character, of the frenzy for hanging
that went on in England during the Eighteenth Cen-

tury? When I say salubrious, of course, I mean in the purely social sense. At the end of the Seventeenth Century the Englishman was still one of the most turbulent and lawless of civilized men; at the beginning of the Nineteenth he was the most law-abiding; *i. e.*, the most docile. What worked the change in him? I believe that it was worked by the rope of Jack Ketch. During the Eighteenth Century the lawless strain was simply choked out of the race. Perhaps a third of those in whose veins it ran were actually hanged; the rest were chased out of the British Isles, never to return. Some fled to Ireland, and revivified the decaying Irish race: in practically all the Irish rebels of the past century there have been plain traces of English blood. Others went to the Dominions. Yet others came to the United States, and after helping to conquer the Western wilderness, begat the yeggman, Prohibition agents, footpads and hijackers of to-day.

The murder rate is very low in England, perhaps the lowest in the world. It is low because nearly all the potential ancestors of murderers were hanged or exiled in the Eighteenth Century. Why is it so high in the United States? Because most of the potential ancestors of murderers, in the late Eighteenth and early Nineteenth Centuries, were *not* hanged. And why did they escape? For two plain reasons. First, the existing government was too weak to track them down and execute them, especially in the West.   Second, the qualities of daring and enterprise that went with their murderousness were so valuable that it was socially profitable to overlook their homicides.   In other words, the job of occupying and organizing the vast domain of the new Republic was one that demanded the aid of men who, among other things, occasionally butchered their fellow men. The butchering had to be winked at in order to get their help.   Thus the murder rate, on the frontier, rose to unprecedented heights, while the execution rate remained very low.   Probably 100,000 men altogether were murdered in the territory west of the Ohio between 1776 and 1865; probably not 100 murderers were formally executed.   When they were punished at all, it was by other murderers—and this left the strain unimpaired.

4

Heroes

Of human eminence there are obviously two varieties: that which issues out of the inner substance of the eminent individual and that which comes to him, either partially or wholly, from without.   It is not difficult to recognize men at the two extremes.   No sane person would argue seriously that the eminence of such a man, say, as Richard Wagner was, in any plausible sense, accidental or unearned. Wagner created "Tristan und Isolde" out of his own inherent substance. Allowing everything for the chances of his education and environment, the massive fact remains that no other man of the same general education and environment has ever created anything even remotely comparable to it. Wagner deserved the eminence that came to him quite as certainly as the Lord God Jehovah deserves that which attaches to Him. He got it by differing sharply from other men, and enormously for the better, and by laboring colossally and incessantly to make that difference visible. At the other extreme lies such a fellow, say, as young John D. Rockefeller. He is, by all ordinary standards, an eminent man. When he says anything the newspapers report it in full. If he fell ill of gallstones to-morrow, or eloped with a lady Ph.D., or fell off the roof of his house, or was taken in a rum raid the news would be telegraphed to all parts of the earth and at least a billion human beings would show some interest in it. And if he went to Washington and pulled the White House bell he would be let in infallibly, even if the Heir of Lincoln had to quit a saxophone lesson to see him. But it must be obvious that young John's eminence, such as it is, is almost purely fortuitous and unearned. He is attended to simply because he happens to be the son of old John, and hence heir to a large fortune. So

far as the records show, he has never said anything
in his life that was beyond the talents of a Rotary
Club orator or a newspaper editorial writer, or done
anything that would have strained an intelligent
bookkeeper.   He is, to all intents and purposes, a
vacuum, and yet he is known to more people, and
especially to more people of means, than Wagner, and
admired and envied vastly more by all classes.

Between Wagner and young John there are infinite
gradations, and sometimes it is a hard matter to
distinguish between them.   To most Americans, I
daresay, a Harding or a Coolidge appears to enjoy an
eminence that is not only more gaudy but also more
solid than that of, say, an Einstein.   When Einstein
visited the United States, a few years ago, he was
taken to see Harding as a sort of treat, and many
worthy patriots, no doubt, regarded it as somewhat
too rich for him, an enemy alien and a Jew.   If
Thomas Hardy came here to-morrow, his publisher
would undoubtedly try to get an invitation to the
White House for him, not merely to advertise his
books but also to honor the man.   Yet it must be
plain that the eminence of Coolidge, however vastly
it may be whooped up by gentlemen of enlightened
self-interest, is actually greatly inferior to that of
either Einstein or Hardy.   These men owe whatever
fame they have to actual accomplishments.   There
is no doubt whatever that what they have is wholly

theirs. They owe nothing to anyone, and no conceivable series of accidents could have made them what they are. If superiority exists among men, then they are indubitably superior. But is there any sign of superiority in Coolidge? I can find none. His eminence is due entirely to two things: first, a series of accidents, and secondly, the possession of qualities that, in themselves, do not mark a superior man, but an inferior. He is a cheap, sordid and grasping politician, a seeker of jobs all his life, willing to do almost anything imaginable to get them. He has never said a word worth hearing, or done a thing requiring genius, or even ordinary skill. Put into his place and given the opportunities that have arisen before him in a long succession, any other ninth-rate lawyer in the land could have got as far as he has got.

Now for my point. It is, in brief, that the public estimation of eminence runs almost directly in inverse ratio to its genuineness. That is to say, the sort of eminence that the mob esteems most highly is precisely the sort that has least grounding in solid worth and honest accomplishment. And the reason therefor is not far to seek. The kind of eminence that it admires is simply the kind that it can understand—the kind that it can aspire to. The very puerility of a Coolidge, in fact, is one of the principal causes of the admiration he excites. What he has done in the world is within the capacities, given luck enough, of any John Smith. His merits, such as they are, are almost universal, and hence perfectly comprehensible. But what a Wagner or an Einstein does is wholly beyond the understanding of an ordinary ignoramus, and so it is impossible for the ignoramus to admire it. Worse, it tends to arouse his suspicion, and hence his animosity. He is not merely indifferent to the merits of a Wagner; he will, if any attempt is made to force them upon his attention, challenge them sharply. What he admires fundamentally, in other words, is himself, and in a Coolidge, a Harding, a baseball pitcher, a movie actor, an archbishop, or a bank president he can see himself. He can see himself, too, though perhaps more dimly, in a Dewey, a Pershing, a Rockefeller or a Jack Dempsey. But he can no more see himself in a Wagner or an Einstein than he can see himself on the throne of the Romanoffs, and so he suspects and dislikes such men, as he suspects and dislikes Romanoffs.

Unluckily, it is one thing to denounce his stupidity, and quite another thing to escape its consequences. The history of mankind is peopled chiefly, not with the genuinely great men of the race, but with the flashy and hollow fellows who appealed to the mob. Every American remembers vividly the contribution that Theodore Roosevelt made to the building of the Panama Canal—a contribution that might have been made by any other American thrown fortuitously into his place, assuming only that the substitute shared his normal American lack of a sense of honor.   But who remembers the name of the man who actually designed the canal?   I turn to the New International Encyclopedia and find nine whole pages about the canal, with many drawings.   There is eloquent mention of Col. Goethals—who simply carried out the designer's plans.   There is mention, too, of Col. Gorgas—whose sanitary work was a simple application of other men's ideas.   There is ample space for Roosevelt, and his blackjacking of Colombia.   But so far as I can find, the name of the designer is not there.   The mob did not admire him, and so history has overlooked him.

5

An Historic Blunder

The Southern gentry made a thumping mistake when, after the Civil War, they disfranchised the blacks.   Had they permitted the latter to vote, they would have retained political control of all the Southern States, for the blacks, like the peasants everywhere else, would have followed their natural masters.   As it was, control quickly passed to the poor white trash, who still maintain it, though many of them have ceased to be poor.   The gentry struggle in vain to get back in the saddle; they lack the votes to achieve

the business unaided, and the blacks, who were ready
to follow them in 1870, are now incurably suspicious
of them.   The result is that politics in the South remain fathomlessly swinish.   Every civilized South-
erner knows it and is ashamed of it, but the time has
apparently passed to do anything about it.   To get
rid of its Bleases, Mayfields, Slemps, Peays and
Vardamans, the South must wait until the white trash
are themselves civilized.   This is a matter demanding
almost as much patience as the long vigil of the
Seventh Day Adventists.

6

On Cynicism

One of the most curious of human delusions lies in
the theory that cynics are unhappy men—that cyn-
icism makes for a general biliousness and malaise.
It is a false deduction, I believe, from the obvious
fact that cynics make *other* men unhappy.   But they
are themselves among the most comfortable and se-
rene of mammals; perhaps only bishops, pet dogs and
actors are happier.   For what a cynic believes,
though it may be too dreadful to be put into formal
words, at least usually has the merit of being true—
and truth is ever a rock, hard and harsh, but solid
under the feet.   A cynic is chronically in the position of a wedding guest who has known the bride for

nine years, and has had her confidence. He is a great deal less happy, theoretically, than the bridegroom. The bridegroom, beautifully barbered and arrayed, is about to launch into the honeymoon. But the cynic looks ahead two weeks, two months, two years. Such, to borrow a phrase from the late Dr. Eliot, are the durable satisfactions of life.

7

Music and Sin

Among Christian workers and other intellectual cripples the delusion seems to persist that jazz is highly aphrodisiacal. I never encounter a sermon on the subject without finding it full of dark warnings to parents, urging them to keep their nubile daughters out of the jazz palaces on the ground that the voluptuous music will inflame their passions and so make them easy prey to bond salesmen, musicians and other such carnal fellows. All this seems to me to be nonsense. Jazz, in point of fact, is not voluptuous at all. Its monotonous rhythm and puerile tunes make it a sedative rather than a stimulant. If it is an aphrodisiac, then the sound of riveting is also an aphrodisiac. What fetches the flappers who come to grief in the jazz parlors is not the music at all, but the alcohol. Drinking it out of flasks in the washrooms, they fail to keep the dose in harmony with their natural resistance, and so they lose control of their faculties, and what follows is lamentable.   Jazz, which came in with Prohibition, gets the blame that belongs to its partner.   In the old days, when it was uncommon for refined women to get drunk at dances, it would have been quite harmless.   To-day even Chopin's funeral march would be dangerous.

The truth is that jazz is probably the least voluptuous variety of music commonly heard in Christendom.   There are plenty of Methodist hymns that are ten times as aphrodisiacal, and the fact is proved by the scandals that follow every camp-meeting.   In most parts of the United States, indeed, the Methodists have begun to abandon camp-meetings as subversive of morality.   Where they still flourish it is not unusual for even the rev. clergy to be taken in byzantine practices.   But so-called good music is yet worse than the Methodist hymns.   Has the world so soon forgotten James Huneker's story of the prudent opera mamma who refused to let her daughter sing Isolde, on the ground that no woman could ever get through the second act without forgetting God?   That second act, even so, is much overestimated.   There are piano pieces of Chopin that are a hundred times worse; if the Comstocks really had any sense, they would forbid their performance. And what of the late Puccini?   If "La Bohème" is not an aphrodisiac, then what is it?   Yet it is sung publicly all over the world. Only in Atlanta, Ga., is there a law against it, and even that law was probably inspired by the fact that it was written by a Catholic and not by the fact that it has brought hundreds of thousands of Christian women to the edge of the abyss.

Old Ludwig himself was not without guilt. His "Egmont" overture is a gross and undisguised appeal to the medulla oblongata. And what of his symphonies and quartettes? The last movement of his Eroica is not only voluptuous to the last degree; it is also Bolshevistic. Try to play it with your eyes on a portrait of Dr. Coolidge. You will find the thing as impossible as eating ice-cream on roast beef. At the time of its first performance in Vienna the moral sense of the community was so greatly outraged that Beethoven had to get out of town for a while. I pass over Wagner, whose "Tristan und Isolde" was probably his most decorous work, despite Huneker— think of "Parsifal"!—and come to Richard Strauss. Here I need offer no argument: his "Salomé" and "Elektra" have been prohibited by the police, at one time or another, in nearly every country in the world. I believe that "Der Rosenkavalier" is still worse, though the police leave it unmolested. Compare its first act to the most libidinous jazz ever heard of on Broadway. It is like comparing vodka to ginger-pop. No woman who hears it is ever the same again. She may remain within the law, but her thoughts are wayward henceforth.   Into her ear the sirens have poured their abminable song.   She has been beset by witches.   There is a sinister glitter in her eye.

8

The Champion

Of the forty-eight sovereign States of this imperial Federation, which is the worst?   In what one of them is a civilized man most uncomfortable?   Over half the votes, if the question were put to a vote, would probably be divided between California and Tennessee.   Each in its way, is almost unspeakable.   Tennesee, of course, has never been civilized, save in a small area; even in the earliest days of the Republic it was regarded as barbaric by its neighbors.   But California, at one time, promised to develop a charming and enlightened civilization.   There was a touch of tropical balm in its air, and a touch of Latin and oriental color in its ideas.   Like Louisiana, it seemed likely to resist Americanization for many years; perhaps forever.   But now California, the old California, is simply extinct.   What remains is an Alsatia of retired Ford agents and crazy fat women— a paradise of 100% Americanism and the New Thought.   Its laws are the most extravagant and idiotic ever heard of in Christendom.   Its public

officers, and particularly its judges, are famous all
over the world for their imbecilities. When one
hears of it at all, one hears that some citizen has been
jailed for reading the Constitution of the United States,
or that some new swami in a yellow bed-tick has got
all the realtors' wives of Los Angeles by the ears.
When one hears of it further, it is only to learn that
some obscure movie lady in Hollywood has murdered another lover. The State is run by its Chambers of Commerce, which is to say, by the worst
variety of resident shysters. No civilized man ever
seems to take any part in its public life. Not an idea
comes out of it—that is, not an idea beyond the grasp
of a Kiwanis Club secretary, a Christian Science sorcerer, or a grand goblin of the American Legion.
Twice, of late, it has offered the country candidates
for the presidency. One was the Hon. Hiram John-
son and the other was the Hon. William Gibbs Mc-
Adoo! Only Vermont can beat that record.

The minority of civilized Californians—who lately,
by the way, sent out a call from Los Angeles for
succor, as if they were beset by wolves!—commonly
lay the blame for this degeneration of a once-proud
commonwealth upon the horde of morons that has
flowed in from Iowa, Nebraska and the other cow-
States, seeking relief from the bitter climate of the
steppes. The California realtors have been luring
in these hinds for a generation past, and they now

swarm in all the southern towns, especially Los Angeles.   They come in with their savings, are swindled
and sent home, and so make room for more.   While
they remain and have any part of their money left,
they patronize the swamis, buy oil stock, gape at the
movie folk, and pack the Methodist churches.   Unquestionably, the influence of such vacuums has
tended to degrade the general tone of California life;
what was once a Spanish *fiesta* is now merely an upper
Mississippi valley street-carnival.   But it is not to be
forgotten that the Native Sons have gone down the
chute with the newcomers—that there is no more sign
of intellectual vigor in the old stock than there is in
the new stock.   A few intransigeants hold out against
the tide of 100% Americanism, but only a few.
The rest bawl against the Reds as loudly as any Iowa
steer-stuffer.

The truth is that it is unjust to blame Iowa for the
decay of California, for Iowa itself is now moving
up, not down.   And so is Nebraska.   A few years
ago both States were as sterile, intellectually, as
Spain, but both are showing signs of progress to-day,
and in another generation or two, as the Prohibition
lunacy passes and the pall of Methodism begins to
lift, they will probably burst into very vigorous
activity.   Some excellent stock is in them; it is very
little contaminated by what is called Anglo-Saxon
blood.   Iowa, even to-day, is decidedly more civi-

lized than California. It is producing more ideas, and, more important still, it is carrying on a much less violent war *against* ideas. I doubt that any man who read the Constitution in Davenport or Des Moines would be jailed for it, as Upton Sinclair (or one of his friends) was in Pasadena. The American Legion would undoubtedly protest, but the police would probably do nothing, for the learned judges of the State would not entertain the charge.

Thus California remains something of a mystery. The whole United States, of course, has been going down hill since the beginning of the century, but why should one State go so much faster than the others? Is the climate to blame? Hardly. The climate of San Francisco is thoroughly un-Californian, and yet San Francisco is almost as dead as Los Angeles. It was there, indeed, that that California masterpiece, the Mooney case, was staged; it was here that the cops made three efforts to convict poor Fatty Arbuckle of murder in the first-degree; it was there that the late Dr. Abrams launched a quackery that went Mother Eddy one better. San Francisco, once the home of Mark Twain and Bret Harte, is now ravaged by Prohibition enforcement officers. But if the climate is not to blame, then what is? Why should a great State, lovely physically and of romantic history, so violently renounce all sense and decency? What has got into it? God alone knows!

9

Honor in America

Some time ago I enjoyed the distinguished honor
of entertaining an American university professor in
my house.   The fellow had a resilient gullet, and in
the course of the evening we got down a quart of
Scotch.   Made expansive by the liquor, he told me
this story:

A short while before, at his university, one of the
professors gave a booze party for a group of colleagues, including the president of the institution.   It
was warm weather, and they sat on the veranda,
guzzling moonshine and ginger-ale.   There was so
much chatter that they didn't hear a student coming
up the path.   Suddenly he was on them, and they
almost fainted. . . .

At this point I asked why they were alarmed.

"Well," said my visitor, "suppose the student had
turned out to be a Christian?   He would have
blabbed, and then our host would have lost his chair.
The president would have been forced to cashier him."

"But the president," I argued, "was a guest in the
man's house.   How could he have dismissed him?"

"What else would there have been for him to do?"
asked the professor.

"Resign at once," I replied.   "Wasn't he under the

obligations of a guest? Wasn't he *particeps criminis?* How could he separate himself from his host? How could he sit as judge upon his host, even if only formally?"

But the professor couldn't see the point. I began to fear that he was in his cups, but it soon appeared that he was quite clear. We argued for half an hour: he was still unable to see the point. The duty of a president to enforce an unwilling and dishonest obedience to an absurd law—this duty was superior to his duty as a guest, *i. e.*, it was superior to his obligation as a man of honor! We passed on to another point.

"What of the student?" I asked. "I take it that he turned out to be a gentleman. Suppose he had been a Christian? Suppose he had blabbed? What would the other boys have done to him?"

The professor stared at me blankly.

"Nothing," he said at length. "After all, we *were* boozing."

This professor, I should add, was a man of the old American stock—in fact, a fellow very proud of his colonial ancestry. When he got back to his university he joined in signing a public statement that Prohibition was a great success there.

I proceed to another case. One day in the Summer of 1924, during the Republican National Convention at Cleveland, I met an eminent American publicist in a hotel lobby there. He told me at once that he was suffering from a dreadful belly-ache. I had a jug in my room, but my own hotel was far away, so I suggested that help might be got from a journalist on the premises. We went to his room, and I introduced the publicist. The journalist promptly got out a bottle and gave him a policeman's drink. The publicist had recovered in three minutes. . . . When he got home, he joined, like the professor, in signing a public statement praising Prohibition.

10

Note in the Margin of a Treatise on Psychology

As I stoop to lace my shoe you hit me over the coccyx with a length of hickory (*Carya laciniosa*). I conclude instantly that you are a jackass. This is the whole process of human thought in little. This also is free will.

11

Definition

Democracy is that system of government under which the people, having 35,717,342 native-born adult whites to choose from, including thousands who are handsome and many who are wise, pick out a Coolidge to be head of the State. It is as if a hungry man, set before a banquet prepared by master cooks and covering a table an acre in area, should turn his back upon the feast and stay his stomach by catching and eating flies.

XVIII. CATECHISM

Q. If you find so much that is unworthy of reverence in the United States, then why do you live here?

A. Why do men go to zoos?

INDEX

305